SLOW BURN

TRACEY BARSKI

contents

To all the girls who never felt like they were wanted. Let
that fire burn.

SLOW Burn PLAYLIST

For those of you who like a little mood music, here is the playlist I used as inspiration for Cole and Jocelyn's story.

ONE

"The fires of suffering become the light of consciousness." - Eckhart Tolle

Jocelyn's mama had once said the women in their family were cursed—destined, even—to get burned. Bonnie Murphy had meant by love, but the truth of the statement went beyond what she could've predicted with her heartbroken lament.

Jocelyn's therapist didn't think the irony was as funny as she did.

Dr. Deborah had, however, encouraged her to go back to Cedar Hollow. Her theory was that visiting the town where Jocelyn had lost her mother might douse the long-flickering flame of obsession.

She probably hadn't meant for Jocelyn to turn it into a veritable amateur investigation into what happened that night, but closure was closure.

Or so Jocelyn hoped.

But sitting in her car outside the empty lot that had been her childhood home, she wasn't as sure. Not with the way echoes of memory slipped in and out of her mind like snatches of a nightmare she would never truly forget.

She was the same age her mama was when she died—twenty-nine—and it felt like the years she'd been given were borrowed ones, always meant to be counted twice.

It was still warm in Tennessee in mid-September, but goose flesh popped up in little constellations across her skin, telling a story of unresolved traumas in indecipherable pictures.

She'd started to write them down, scribbling in a journal she'd bought at Dr. Deb's urging so she could recount the things she remembered from that night.

A fire had burned in her heart for two decades, ever since the conflagration that stole her mother and her home had licked at her bedroom door. One year ago, she'd moved from writing down memories to taking notes as she researched, spending hours looking at reports and articles, not-so-subtly grilling her grandmother, and admitting to Dr. Deb that she wanted to go back to Cedar Hollow to experience the town from adult eyes and maybe get the dreams from her head.

Deb had encouraged her in that. But she didn't know about the research.

John Hauser's award ceremony had been the perfect excuse to make the five-hour trek from Asheville, North Carolina to the rolling hills of Middle Tennessee. She'd been invited, after all, though it was unclear how genuine Ellen Hauser had been when she'd sent the official invitation on that shiny card stock in her last letter.

Because Mama had been raising her on her own, aside from Nan, Ellen was pretty much the only mother Jocelyn had known once hers had been taken from her, and she owed John the honor of the day.

Starting the car and chewing her lip, she worked to tear her gaze away from the empty lot. Kudzu ran wild along the back fence, coiling around the trunks of the nearest trees, branches drooping with the weight of the invasive plant. It threatened to take over everything in its path, including the empty lot where the house had once stood. Why had nothing been built in its place? The neighborhood was older, a little more rundown, but certainly not forgotten.

But she knew better than anyone that the fire on Hill Drive was a blemish on the town's history. Maybe it remained a scar as a reminder for anyone who drove by.

She left the window open and skated her palm over the wind as she drove back toward First Street, the buzz of cicadas a soundtrack of nostalgia. The affectionately tended maples lining the road back to downtown were starting to give up their green; reds and oranges and yellows fluttered in the light breeze like hands waving as she passed. It was that in-between part of the season where summer hadn't fully let go, but autumn was starting to whisper its name.

Enough of the town had changed to mismatch what she remembered of her days as a girl there. New restaurants, revitalized store fronts, offices, and even a trendy little boutique beckoned tourists passing through on their way to the nearby Falls or old Civil War battlefield sites marked by aged metal placards and old pyramid-stacked canon balls. Some of those very brick buildings bore the marks of prestigious historical status, listing out names of families whose legacies still walked the sidewalks.

First Street was a straight shot through the heart of the town, the artery that led to longer, lonelier stretches of highway outside city limits. Thick tunnels of trees and rolling hills led to the more rural areas of the county.

Past the line of businesses along First Street sat a lovely square of buildings as old as they were stolid. In the center, a patch of open space large enough to hold small assemblies pulled people in for picnics and romps in the grass.

She recalled the festivals from long ago—staples of small towns with nothing better to do than celebrate every little milestone even if it was power-washing the courthouse's brick facade to rid it of the mildew propagated by the quintessential southern humidity.

People would line the sidewalks with their rows of booths and tables, stringing lights and decorations from lampposts, spending just as much time gossiping as they did selling whatever they were offering that season.

No gossip-mongers lined the streets now, but a small platform had been set up on the eastern edge of the grassy inner square with a skinny podium jutting up. Chairs sat in neat rows, dozens-deep, and already a decent crowd had gathered.

Despite the congregation, she had little trouble finding a parking spot. The weather was pleasant enough that a lot of people had likely walked to the square.

Her fixation on the house fire twenty years ago had lured her with easy determination across hundreds of miles, but either the ill-begotten visit to the lot had settled the dread like a boulder in her stomach or the thought of facing the townsfolk she'd spent two decades vilifying set an uncertainty in her bones.

Either way, reluctance pressed her deep into the faux leather of her seat as her hands twisted around the steering wheel. It would've broken apart in her hands if she let the anxiety have its way.

She'd already been to the Cedar Hollow Inn, calling on Sally Anne—her mother's best friend once upon a time—for an early check-in since she and her husband owned the place. Sally had happily obliged, though Jocelyn hadn't missed the concern written across the other woman's face.

It didn't take long for Sally to express the worry that Jocelyn's presence would cause a bit of a stir. A population of scarcely ten thousand meant that newcomers got noticed, and someone whose history was as deep and bruised as Jocelyn's was with Cedar Hollow guaranteed her visit would be the talk of the town.

But Jocelyn was okay with talk, especially if it meant the secrets she knew were buried would slip out.

She wasn't there to make friends.

She'd come to shake up some ghosts.

Someone needed to pay for killing her mama.

Two

"Where there is smoke, there is fire." - Proverb

There was little Cole Hauser and his daddy had in common aside from their devotion to their small town and the love of a challenge.

Today's battle? This damn suit. He'd wrangled himself into it like a possum at a dog show. Sure, it was the only thing halfway respectable for a day like this—his daddy getting honored in front of half the county—but that didn't make it feel any less like slow-cooked punishment. Most days, Cole wore jeans and a t-shirt with The Hammered Nail's logo on the front, not a three-piece like he was posing for a bank ad. His only saving grace was having this ceremony in September and not the infamous oven that was Tennessee in July.

That would've been his daddy's pick, no question—though none of this was his doing. Still, he'd have eaten up the heat like molasses on a biscuit. That thick, sticky kind of summer that had your clothes clinging was like sweet nectar to a honeybee for him.

Maybe it reminded his pop of those moments when fire licked at his boots and tugged at his coat, trying its damnedest to take him under in the blaze he'd spent his whole working life beating back as a firefighter.

Until today.

Today, John Hauser was walking away from all of it. No more early alarms or late-night calls, no more soot-stained gear or secondhand smoke in the laundry room. Just a plaque and a podium and a whole town watching.

He didn't look like he was done, though. Standing on that stage, John was as solid and sure as ever. Broad as a barn and sunbaked from years in the heat, he had that same steel in his spine. And when he found Cole's mama in the crowd, they shared a look that said more than words ever could. It was the kind of look you earned after thirty-some years of standing side by side through just about everything.

Usually, those silent communications had to do with Cole—what to do with the son who never quite settled down. But this one? This one was all for them.

It didn't happen often, but pride puffed up in Cole's chest instead of that old bitterness as his daddy strode across the stage like he had every right to be there. And hell, he did. The proof was in the number of people in the crowd.

Pop took his plaque and shook Mayor Abbott's hand, then turned to his audience, cheeks flushed with the embarrassment that came from being recognized for something he'd done out of duty rather than for the accolades.

Folks whooped and hollered as he ducked his head, trying to wave off the mayor's attempt at drawing him to the podium. Despite his efforts, Mayor Abbott managed to get John behind the mic, and Cole's daddy stood there like someone had asked him to perform brain surgery.

From behind came a low, slow chant of "speech, speech, speech!"

Cole glanced back, first spotting the fire chief staring forward. Eric Ward was characteristically stoic in his starched uniform, an extra stiffness in his posture. Lydia Abbott, his sister, sat beside him instead of his wife—no surprise there. The divorce had finally stuck this time. Lydia looked about as happy to be there as her brother. Her husband was, also characteristically, missing.

It was the group behind them—other crew members from the station—who were getting rowdy and chanting the word with increasing volume and intensity. Despite everything between Cole and his daddy and the urge to tear off the damn suit, Cole couldn't help cracking a smile.

It disappeared almost as quickly as it came. His attention snagged on the feminine figure lingering toward the back of the crowd. Glimpses of a yellow sundress flashed between shifting bodies like heat shimmer off hot asphalt. He reacted like a man who'd broken down on an abandoned road in the dead of summer even before he fully registered that he recognized her.

He'd seen her face often enough, even if they'd never met. Being five years older meant his circle had never overlapped with hers. But amid the clutter of family snapshots and sentimental knick-knacks, her picture had been a constant on his parents' mantel the better part of two decades.

The story of why was as familiar as a lullaby. Because Jocelyn Murphy was tied to his family, whether she wanted to be or not. After all, his daddy had saved her life twenty years ago, almost to the day.

She didn't look like the girl in that picture anymore. She was older now, more guarded. Beautiful in a way that had nothing to do with softness and everything to do with the flint in her eyes. Cole struggled to swallow past the dryness in his throat as he cataloged the changes in her since the last photo was placed in the same old frame on the mantel.

He turned to his mama, mostly to keep from staring. "Jocelyn Murphy's here," he murmured.

Ellen lit up. "Is she? Oh, I hoped she'd come." She craned her neck, waving until she caught Jocelyn's eye.

There was a ripple effect, and several others turned to look, too.

Pink tinged Jocelyn's cheeks as folks traded whispers, the added color like a punch to Cole's gut. The visceral reaction almost knocked him over. She waved back, then shifted to fiddle with a piece of her dark hair that'd fallen from her updo, clearly uncomfortable with all the focus that had landed on her.

Ellen ignored the whispers of the townsfolk. "I wish she could sit with us." She bit her lip. "Do you think your daddy can see her?"

Cole's gaze swiveled back to the stage where John was reluctantly clutching the edges of the podium, another flush creeping up his neck.

"Probably can't think beyond whatever he's trying to cobble together for a speech," Cole answered with a smirk.

John cleared his throat as if he'd heard his son's comment. "Thanks, everyone. Really. It's too much, but I appreciate it."

His voice over the loud speaker had the side conversations about Jocelyn Murphy dying down, even if Cole's awareness of her presence did not.

"I never aimed to be anybody special," John continued, staring down at the podium. "Just showed up and tried do the right thing. Hope I got it right more often than not."

Straight-forward. Very John Hauser.

He did a little salute with the award and shook the mayor's hand again as everyone started clapping, a raucous sound that made Cole's hands itch to do anything else but add to the clamor.

With subtlety in mind, he turned to look for Jocelyn in the crowd, but the crew from the station blocked his view as they filed out of their row to rush the stage. Dozens of hands patted his daddy on the back, even while the guys razzed him for being so nervous. He grinned, the ribbing relaxing him, and Cole was reminded that his pop had built himself a kind of family at that station, one he'd never quite got a piece of.

Cole slipped an arm around his mama's shoulders, guiding her into the aisle as she dabbed at her eyes with tissues, beaming so bright it almost hurt to look at her. That was the best part of it all. Her pride was its own glow.

She waded through the crowd to rescue John from all the attention, which kept a steady tinge of red under his already ruddy complexion. Cole followed, though he searched for the dark-haired woman who'd lingered in the back so uncertainly. Like that lost man on the abandoned road, his wish to find her brought the mirage back into view.

The most surprising thing about Jocelyn's appearance, and the reason he told himself he couldn't keep his eyes away, was the fact that she was a grown woman now, a walking contradiction to what he'd believed about her for years. Always relegated in his mind to that little girl in the story, the whispered-about black mark on his town's history, it felt impossible to match this woman to the image that existed in his memory.

Someone bumped him, breaking his concentration, and he turned to see his daddy reach for his mama's hand and tug her into his side. Cole knew the move for what it was—an attempt to deflect the spotlight. As much as Pop hated it, his mama loved the fuss, and John was letting her bask in the shared accomplishment.

People pressed forward, trying to get closer to shake John's hand. A few settled on shaking Cole's or cuffing his shoulder, offering congratulations as if he had anything to do with it. It restarted the buzzing under his skin, and he tugged at his sleeves, trying to fade into the background.

And then there was Jocelyn, closer now even as she still fiddled with the loose lock of hair. She looked like she didn't want to be seen but didn't quite want to disappear.

"Is that Bonnie Murphy's girl?"

The voice was familiar enough, and Cole wasn't surprised to see Edith Wetzel lean in to Harriet Munson like this was the biggest news since the preacher's wife left town. Edith flapped a paper fan incessantly, making wisps of her hair flutter around her face.

"Spitting image," Harriet said.

"Never thought I'd see her around here again, bless her heart." A judgmental sweep of the gaze sent Edith's ridiculous spider-leg eyelashes brushing against her cheeks. "I hope she doesn't ruin the fall festival."

Harriet gasped as if someone had just spit in her prize-winning potato salad. "Heaven forbid!"

Almost like they knew he was watching, both women looked at Cole with a scheme already brewing. Since he was part of the setup committee for the festival, he'd likely be hearing the plot they'd hatch before the day was through.

He'd have to shut that down quick. Wouldn't stop the jaws flapping, but it might send a message to anyone looking to drag him into it.

Wishful thinking.

He shifted his attention back to Jocelyn, hoping that was message enough for the old biddies. She was taller than he realized, and he himself was a tall man. Her hands clutched at the purse she held, her nerves becoming more obvious the closer she got to his folks.

If she'd heard the women, she gave no indication. It was a mild enough conversation, easily ignored. But Jocelyn had been gone from Cedar Hollow for two decades, and gossip could ignite faster than dry tinder in a small town, and it often burned viciously. It would take some thick skin if she planned to stay longer than five minutes.

Big assumption on his part, but it seemed damn wasteful to drive the hours it took to get here and only stay for this one event. And just like that, the shrewd glint in her eyes made sense.

He folded his arms across his front as Jocelyn stepped up to his mama, who reached out to draw her in for a hug.

But almost as if he'd televised his inner monologue, Jocelyn's dark eyes shot straight to his, and he could swear her chin lifted a fraction of an inch, issuing a challenge that was a siren song to the very core of his makeup.

Aw, hell, he was in trouble.

THREE

"The wind forgets, but the flame remembers." -
Matshona Dhliwayo

The things they said about small towns may have been true, but the overly romanticized presentation set an unrealistic expectation for those who'd never truly experienced it. The way people whispered and stared at Jocelyn was downright un-Christian instead of endearing, but it was nothing she hadn't expected.

Nan hadn't thought going back to Cedar Hollow was a good idea, and not just for that reason. It was where she was born, where she'd been raised, and where her remaining relatives still resided, but she'd cut herself off from the history—happy and heartbreaking—a long time ago. The grief made it unbearable for her to set foot in this tainted town.

It held plenty of ghosts for Jocelyn, too. But it also guarded the secrets that had taunted her for years, buried in the ashes and rubble of a burned house that haunted her dreams several nights a week.

Jocelyn expected the searing grief to scrape at the inside of her chest, to knock the wind from her lungs. But it only simmered, hissing for the relief her search for answers would bring.

Then maybe she could let it all go.

"Jossie, why are you asking these questions now?" Nan had asked, irritation spiking her smoker's rasp when Jocelyn had told her.

"You know it doesn't add up, Nan." Jocelyn's own frustration had risen. *"Don't you want to figure out why?"*

Nan had grown quiet, sad. *"It hurts too much, Honeybee."*

Jocelyn had tried to drop it for her grandmother's sake, but journaling every detail she could remember had filled her to the brim with questions she could no longer ignore.

And since Dr. Deb thought the questions were worth exploring, Jocelyn had ignored the guilt, Nan's discouraging comments, and her own good sense, and made her way across state lines, from North Carolina to the southern edges of Middle Tennessee.

Then she'd arrived at the ceremony, the crowd of people that seemed so *cohesive* filling the seats neatly lined up in rows, reminding her what it was to be an outsider.

It was not a new experience, but she'd held some delusion that she would suddenly feel a rightness in the town where her family had deep roots.

All she actually felt were the stares. The ones that rolled the knowing sweep over her, making it clear she wouldn't be flying under the radar. The child of an unwed mother could inspire those judging looks in this part of the Bible Belt.

Ellen Hauser's was the only face that held joy at seeing Jocelyn, which sent a measure of comfort through her, even as Ellen's son, Cole, had stared with no discernible reaction. His gaze was heavy all the same, tracing along her face, pulling the warmth into her cheeks unbidden.

Jocelyn had never met Cole, but in the letters Ellen had sent over the years, she'd talked often of her only child—his years of struggle as the town's bad boy, her elation when he'd started to turn things around and became a respected local business-owner.

And though Jocelyn had never seen so much as a picture of Cole, she knew without question who he was. The way he'd leaned in close to Ellen during the ceremony, how he'd dropped his arm around her shoulders—all a dead giveaway. But it was his appearance that sealed the deal.

John Hauser's face was forever burned into Jocelyn's mind, so she found the similarities in their features instantly, like a snapshot of John had been laid over Cole. There was more of an edge to Cole's looks, though, that glimmer of the bad boy still in the depths of his pale eyes as he looked her over.

It was a whirlwind of people and movement once she hugged Ellen and John, who was instantly swept into conversation with others. Too busy for a proper catch-up, and Ellen gripped her in another embrace before she could leave, insisting on inviting her to their house later so they could actually chat.

Jocelyn tried to brush her off. "I'll be here for a couple of days. We can catch up another time."

Ellen had flapped a hand at her. "Hush now. You know good and well you're stayin' for supper. We'll feed you and welcome you proper."

There was little room for argument, though Jocelyn caught the sour looks from others as she turned, cheeks burning again, to walk back to her car. She'd lost sight of Cole in the crowd, happy to have at least one pair of eyes off of her.

It was under the blanket of heat in her car that she felt the full intensity of her erratic heartbeat. The impact the judging looks had made on her body left invisible bruises she felt to the bone.

"What are you doing here, Jossie Girl?" she asked herself.

And then the worn notebook that sat in the passenger seat caught her eye, the edges of the soft cover curling up from constant use.

Sweat rolled between her shoulder blades, tracing the length of her spine, and she shifted on the sticky faux-leather seat. Answers. That's what she was here for. And she intended to get them.

She drove around in the air conditioning for a while, walking herself through calming rituals she'd developed with her therapist over the years so that, when it was time to head for the Hausers', she'd feel much more in control of her mind and emotions.

She eased off the gas and let the car coast as she wound through the country roads sweeping up and around the lush hills. There was no rush. Just letting the streets rise up under her, familiar and strange all at once, was all she needed to settle herself.

Through breaks in trees, houses peeked from precarious perches on slopes. On the corner, someone had painted the windows of a house-turned-hair-salon with pumpkins and leaves, like that could convince the heat to go. And just like that, she found herself emerging from the rural back into the town proper, where the houses were stacked closer, if not neatly.

Her GPS had her making turns through unfamiliar neighborhoods until it announced she'd arrived. She knew the Hausers' address by heart after twenty years of correspondence, but she'd been gone from Cedar Hollow too long to remember the layout of the residential areas. Not that nine-year-olds paid much attention to those kinds of things in the first place.

She took a breath and got out of the car, gaze never leaving the two-story brick house that sat nestled amid huge white oaks and dogwoods that shifted in a hot breeze. The movement offered no relief from the humidity that had grown heavy in the air as the day had aged.

She blessed the air conditioner stationed against the side of the house, its rumbling growl proof that there'd be comfort inside.

The door opened before she could knock, and Ellen's smile greeted her with such warmth that Jocelyn almost forgot the reason she'd come to Cedar Hollow in the first place. She and Ellen had built enough of a friendship that it felt a little like visiting an aunt instead of someone Jocelyn hadn't actually seen since she was a child.

"Well, hey there, Honey! Get on in this house before we melt on the porch," Ellen crooned, her fingers wrapping around Jocelyn's wrist to tug her into the entryway.

Before she could get her bearings, Ellen pulled her in for a hug, her chestnut hair tickling Jocelyn's chin as she tucked in against her.

"I'm so sorry I didn't get to talk with you at the ceremony, but this is much better than standing in that hot sun anyway!" She pulled back and held Jocelyn at arm's length. "My, you are a beauty, Jocelyn. So statuesque."

Cheeks burning at the unexpected compliment, Jocelyn couldn't collect her thoughts in time to thank Ellen for it before the older woman led her deeper into the house.

Everything had that lived-in feel, rooms cluttered with a mish-mash of antique furniture in a variety of finishes that somehow seemed to fit with the shining wood floors and crown molding and trim. The house was likely built in the early part of the 20th century, and little had changed of its bones, cared for lovingly by this woman who seemed as sturdy and constant as her home.

The air was as blessedly cool as Jocelyn had been hoping, and it helped dry the sweat that had gathered in unmentionable places on her body from the weather and her nerves.

She only got a glimpse into the sitting room to the right and a peek toward the stairs down the hall before following Ellen into the kitchen on the left. She was about to offer to help with the meal when the back door slammed open, hitting shelves of canned goods tucked in a little alcove toward the back of the room.

Cole brushed bronze curls from his forehead, his lips rolled inward in annoyance.

"Grill's going, Ma, but Pop isn't back yet with the steaks." He stomped up the three steps from the back door into the kitchen and stiffened for a second when he spotted Jocelyn.

He'd exchanged the suit for loose-fitting jeans and a gray t-shirt that pulled across broad shoulders. The suit hadn't seemed like his style, and his appearance now fit the image of what Jocelyn imagined a bartender looked like. Never mind that he was the owner of that bar.

"Mind your manners, Cole. Say hello," Ellen scolded when he remained silent.

He shifted to her and ran his knuckles along the stubble that shaded his jaw. "Uh, right. Hello, Jocelyn." He took a halting step forward and offered his hand like he was unsure of the move.

Jocelyn took it and smiled. "Nice to meet you, Cole."

His hand was wide and rough, swallowing hers in its calloused warmth.

Ellen watched them closely as they both fell awkwardly silent. Then she took a breath. "How long are you in town, Jocelyn?"

The question caught her off-guard, her pulse spiking for a second. "Oh, I hadn't decided yet," Jocelyn hedged. "Uncle Joe still lives around here, and I'd planned to visit him for a bit."

Cole glanced at his mama, but Ellen didn't meet his gaze as her smile tightened. The lie was thin, Jocelyn knew. Uncle Joe was Nan's much younger brother, and he was a well-known deadbeat drunkard. Nan and Joe didn't speak, so he wouldn't even know Jocelyn was there, let alone that she planned to visit him. If she even did. It wasn't likely he'd have any answers for her.

"I'm sure he'll be happy to see you," Ellen said with false cheer.

Cole snorted and folded his arms across his chest.

"Steaks incoming!" a voice bellowed from the front of the house.

Jocelyn turned when John came shuffling into the kitchen, his big frame eating up space. With all four of them in there, it was beginning to feel small.

"Jocelyn!" John hollered, shoving the grocery bags into Cole's arms so he could scoop her up. The bear hug eased the hollow ache inside her that her father's absence had carved out long ago.

He released her, grinning as he looked her up and down. "All grown up!"

"Thanks to you," she replied.

He scoffed, waving her off.

Behind him, Cole brought the groceries to Ellen.

"John Hauser, what on earth is this?" Ellen asked, rifling through the first sack. She lifted the tub of ice cream and turned to look at her husband with a brow raised.

Pink crept up the back of John's neck. "We're celebrating, aren't we?" He shot Jocelyn a wink, and Cole shook his head, smirking from behind him.

"You just had that appointment with Doc." She wagged her finger in his face as he crowded close to her, pushing Cole out of their corner and toward Jocelyn.

John's hands landed on Ellen's hips, and he leaned down to kiss her. "Special occasions, El."

She squinted at him. "Special occasion, my foot. You said the same thing last Thursday when you lost twenty dollars to Jimmy Ray."

Cole settled closer to Jocelyn, an amused smile dancing along his mouth.

"I didn't buy the pie!" John argued. "That was all Sissy's doin'."

Ellen slapped at his chest. "And who forced you to eat it?"

"I was bein' polite."

"Pop's supposed to cut down on sugar," Cole murmured.

Jocelyn nodded, expecting as much, but it was hard to look away from the easy affection that bounced between John and Ellen, aching at the what-might-have-been of a scene like that.

"Cole, go on and pour Jocelyn a glass of lemonade and settle in the front room 'til supper's ready," Ellen suggested, her reproachful look still directed toward her husband.

"Please, Ellen, let me help," Jocelyn offered, though Cole pushed away from the wall and walked across the kitchen to do his mama's bidding.

"Oh, no, Honey. You just relax," Ellen said, handing the bag of steaks to John so he could work on seasoning them for the grill.

"But—"

"She doesn't abide arguin'," Cole said softly as he poured the lemonade.

Ellen turned to pat his cheek affectionately before she set to work on whatever fixings she'd planned for dinner.

Jocelyn couldn't help feeling like Ellen was dividing them this way on purpose, and the pinch at the edges of Cole's mouth said he suspected it, too. He still managed a gentle smile as he tipped his head for Jocelyn to follow him across the hall, two glasses of lemonade in his hands.

The floor complained as they shuffled along through the wide cased opening into the modest living room. A small fireplace sat to the left, its mantel crowded by snapshots of memory, frames overlapping each other so it was hard to differentiate any single image.

One picture stood out, though, drawing her forward. The last one she'd sent several years back, not long after she'd graduated college. Tilting her head, she took in the self-conscious smile, the uncertainty that plagued her twenty-two-year-old self obvious in her face. So much and so little had changed.

There were several of Cole through the years. His rebellious stage, not smiling at the camera, his curly hair long and swept across his forehead, hiding half his face. His high school graduation, a picture of him in front of the restaurant and bar he now owned.

Cole set the glasses on the coffee table and settled on a big leather couch the color of butterscotch candy. The weight of his gaze was hard to ignore.

"It's an honor to have my photo up here with all these family memories," she said, desperate to fill the appraising silence.

He leaned into the couch, stretching his arm across the back in a casual way. Very little in his contained stillness seemed casual, though. "Been a picture of you in that frame since that day."

She didn't know if he expected her to react to that or to the reminder of what happened twenty years ago—if he expected a reaction at all. Was he bothered that her picture was included with all the images that cluttered the shelf? It was hard to read him, and it unsettled her. She thought maybe there was a question he wanted to ask, but he didn't voice it.

"It was an impulse," she said, forced into the confession by his silence. "Sending my picture in my thank you letter to your dad."

His eyebrows shifted up a fraction, but he said nothing to prompt her. Another wave of uncertainty danced through her.

"He deserved it—my gratitude. But I also had a lot of feelings back then." *Still do,* she thought. "And I didn't have anywhere to put them. Moving away from everything I'd known after losing my mama like that made me latch onto whatever I could. Writing letters to your parents helped me get my bearings."

The words poured out, more than she'd meant to share, but she stopped before she admitted the most embarrassing part to Cole: that she'd briefly developed a crush on his dad. It was a silly thing a kid in elementary school might do, and certainly understandable from an adult perspective. But it was still uncomfortable to acknowledge that was part of what prompted her to write.

The memory of being cradled against the strong, broad chest while she screamed for her mama was what pushed her to stuff that picture into the envelope. The blue eyes that had held such sympathy, the way he'd said, "You'll be alright, baby girl," in that masculine southern drawl, the faintest molasses in his baritone, had solidified her life-long admiration, though she'd moved on from the childish crush.

"Ma's always enjoyed your letters," Cole said. His eyes were so much the same as his dad's—mournful azure pools that seemed to pierce down to the marrow. A smile tugged one side of his mouth up. "She talks about you often."

Warmth filled Jocelyn's chest, and a twin bloom of anxiety formed in her stomach. Although she cared deeply for his parents, and maybe by extension him, she knew that what she was doing here would ruffle some feathers.

Maybe even theirs. But it was worth burning bridges if it meant getting answers, and she could finally put her mama's memory to rest. Twenty years was a long time to wait for the truth, and too long for those responsible to live scot-free.

Cole's gaze sharpened as if he could sense something hidden behind her expression. Maybe it was in her body language. She *was* twisting the high school ring that'd belonged to her mama around her right ring finger. It was one of few things Jocelyn had of hers after the fire destroyed everything else, and that was mostly because it had been at Nan's house, abandoned after her father had broken her mama's heart years before.

Jocelyn wore a pair of her earrings, too. She'd brought everything she still had of her mama's, hoping those few items would help tether her to the town Bonnie Murphy had grown up and died in.

Jocelyn's heart started its rattling again as she and Cole stared at each other. Her mind screamed that he knew what she was up to, that he thought she was a horrible person for wanting to stir things up, that he might hinder her, or that he'd hate her.

It wasn't until Ellen came into the room with a bowl in each hand that Cole's intense gaze left her.

"Steaks'll be a minute yet," Ellen said, smiling at Jocelyn. "So here's a little somethin' to tide us over."

At first, it seemed like she was oblivious to the string of tension in the room until Jocelyn caught the searing look she sent Cole's way. It only served to pluck that taut string, making it sing discordantly, and Jocelyn shifted from the discomfort.

It's not about them, she reminded herself, even as a part of her shied away from saying something that might ruin what she and Ellen had forged over the years. Jocelyn had been without a mother this long. What difference did it make if she ruined a surrogate bond that had only existed on paper anyway?

Despite Ellen's look and the arrival of snacks, no one said a thing. Ellen cleared her throat a couple of times, and Jocelyn's skin started to hurt from the pressure of the unspoken.

"Gotta let those steaks rest a minute," John said as he lumbered in, heavy as a bear in boots.

It'd been years, but Jocelyn remembered the way he moved, how it felt to be carried by someone that big and capable.

His head tilted as he took in the coiled silence that enveloped the room. "Cole, you been runnin' your mouth?"

It sounded exactly like an accusation. Enough to make Jocelyn look between them, but Cole didn't even flinch. He was still staring at her.

"Jocelyn?" John turned to her since Cole didn't seem to plan on responding.

A debate raged inside her. She'd already lied once, even if they had known from the get-go that she wasn't there to visit Uncle Joe.

Ellen and John watched her now, too, but with benign interest. It was Cole's intensity she couldn't shake, though. His eyes blazed along her face like he could read every thought that went through her mind there, and he was just waiting for that shoe to drop.

"You deserve to know, I suppose," she said, resigned.

Ellen sucked in a breath, folding her hands in her lap like they were about to pray for the meal. John's brows lifted, but there was no worry in his expression.

The bound energy that buzzed like some kind of frequency off of Cole wound tighter, urgently buffeting Jocelyn. She fought an urge to put her hands up as a deflection, reminding herself the onslaught wasn't physical and that she wasn't responsible for how they might take the news.

"The real reason I'm in Cedar Hollow is because I'm looking into my mama's death." The words, spoken so matter-of-factly, bolstered her. "It's always felt like something wasn't right, and I want to know why."

Ellen and John exchanged a tight look she didn't miss but Cole did because he was too intent on her.

But that look, the silent communication in it, twisted something in her chest. "And I want you to know because

I'm going to be digging deep, might stir people up. I can't abide the secrets."

John's big hand rubbed the back of his neck as his gaze shifted away, and oh, that twisting got more painful.

"So if there's something you're hiding," she said, forcing the words over the pain, wishing they weren't necessary, "I'm going to find out about it."

Cole sprang up from the couch. "The hell's that supposed to mean?"

"Cole," Ellen said, her hand shooting toward him.

Jocelyn didn't look away from Cole. "It means nothing if no one is hiding anything."

He cocked his head, jaw tight. "Are you accusing my parents of somethin'?" There was anger in that question, but also something else. Disbelief. Betrayal. Maybe even a little fear.

Jocelyn lifted her chin but was unable to keep from folding her arms across her chest as if it might ward him off.

"Cole, please," Ellen said again.

John was quiet and still.

"Ma, you're hearing this, right?" Cole's frustration filled the space, burned Jocelyn's skin. He turned to Ellen, and then his whole body clenched as he shifted his attention to his father. "Pop?"

John didn't respond, didn't look at him. His breath came heavier than it should've, his silence answer enough.

The disappointment dropped like a boulder in her stomach. The warning had been a courtesy, but she hadn't expected it to go this direction. It shouldn't have been surprising. Too many times, she'd experienced the letdown from those closest to her, and a part of her knew there had to be something there. John had been the perfect paragon of heroism. Of course he couldn't stay on that pedestal she'd set him on.

She swallowed the urge to cry. "I'll get out of y'all's way," she murmured as the Hausers continued to breathe life into the tense moment between them.

No one moved a muscle as she rushed through the entryway and back into the warmth of the afternoon.

Four

"But anger is like fire. It burns it all clean." - Maya Angelou

Heat tore through Cole every time he replayed the conversation they'd had in the living room the night before. The scene rolled through his mind like a movie put on a loop, and he couldn't stop hearing the edge in Jocelyn's voice—sharp and sure, not at all what he'd expected from her.

He'd been knocked sideways already just by her presence; she was the kind of woman that made a man's throat go dry—curves, grace, a fire in her eyes that stirred him up.

But that warning? It hit like a punch he hadn't seen coming.

His mama had gone quiet after Jocelyn left, lips pressed in a tight line as she sat beside his daddy. And Cole had stood by the window clenching his fists like that might keep him from breaking something. Her car was already gone, but he'd stared down the spot where it'd been like he could make her feel his anger.

"John," Ellen had said, soft but steady. Not upset about Jocelyn's insinuation. Not even surprised.

That had stung more than he liked.

He'd spun on his heel to face them, anger fanned by frustration and uncertainty.

Ellen was looking straight at his daddy, who hadn't said a damn word. John's eyes were locked on his hands folded between his knees, shoulders rounded by... shame.

"Pop?"

John lifted his head and let out a sigh like he'd been holding it for years. "I'm sorry, Cole."

"Sorry for what?" Cole had demanded. Even now, his gut tightened, dread clawing up his throat remembering.

"I haven't been straight with you about some things."

His mama's hand had run circles along his daddy's back as she sat quiet and resigned. Which meant she'd known for a long time. Of course she had. Betrayal had pierced him then, and it drilled into him now. He hadn't been ready for it.

Still wasn't.

But the trees out here didn't give a damn. They just stood tall and steady, and that steadiness kept him from snapping in two.

Still, the hammer felt too light in his hand as he squared up the studs, framing out the wall that'd stand between the kitchen and living room. It was all just wood and nails for now, but something sturdy and reliable would stand here one day. And right then, he needed sturdy and reliable.

Evenings or early mornings offered the only bearable times to be out working on the house, which was barely more than a slab of foundation at the moment. Good thing it wasn't much more than concrete because his hands itched to tear something apart.

Hammering the shit out of this frame was a good second option.

When something rattled loose in him—anger, nerves, whatever—he ended up out here on this patch of land that'd been in his mama's family for generations. It belonged to him now, after his granddad had moved to an old folks' home.

Right now, it was the perfect place. No cell signal, no distractions. Just quiet.

He was supposed to be up at the high school, hammering together booths and platforms for the festival. Could've offered the same busyness to soothe, but he didn't have the patience for small-town chatter, not when everything in him felt half a step off. Not enough for most folks to notice, but he sure as hell did.

Problem was, it pissed him off how something like this could get under his skin that easy. Felt damn near dramatic, and that just made it worse.

He wanted to lay the blame on Jocelyn's doorstep, but it was more than that.

Cole had never fully shaken the resentment toward his daddy's job. It'd taken John from them more than it gave. While his daddy was off pulling shifts at the station, it was just him and his mama for days at a time.

Sure, what his daddy did was noble—important, even—but there were times it felt like he had a whole other family. A crew of men Cole had called uncles that he'd envied deep down. Those boys had gotten John for full days and nights, built something with him Cole could never touch.

To a kid starving for time, it looked like a feast behind glass.

By the time Cole hit middle school, he was already a handful—bitter as week-old coffee and twice as hard to swallow. He was fourteen when his daddy pulled Jocelyn out of that fire—the one that took her mama. Whole thing threw Cedar Hollow into the spotlight. News crews swarmed the station, their house, the scene. And Pop? He got pulled even further away. Giving interviews, shaking hands, getting honored like a damn hero.

All it did was make the gap at home wider.

Cole understood the weight of it, an ordinary man saving a life. That kind of thing stuck with folks. Made them see you different. But he resented it all the same. It turned his daddy into something untouchable. The Hero. The man who always did right.

Took him a long while to see how much that fed the anger he carried. Longer still to work his way through it and come out the other side—if he even was.

Maybe that was why his parents didn't tell him about John's addiction until last night—how close it came to taking everything from him. He and his daddy had only just started rebuilding from the wreckage between them, and this new truth was near to knocking the whole thing sideways.

So yeah, Cole got it. Sort of.

His jaw ached from grinding his teeth, and the hammer damn near slipped out of his hand, missed smashing the other one by an inch.

He let out a string of curses and dropped the hammer, running both hands through his hair like he could get a grip on more than just the mess in front of him. That old anger still burned hot—same as it did when he was a kid. Felt like fire under the skin, hard to hold and harder to put out.

Maybe that was why he hadn't followed in his daddy's footsteps. Fighting fire felt too much like what he'd been doing his whole life inside himself.

Cole spent years hearing folks whisper how they couldn't believe he was the son of such a good man. The kid getting suspended for pulling fire alarms, vandalizing half the town, shoplifting at the general store, drinking before he could drive, and chasing skirts—or slipping 'em off any girl who'd let him.

It was a hell of a long way from where he stood today as a man who'd built himself a damn good business, never missed a payment, and could be counted on to lend a hand whenever the mayor cooked up some fool town shindig. But deep down, he was still the same ornery cuss he'd always been.

And maybe that was what kept the rage going.

The sun had burned through the morning haze, turning the treetops gold, and he quit what he was doing to walk his property, hoping it'd clear his head before he had to go back and open The Hammered Nail for the Sunday after-church crowd and all the tourists who flooded their little town this time of year.

Thirty minutes in, and he gave up, heading back to the restaurant sooner than he'd like. He pounded up the back steps to his place above it to throw on his running gear. Since he couldn't shake that damn buzzing in his head, he figured to try beating the hell out of himself on a long run, even if he couldn't stand the actual running part. It was what it did for him afterward that made all that misery worth it.

Seven miles down and a cold shower later, he felt halfway human again, if not exactly calm. Coming down to the bar, he ran his hand along the banister he'd fixed up himself, checking his work without even thinking about it while he listened for voices coming from the kitchen.

The Nail used to be a sad-sack saloon whose owner had run it into the ground after inheriting it from his grandfather, who'd—rumor had it—won the thing in a poker game decades back. It had lasted longer than expected as a haunt for derelicts before its doors closed when Cole was a teenager.

After high school, when Cole was bouncing from one dead-end job to another, those boarded-up windows caught his eye more than once. For ten years, he'd walk by and cook up bigger and bigger schemes for what he could do with the place until his eyes had grown too big for his stomach.

Once he scaled back on the ideas, realizing he didn't have to think so outside the box, he'd stewed on the idea of a bar and grill for a year before he approached his cousin Terra to go in on buying the place.

Walking through the wall of heat created by the kitchen like some sort of humid curtain, he emerged behind the bar to survey the atmosphere they'd curated, that sense of pride filling his chest like a balloon.

He'd done most of the renovation himself. Busting his hide for contractors right out of high school had its perks.

There was an extra measure of satisfaction knowing that this was the result of his literal blood, sweat, and tears, especially when a lot of the space was already occupied only forty minutes after opening for the day.

He sidled up beside his cousin Terra, who was busy pouring a Belgian beer they had on tap for the month. "How's it going?"

She didn't glance up. "Steady. I figure we'll get slammed soon. Lunch rush."

It was a standard report, nothing surprising for a weekend. The tourists always came through for the trails and waterfalls—big draw every year. The falls really were something to see, and the cool mist was about the only mercy this late-summer heat offered.

"Need help?" he offered.

"I got it, Cole."

Terra didn't ask for or receive help unless she really needed it. Pushing forty, raising two boys on her own, she was built tough as nails. Didn't mean she didn't have a heart buried under all that steel, but she kept it tucked away. He respected that about her. It made her a damn good partner to run a business with.

Since she'd given her answer, he moved on, making the rounds. Folks expected smiles, handshakes, a little small talk. Not his strong suit, but owning a business meant he had to play along.

"Cole, that was such a nice ceremony for your daddy yesterday," Sylvia Dayberry said, leaning forward to snag a fry off her husband's plate. Walt just smiled like a man used to losing battles.

Cole's gut tightened. He forced a nod. "It was."

"He sure deserves it." Her hand went to his forearm, giving it a light squeeze.

He nodded again, swallowing a surge of heat crawling up his throat. She meant it. Everybody loved his daddy. The man had poured himself out for this town—ran calls at the firehouse, patched roofs for widows, organized clean-ups, hauled lumber for the community center. Hell, he even checked on neighbors just because he could.

But the new secret Cole carried about him was a bitter taste he couldn't spit out.

He drifted, doing the rounds on autopilot, until—

"Cole, just the man I was hopin' to see."

He caught his grimace before it broke loose and turned. Henry Wetzel was waving him down.

"Henry," he said mildly, glad that at least Edith wasn't with him.

"The girls were telling me y'all had a special visitor at the house yesterday after the ceremony."

Apparently, Edith not being there didn't matter.

Cole took a slow breath, bracing his hands on his hips. "That's right. Jocelyn Murphy came all this way to honor Pop."

Henry shifted but pressed on. "How long is she staying?"

Cole sucked his teeth, let the silence drag a beat. "Don't know. Why?"

Henry's gaze darted around, his face souring. Age sat heavy on him, sagging his lids over those small, dark eyes, though he was somewhere around his pop's age. "Well... she isn't exactly a welcome sight."

Cole resisted the urge to roll his eyes, but only just. "Sounds like a personal problem, Henry."

Henry leaned in, shoving his plate aside. "We're just worried what it means for the festival."

There it was. Cole's hand went for Henry's empty glass, more for something to do than anything. "Why would it mean anything?"

"Well, you know how the ladies get." He waved a pudgy hand like female feelings were gnats in the air. "The festival matters—heritage, tourism, all that."

Cole's jaw ticked. "Tourists don't give a damn about Jocelyn bein' here." Locals, though... They'd eat themselves alive if she so much as breathed wrong.

Henry winced as if a phantom of his wife had slapped him. "Now, listen. You know who her mama was, right?"

Cole leaned heavily on a long-suffering sigh, jaw shifting forward.

Henry was undeterred. "She was from the wrong side of the tracks, as they say. Lots of family scandal. You know

Bonnie's mama and daddy got married just because she was pregnant, and then he up and left when Bonnie was barely a baby? And her grandaddy was the town drunkard. Apple don't fall too far from *that* tree." His brows bounced with the words.

A slow, mean burn settled in Cole's gut—sparked by that pile of judgment he hadn't invited. "Didn't sign up for the biography."

Henry held up both hands. "Alright, alright. I know your mama's close with her, and your daddy, too. I figure they probably won't be too happy to hear about any schemin'. But we all know how you feel about... things. Maybe you can find a way to, I don't know, encourage her to move along?"

Cole's whole body clenched. Henry had pressed the right button there, and that just pissed him off more. "What makes you think I could do any damn thing?"

"Because she's young, she's pretty, and you are—" He gestured at Cole.

"Young and pretty?" he supplied, tone flat. The last thing he needed was to spend his time trying to convince Jocelyn Murphy of anything.

Henry grinned. "Exactly."

Cole squinted. "Don't you reckon me trying to charm her would backfire?" He lifted a brow. "Curse of being too good-looking."

Henry's grin flattened, his brows following suit until they folded into a deep furrow.

"Best let it be," Cole said, spotting his mama stepping through the door. Should've figured she'd show. She always gave him a little space when he was heated but never too much that anyone could forget about it.

"Cole—" Henry started.

"We'll talk later," Cole cut him off, already moving.

"There's my boy," his mama said, and he bent to kiss her cheek.

"Hey, Ma."

FIVE

"Fire is never a gentle master." - Proverb

Though Jocelyn had seen it in news reports and pictures growing up, she had never stepped inside the Cedar Hollow fire station. The brick building loomed before her, older than most of the city itself.

Standing there stirred her resolve. The visit with the Hausers had shaken her confidence, but two days of lying low had steadied her, and she needed to get her focus back.

She hitched her purse higher and pushed through the administration doors. Passing the bay where the engines were parked, a glimmer of childlike curiosity tugged at her. She understood why kids loved school tours here—the unknown world behind those doors held its own kind of power.

"Help you?"

She jerked upright at the voice. A woman stood with a file in hand, sandy brows raised. She was probably in her mid-forties, fit despite being a little top heavy, with blonde hair pulled up into a tight ponytail. Wispy bangs fell across her tanned, gently lined forehead.

"Um, yes," Jocelyn began. "I wanted to speak with the chief."

The woman's shoulders rolled back, making the buttons on her crisp uniform shirt pull tight across her chest. "About what?" Her gaze raked over Jocelyn from head to toe, like she was trying to place her. If she'd known Jocelyn's mama, she didn't seem to make the connection.

Jocelyn couldn't help shifting under that tight appraisal. "I had some questions about a fire from about twenty years ago."

If possible, the woman's squint got narrower, her brown irises nearly disappearing. "Why on earth—" Those eyes popped wide. "You're the girl from the Hill Drive fire."

Jocelyn's fingers curled involuntarily into her palms, but she managed a nod. "I want to understand what happened. Were you there?"

Sympathy softened the lines in the woman's face, and she melted in a maternal sort of way. "No, I wasn't. I came to this station about seven years ago from Knoxville. Big fire fatality in a town like this, though, you hear about it, even years later."

A bitterness cloaked Jocelyn's heart. "Fatality," she repeated. "That was my mama."

"I'm sorry, Honey." The woman gestured toward a row of chairs. "Let me see if the chief's available. I'm Amber—I handle admin around here."

"Jocelyn." She managed a thin smile as Amber disappeared toward the offices.

The plaque beside the door announced it belonged to Chief Eric Ward. The name tickled in the back of Jocelyn's mind, but she wasn't sure why.

The other office was marked for the deputy chief, Gabe McCann, and she wondered if he'd also been around that night.

Amber returned with a rangy, copper-haired man in tow. Chief Ward's still-handsome, weathered face shifted with something more than just recognition. She couldn't be sure what it was—maybe nervousness? If he had been there that life-changing September, he'd know exactly who she was.

"Jocelyn Murphy," he said, his quick gait eating the distance between them in a matter of seconds.

She stood as he stretched his hand to her. "Hello."

"God, you look just like Bonnie," he murmured.

The words burned against her skin, and she resisted the urge to jerk her hand back.

Ward dropped her hand, shaking his head. "Sorry. I know it's probably painful to talk about her."

Jocelyn took a breath, smoothing her expression, though a storm brewed in the back of her mind. "I forget what it's like to talk to people who knew her."

He nodded. "Y'all moved away, didn't you?"

This was at least neutral territory. But if she was going to pursue this case, she needed to get her head on straight and face it all without tripping up. "Yes, Sir. Nan had a friend out in North Carolina who helped us get settled."

"I've been out that way a few times. Let's talk in my office."

Jocelyn ran her hands down the skirt of her dress and nodded, following him back. Amber gave her a reassuring touch on the shoulder as she passed like she had some understanding of loss.

Ward's office was spare and immaculate, blinds raised to let in full daylight. Awards and diplomas lined the walls, but only one photograph sat on the desk—a dark-haired woman with sadness carved into the lines of her face.

He caught Jocelyn looking, and his right hand moved to his left, as if feeling for what was not there—a wedding ring. It had been there not long ago, though. A tan line remained, as did a faint indentation in his skin. Trouble at home, then.

"So, Jocelyn," he said, scooting a pile of papers out of his way, "what did you want to talk about today?"

His discomfort matched her own, if for different reasons. Faced now with her opportunity to ask her questions, she found herself floundering in uncertainty.

But she swallowed, steeling herself. "As you know, I was young when... the fire happened. I don't remember a lot of the details. Bits and pieces, of course, but I'm trying to understand what really happened that night."

Ward studied her, but she wasn't sure what he was looking for. Maybe he was still thrown by her resemblance to her mama, maybe by the fact that she was almost the exact same age.

He dipped his chin once, apparently approving of whatever he saw in her expression. "Alright. We'll start with what I know. You can ask me any questions you have, and I'll answer what I can."

Jocelyn nodded, rubbing her fingertips along her thumbs. She had to prepare herself.

"I was about ten years into my career with the department," Ward said. "Think the call came in around ten p.m.? Some of us had turned in, but I wasn't asleep yet." He looked at the desk between them as he thought back. "I remember we rolled out fast, headed down First Street. When we turned onto Hill Drive, we could see the flames before we even got there."

Hearing it from this side felt a little less like walking through her own trauma. It was just a recounting of a story. But it still pumped her blood faster.

"That was a concern," he continued. "Dry year, trees too close. If they caught, the whole block would've gone." He caught the way she was staring at him and paused.

She had never considered the possibility of the fire spreading. As a child, her whole world had been that little house, already ancient even twenty years ago. Run down, though Mama had wanted to fix it up a bit. Their landlord wouldn't allow it. But the fact that it wasn't only about her home, or her mama, made her realize how narrow her focus had been until now.

Ward leaned back, clearing his throat. "John Hauser had been nearby. He'd already gotten you out by the time we arrived."

That was a memory that still had teeth. Being huddled in John's arms, watching the flames consume every inch of that house when the sirens screamed behind them, the flashing red painting the trees. She remembered thinking the light was there to outshine the burning shade of angry that fire seemed to wield.

In memory, the fire always felt angry, consuming out of spite.

It had always seemed miraculous that John had been there, but it struck her as odd now. Jocelyn frowned. "Nearby?" she repeated. "Doing what?"

Something in Ward's face shifted, expression tightening. "Was his day off." He shrugged. "Said he was out walking.

Saw the fire, saw you in the window. It's in his nature to step in."

His words sounded like a compliment, but something about them felt like stiff bristles along her skin.

"It's what any of us would've done," Ward added. "Thank God he was there."

She swallowed, thinking about what might've happened had he not been. Then her heart ached for what might've been if only he'd gotten there ten minutes sooner.

"By the time we pulled in," Ward said, voice softer, "the house was engulfed, burning too hot and high to get into. We knew your mama was..." He paused, head lowering.

A fist of emotion pressed against her sternum. By that point, only minutes after she'd been pulled out, her mama was already gone. Jocelyn had lost her before she'd even woken up.

"By then, it was only about containing the fire and keeping everyone safe."

This she knew from reading the news reports about it. It was too far gone to do more than wait it out. But there was still that question that plagued her, that had haunted her steps since she was that little girl in the window.

"What I don't understand is why she didn't wake up when the fire started."

He shrugged like it was a simple matter of a misunderstanding and not her mother's life. "The fire started in her room. Candle by the window caught the curtain. Medical examiner found alcohol in her system."

Jocelyn's temper had her heart thumping harder. "I remember her drinking a glass of wine before I went to bed, but that was it."

"Might've had more after." His fingers curled slowly into his palms, though his gaze was steady on hers.

Jocelyn's body went rigid with her rising anger. "Even so, if something had caught fire, she would've tried to put it out. And if she couldn't, she would've come to get me. She would've gotten us out."

The tension wound tighter through her, but he expelled a breath, loosening his fists.

"I'm sorry, Jocelyn." He shook his head. "I don't have an explanation for that. If all that were true, that's what would've happened. I wish it'd gone that way. Honestly, I do. But the best we could figure, she was too intoxicated to wake up."

The burn of tears stung in Jocelyn's eyes. It was stupid to get hung up on that, but it still didn't make sense. It didn't seem right.

"Why don't we call it a day?" Ward suggested. "This is hard, and I want to make sure I give you the right answers. Let's meet again on Wednesday after I've had time to look at the reports. Does ten a.m. work for you?"

She couldn't force words past the lump in her throat, so she simply nodded and stood, letting him guide her from his office.

Six

"The fire doesn't make you what you are; it reveals what you were." - Jack Hyles

C ole was about ready to lose his damn mind.

Everywhere he turned, folks had Jocelyn Murphy's name on their lips—whispering about how she was here to ruin Harvest Fest, acting like she was some storm blowing in to tear the town apart. And for some reason, everyone thought *he* had the inside scoop.

The number of times he'd been stopped in the past two days, he might as well have been wearing a sign that said: *I know everything there is to know about Jocelyn Murphy. Please ask me.*

And it wasn't just Henry Wetzel.

Kiki Womack marched into the bar at half-past one with her chin jutted so far forward she looked like a bulldog spoiling for a fight. She didn't even pretend to glance around for a table, just made a beeline straight for him. Cole stuffed his stylus behind his ear like an old-school reporter, setting his tablet aside. He'd been trying—and failing—to run through inventory before the next rush.

"Miz Kiki," he said, leaning both hands on the bar, already braced for the ambush. His tone carried a layer of exasperation he didn't bother to hide.

She wedged herself between two stools, glaring up at him with the look that had made him quake as a boy. Even now, a chill crawled up his spine, reflexive as a kicked dog.

"That Murphy girl went into the fire station to talk to Chief Ward," she huffed, her hair unmoving under the assault probably thanks to half a can of hairspray.

"Not illegal last I checked," Cole said evenly. Truth was, he didn't give a damn what Jocelyn did, but Kiki was in his mama's book club, and crossing her meant grief for Ma. Kiki Womack was a copperhead—best left alone unless you had a stick in your hand.

"I know Henry Wetzel talked to you about this."

Cole cut her off, patient to the point of sarcasm. "And Edith, and Wheezy Harrington, and Beatrice Eckstrom. I'm keepin' a list if you'd like to see it. Most run with you, though, so you probably knew already."

Her lips pinched flat as she ignored that last bit. "How many more of us need to complain before you do something?"

"Ma'am," he said, trying for polite but slipping into petulant, "I am one man. With *zero* sway. Why y'all keep comin' to me about this, I'll never understand."

That only poured gas on her fire. She jabbed a finger close to his nose. "You best have pride in this place that took you back after all your many failings, young man. We need this festival to go well—all of us."

Words dried up on his tongue as she spun and stormed out. Sweet Southern exterior or not, Kiki had venom—and he'd just gotten a mouthful of it. He half-wondered if her late husband hadn't just keeled over one day from too many doses.

But the worst part? Her words had landed. Right in the spot he hated most—the part of him that *did* feel like he owed Cedar Hollow for taking him back. The prodigal screw-up. The one who'd burned every bridge once, then came limping home.

"You don't owe this town a damn thing, Cole," Terra muttered from the end of the bar. His cousin knew exactly which bruise Kiki had pressed on. "Festival ain't your responsibility. And it sure as hell ain't dependent on whether Jocelyn Murphy sticks around."

Didn't matter. He still felt the sting.

By the time the lunch crowd thinned, he was half-convinced he ought to march to Jocelyn's hotel and run her out of town with a pitchfork—if only to get the locals off his back. His head ran through every ugly angle: he could be rude, push her away, maybe even lie about something his mama'd said that'd cut her off quick. But the thought of wounding his mama like that had him stopping short.

She had made it clear the day before—she understood his feelings, but she and his daddy loved Jocelyn and wanted her to find peace. That was enough to keep him in line.

So he busied himself with inventory, taking orders, and running dishes until the tension in his shoulders eased.

Then the front door opened.

Cole didn't even have to look to know who it was—something in him just *knew*. And when his gaze landed on Jocelyn, every bit of noise in the room drained out like a damn movie scene.

That sundress she wore wasn't doing him any favors, but it was the way she carried herself—braced and uncomfortable—that struck him harder than the curve of her waist.

Then she walked straight to Frank Leone at the bar. The man went pale as milk, blinking like he'd seen a ghost. Cole tensed, half ready to call an ambulance.

"Cole?" Dave Hume's voice cut in, snapping Cole's focus back.

"Yeah—hang on." He didn't even look at Dave, who'd been in the middle of ordering dinner, before moving toward Jocelyn and Frank.

The conversation was too quiet to hear, but the strain in their faces was enough to draw the attention of others around them. Even Terra was watching, her sharp gray gaze flicking between Cole and the pair at the bar.

Frank didn't last long. He shot up from his stool, leaving his half-full beer on the bar, and stormed toward the door. Jocelyn stayed behind, sinking into the empty stool like the air had been punched from her lungs.

Cole approached before he'd thought better of it, and the first words out of his mouth were the wrong damn ones. "First you threaten my pop, and now you're chasin' off my customers?"

The way her body tightened, shoulders to neck, had him hating himself instantly. He slid between two stools—one over from her because he needed that space—and leaned an elbow on the cedar bar like he wasn't rattled.

"I didn't threaten anybody." Her voice was sharp but not cruel. More blunt than biting, like she was holding something back. Tears, if he had to guess.

It made him want to apologize immediately, but the rebel in him wouldn't allow it. "Not in so many words."

When her eyes met his, dark and unguarded, he had to look away. He directed himself to the liquor shelf behind the bar, ticking through the bottles, cataloging which needed restocking. The routine grounded him, gave him something solid to hold onto while every inch of his body reacted to her presence like she was a live wire.

"I came at y'all from left field," Jocelyn admitted, her voice softer.

Even the lift and fall of her shoulders was a rush on the air that vibrated against his skin.

"I owe your dad my life," she went on. "I thought it was the right thing to be upfront about why I'm here."

Cole inhaled, catching the scent of fried chicken, beer, and something warm and sweet that could only be her. Vanilla, maybe. He shoved the thought away before it dug in.

"Honorable of you." He tapped his fingers against the bar, keeping his hands busy when all they wanted was to reach out, to undo that ponytail and lose himself in the softness of her hair.

Redirect. *Redirect, damn it.*

"Hungry? Whatever you want, on the house." He pushed away from the bar before he lost every ounce of control.

She gave him a long, narrow look, eyes sharp but sparking with something else underneath—something that pulled at him, dangerous and magnetic all at once.

That was all the proof he needed to back off. Folks wanted him to scare her off, but he knew better now. If he kept leaning in, he wasn't going to drive her away—he was going to get tangled up in her. And he wasn't sure he had the strength to untangle himself after.

He lifted his hands in surrender. "Consider it an apology."

Her eyebrow arched, one dark slash above those alluring eyes. "Not sure I deserve an apology."

"Then call it a welcome gift. A courtesy." He shifted closer, playing with fire as he bent just enough to murmur near her ear: "Don't make this harder than it needs to be, Darlin'."

He thought he saw her shiver, though she tried to hide it.

For a half-second, he felt like he had the upper hand. But the truth hit harder than whiskey—he wasn't in control at all.

He was already undone.

SEVEN

"Keep a little fire burning; however small, however hidden." - Cormac McCarthy

F rank Leone's reaction to Jocelyn had been as visceral as it was surprising. He'd called her *Bonnie* at first—just like Chief Ward had—as if the name clung to her face the way grief clung to his eyes. For a moment, she'd felt the old ache of being her mother's mirror, a truth she could forget in the years away from anyone who had actually known Bonnie Murphy.

Nan was the only one who'd ever said so, and even then, only rarely. When she did, it came with the weight of loss, her weathered hands somehow so silky soft against Jocelyn's cheek like she was stroking memory itself rather than the girl in front of her.

When Frank whispered Bonnie's name, pale and stricken, Jocelyn couldn't help but wonder if he truly saw *her* or the ghost of the woman he'd once loved. Either way, his rebuff made more sense.

Maybe she shouldn't have cornered him in public. Twenty years seemed long enough to wear down grief to something smoother, easier to carry. One would think. But devotion left sharp edges long after the world expected otherwise—and Frank had been her mother's boyfriend for two years before the fire took her.

Jocelyn would leave him to his ghosts for now and soothed her bruised pride with the plate Cole had offered on the house.

As she picked at the last of her food, sulking, Cole's arm crossed into her vision, the tanned skin corded with muscle and veins like a road map that pulled her eyes upward against her will. He didn't look at her as he collected Frank's half-drunk beer, though the slight frown at his mouth betrayed his thoughts.

"Did he pay for that?" she asked.

Cole's gaze flicked to hers, sharp and brief. "No."

"Let me cover it. I'm the one who chased him away."

His mouth curved—not quite a smile, more like the idea of one—and he leaned forward, forearms braced on the bar in a way that crowded the space between them. "Frank comes in here regular enough. I'll catch him next time. Or I'll eat the cost. Don't worry about it."

Then he took her empty plate, too, disappearing toward the kitchen. The casual kindness scraped at her. She didn't want to owe him anything. With a stubborn pang, she slapped a twenty on the bar before leaving.

Cole's gaze followed her out. She felt the weight and the warmth of it even before she turned and caught him. He didn't look away.

Outside, she drew in a deep breath, though it wasn't enough to quiet the thrum beneath her ribs. Cole Hauser carried an intensity that made her chest tight, and she wanted no part of it. Women in her family had a disastrous instinct for men. Bad taste, bad timing, bad luck—it didn't matter which. The result was the same.

Her father, Daniel Abbott, was proof enough. Not a deadbeat exactly, but worse in some ways—willfully oblivious. He hadn't even known she existed until kindergarten, by which point he already had a wife, a daughter, a whole separate life that had continued to move without Bonnie or Jocelyn in it.

Nan hadn't fared better. Her own father had been a cruel drunk, and her husband—if you could call that five-minute relationship a marriage—had high-tailed it as soon as Bonnie was born. Generations of Murphy women repeating cycles like a song no one knew how to stop humming.

Wisdom said distance from Cole was safest. Wisdom said to focus on the fire, on the truth. Wisdom was the only thing that ever saved her from her own emotions.

And yet.

Later, in her hotel room, her thoughts circled Frank again, his ghost-struck expression gnawing at her, until sleep pulled her under and into the fire's red maw. She woke choking, heart thrashing, and for a moment she was nine again—smoke curling under her door, angry flames clawing between the wood and the floor like a beast looking to devour.

She managed to breathe through it, but the fear still pressed down, an echo that hadn't dulled with time. That night, as a child, she'd called for her mama through toxic air, until John Hauser broke through her window, glass raining like stars, and carried her out. Even now she could feel the rough strength of his arms, the sheer miracle of breath returning.

When the nightmare refused to fade, Jocelyn got up and pulled her battered notebook close. She retraced her notes and timelines like a ritual, pressing facts and memories into place. But each line reminded her of absence and grief.

The day her childhood ended, she hadn't even been with her mother. Nan had picked her up instead, an apology falling from her lips as soon as Jocelyn had climbed into her beat-up minivan.

"Last-minute change, Honeybee," Nan had said. "You're coming home with me."

Jocelyn had accepted it, content to spend the evening in Nan's cramped apartment. That was as much a comfort as her own space.

When she'd gone home, her mama had been alone. And sad. Jocelyn remembered asking about Frank. Mama'd brushed the question away too quickly before offering her a piece of fresh-made lemon pound cake. Jocelyn had let it go then—child that she was.

She'd had cake, and Mama had sipped her wine.

And then she was gone.

As an adult, she saw the cracks. The distance. Something had happened, and Frank Leone was the thread she needed to tug.

Cole had said he was a regular at The Hammered Nail, but that was likely an evening ritual. She'd have to bide her time until he showed up again, even if it meant she'd haunt the place every evening until he did.

Part of her wanted to hide in her hotel room forever. She hadn't missed the looks and the whispers of the locals whenever she went out, but those things couldn't be a deterrent if she wanted what she came for, no matter how they stung.

Determined to prove just how untouched she could be, she got up, got ready, and found herself out on First Street. She wandered with no real intention of buying anything, only catering to the need to keep her mind from spinning endlessly over Frank's pale face and Cole's weighty stare. Window displays became her refuge—bright distractions against the burden she carried.

When the bell over a shop door jingled and a couple emerged, voices sharp with an argument, it took her too long to recognize them. Daniel and Lydia Abbott. Her father and his chosen family.

Her pulse kicked hard, and she ducked into the nearest boutique, slipping behind a mannequin like a child hiding from monsters. It wasn't fear so much as unwillingness. She had no energy to confront the people who had built a life around erasing her.

From her hiding place, she watched them pass, their clipped words heavy with a kind of practiced resentment. Not a rare fight, then, but the sort of chronic friction that wears people down grain by grain. A strange pang stirred in her chest—anger, pity, maybe both—but she stuffed it down and turned away.

Might as well get something out of this turn of events.

The boutique smelled of warm vanilla, enveloping her in sweetened nostalgia. It was her mother's favorite scent, and that detail alone softened her enough to step toward the racks. She let fabrics whisper through her fingers, indulging in the quiet pleasure of texture and color, until a voice startled her.

"Hello! Sorry for keeping you waiting!"

Jocelyn turned, heart stumbling, and froze. The woman who entered from the back carried her own ghost—familiar but altered by time. Natasha Abbott. Her half-sister.

They stared at each other, the moment stretching like warm molasses.

"Um, hi," Natasha said, her voice unsteady.

"Hi," Jocelyn echoed.

Memories sifted up like dust motes. They'd gone to the same school for a time but had never spoken beyond the unavoidable. Lydia had seen to that. And now, here they stood, grown, opposite in almost every way except for the faint trace of Daniel Abbott in their long frames.

The contrast between them struck Jocelyn hard: her own chestnut hair, her mother's brown eyes, against Natasha's salon-gold waves and pale blue stare. Two women made from different halves of a man who had never known how to hold them both.

"What brings you in?" Natasha asked, smiling with a practiced warmth that didn't seem false but did feel... cautious.

Jocelyn hesitated, then gestured vaguely toward the door. "I was just..."

Natasha's brows rose when she didn't finish.

Jocelyn waited another beat but couldn't bring herself to lie. "Hiding."

"Hiding?" Natasha repeated.

She exhaled. "Yeah. From... your parents." Her fingers curled into her palms. "They were arguing."

Natasha sucked in a breath, her cheeks flushing. "Oh."

"I didn't want to make things weird...er."

Natasha reached up to tug on a shiny gold hoop at her earlobe. "Well, they make it weird enough for everyone." Her mouth tipped sideways. "They do that. A lot."

The honesty loosened something in Jocelyn, but not enough to quiet the ache beneath it. She wanted to say more, to explain herself, but words tangled.

Natasha, thankfully, shifted the conversation. "Anything strike your fancy? I can help you find something."

The moment rebalanced, and Jocelyn let out a breath. "I haven't had a chance to really look yet."

Natasha moved easily, flipping through a few pieces on the rack, glancing at Jocelyn sidelong. "I've got some linen pants in longer inseams. Figured you might understand the struggle." She gestured down her body.

Jocelyn gave a startled laugh, surprised at how natural it felt. "Yeah. We definitely have that in common."

The words hung between them, heavier than they sounded. A reminder of what they shared and what had always separated them.

"That would be great," she hurried to add.

Natasha nodded with a smile and headed back to where she'd come from. Jocelyn released a captive breath. After twenty years, this was a hell of a way to run into her sister.

A sister who was a stranger.

Circumstances had made it impossible to have a relationship before, but it hadn't stopped her daydreaming as a kid. Connection had always been something she'd longed for and feared in equal measure, and this was no exception. This time, the stakes were higher, and she was just waiting for it all to come crashing down.

"I can get you a dressing room to start," Natasha said, walking back with a couple of pairs of beige colored pants draped over her arm. "I guessed on size since I forgot to ask, but I'd imagine it's close to mine."

Jocelyn nodded as Natasha led her to the dressing rooms. She slipped inside wordlessly, closing the door, and changed slowly, letting the fabric slide over her skin, airy and soft. The pants fit perfectly, and with that came the sharp pang of recognition—same body type, same blood-line. She stared at her reflection, unsettled, feeling both invaded and exposed.

By the time she stepped back out, Natasha had drifted behind the counter, busying herself with hangers.

Jocelyn held up the pants. "I'll take these."

Natasha beamed. "Great. I'll give you the employee dis-count."

"You don't have to do that," Jocelyn protested. "Won't you get in trouble with your boss?"

Natasha's laugh was light, real. "I am my boss."

The revelation knocked the breath out of Jocelyn for a moment. "You own the shop?"

Her shoulders scrunched in a self-deprecating shrug, but her smile was quiet pride.

"That's... amazing," Jocelyn said softly, meaning it.

Natasha beamed at her again.

Jocelyn paid quickly, too aware of her own awkwardness.

"Thank you," she said, taking a hold of the bag as Natasha passed it over. Her fingers wrapped tight around the shopping bag as if it could anchor her.

"Anytime," her sister said, the sincerity plain in her steady gaze.

Uncertainty pirouetted through her like an untrained dancer, but she headed for the door. The bell jingled again as she stepped outside, and she nearly dropped the bag.

Lydia Abbott stood in front of her.

The other woman's surprise smoothed in an instant into a practiced grace, that mask of southern poise Jocelyn had hated as a child. Behind it, though, Jocelyn saw the flicker—the same one she'd seen years ago, every time Lydia had looked at her like a problem that wouldn't disappear.

For one breath, Jocelyn thought she might crumble under the collision of past and present. But then she lifted her chin, bracing herself like she always had.

"Hello, Lydia."

EIGHT

"Stars, hide your fires; let not light see my black and deep desires." - William Shakespeare

Cole grunted as he hauled a case of liquor bottles off the edge of the delivery truck, carrying it in through the front door. The alley between his place and the next was too narrow for the lumbering vehicle to squeeze through, so the front was the only way in.

He didn't mind the work. It gave his hands something to do, especially after Daniel Abbott had already stopped by that morning to bug him about selling his land—a familiar song and dance—and soured his mood. Luckily, Terra had backed him in sending Abbott on his way by demanding he help bring the morning load in. Not that she needed Cole's help to get inventory shelved; the delivery guy was doing most of the heavy lifting with his hand truck anyway.

When Cole stepped back onto the sidewalk, he stopped dead. Jocelyn was across the street, walking away from Natasha's boutique with quick, clipped strides.

Every time he saw her, it was a sucker punch to the gut—enough to rile his already short temper.

Until he caught the glint of her tears.

That had his boots moving before his brain decided anything. He crossed the street in two long strides.

"Hey," he called, jogging to close the gap. "You alright?"

Her chin trembled, another right hook to his stomach. "Fine," she managed, but it wobbled so hard, he worried she might lose her balance.

"Come on." He wrapped a hand around her arm, ignoring the heat that shot into his palm at the feel of her skin. "Don't make me drag you—we'd get the rumor mill rolling."

She shot him a look but let him steer her toward the only decent coffee spot in town—Gert's place, just a couple doors down.

The next town over had a chain grocery store with a Starbucks inside, but folks in Cedar Hollow would never be caught dead buying that over-roasted bean water. Not with Gert pouring shots of espresso at Southern Comfort.

He found a corner table, just in case Jocelyn wanted space to cry it out, though the place was quiet this late in the morning—after the work rush and before the teens that swarmed once school let out.

He opened his mouth to ask, but she beat him to it: "Iced latte."

The misery in her voice twisted him up, but he gave a short nod and went to order. Gert—half-covered in tattoos, dreadlocked, and entirely out of place in small-town Tennessee—gave him a pointed look toward the table. He didn't bother explaining, and she left it alone.

They'd gone to high school together, raised a little hell in some of the same circles. Both of them straightened up around the same time, though she'd lit out for some hippie farm up in northern California before drifting back home to take over her aunt's old bakery. Turned it into the coffee shop folks kept in steady business.

Most everyone kept their mouths shut about her appearance these days. There were the gossipy old biddies who kept their pearls nice and shiny from clutching too often, but nobody with sense paid much mind.

When he came back with the latte and his own Americano, Jocelyn had dried her tears, but her attention was still fixed out the window. He slid her cup over and sat.

"If I ask again if you're alright, would you give me a straight answer?" he asked, brow raised.

She looked down at the cup in her hands. "You already know the answer, whether I say the truth or not." Finally, she lifted her face, meeting his scrutinizing look with a certain glint in her eyes.

Damn, she was beautiful like that—heat in her gaze, steel in her spine.

"What got you all worked up?" he asked. He'd already noticed the boutique bag by her feet; maybe she'd run into Natasha. He couldn't picture Natasha being unkind, but stranger things had happened.

Jocelyn blew out a breath, the sound wobbling. "Oh, just Lydia Abbott."

That tracked. Lydia wasn't one for outright rudeness, but she could be as vicious as Kiki Womack. Just more subtle.

"What'd she say?" Cole's tone was flat, but his blood was already warming at the possibilities.

Jocelyn rotated her coffee on the table to keep her hands busy. "She made a comment about how much I look like my mama." Her lips flattened. "'I suppose some things just can't be helped,' she said."

Cole's jaw ticked, but before he could speak, Jocelyn added, "It is what it is. She made it clear she suspects why I'm here."

"What makes you say that?" His hand was tight around his own coffee cup, the heat seeping into his palm steadying his mind.

"'Your mama had secrets, Jocelyn. Some women do.'" She nailed Lydia's nasally drawl. "Like I should let them lie."

"You're not giving up, are you?"

She jerked to look at him, brows up.

"Ma thinks you deserve your answers."

"Do you?"

The question hit him square in the chest. He shifted in his seat. "Isn't the case closed?"

Her gaze stayed locked with his a beat longer before she looked away. "Never felt like it added up."

Cole tapped a rhythm against the side of his cup, curiosity getting the best of him. "Like what?"

She pulled her bottom lip between her teeth, drawing his attention to her mouth. He'd been ready for a list of reasons, but his mind went tripping over the thought of what those lips might feel like against his.

"It doesn't make sense that my mama didn't get out of her room that night." Her eyes narrowed on that coffee cup, the clear plastic sweating almost as bad as he was trying to steer his thoughts somewhere safer. She worried at the edge of the lid with those long, easy-moving fingers of hers.

Leaning in, he focused up. "Alright, Darlin'. I'll bite. Why?"

Taking a breath, she began: "The fire started in her room. They said a candle caught the curtain."

He didn't know much about the nitty-gritty of the fire. He'd been fourteen at the time and already on his path of destruction. The hubbub surrounding that night only sent him down faster.

"Okay," he said, trying to understand the importance.

Her focus remained on the coffee she hadn't even taken a sip of. "But she didn't keep candles over there."

"Maybe she moved it."

"Maybe," she acknowledged, but he heard the doubt there. "But how come she didn't notice?" Jocelyn cut a look to him. "Do you know how long it takes for a house to go up?"

It was clear the question was meant to be rhetorical, this line of thought obviously well-worn.

"Ten minutes?" he tossed out anyway.

She smiled a little, having expected that. "A new build, yeah. Less, actually."

Because he was a firefighter's son, her knowledge trumping his irked him. There was one thing he knew for a fact: very few houses in Cedar Hollow had been built later than the 1980's. And even though he didn't know much about the fire, he did remember that house. It was older than most.

"That house wasn't new."

Her smile grew, even if it was grim. "No, it wasn't. It would've taken closer to twenty minutes for it to be fully engulfed."

He squinted at her. "Wasn't it at night? She might've been asleep."

"Chief Ward said the call came in sometime around ten. I woke up around then, and your dad got me out before the fire truck arrived. By the time they pulled in, the whole house was on fire, and they couldn't get in."

He tapped the tabletop with a finger, trying to nail what it was she was getting at. It felt just out of reach, so he grasped onto the details he could follow. "So probably started sometime around 9:30-9:45."

She was excited now, pink brightening her cheeks and lighting up her eyes. "Right. Tell me, what time would the average adult go to bed?"

He clicked his tongue, her point solidifying. "Around that time—*if* they're early-risers."

She was leaning forward now, too, breathing his air. "My mom was a night owl since she usually worked the later shifts at the diner."

He shifted back, not wanting to let her proximity get to his head again. "You don't think she was asleep."

"No, I don't. Ward tried to feed me some line that she'd been drinking. I'd seen her drink a glass of wine myself, but that was a pretty regular thing for her, and she didn't like being drunk."

It was only a faint shadow, the doubt easy enough to ignore. Plenty of others had. "Then what do you think happened? She was there when it started, didn't try to put it out, didn't come for you."

Her shoulders lifted. "That's why I'm here. To do the math myself—because none of it adds up."

He studied her. "*None* might be stretchin' things."

The brightness in her face dimmed like a lightning bug going out as her walls slammed back into place.

"I'm just playing devil's advocate, here, Darlin'," he said, softer now, a little mad at himself for putting out that light. "Hell, all I know about that fire is everyone wanted a piece of Pop. It stole him away from me for a long time." He hadn't meant to say that last part and looked away when her expression softened.

She took the hint and sipped her coffee.

"I'm just sayin'," he went on after a minute, guarded again, "folks agreed with what was in those reports for a reason."

Her scowl said she didn't think they should've. "Yeah. They would."

The bitter words stung his skin, wending their way into his chest, oddly deep. Like she was indirectly accusing *him* of something, though she wasn't. Couldn't be.

"That supposed to mean?"

Her chin jutted forward. "You know what they called my mama?"

A flash of irritation shot through him. Layers of cemented anger and resentment were coming to the surface, decades of history that she was holding onto like he should take it, too. But he had enough of his own to lug around.

"No, can't say as I do." He sure could guess, though, based on Henry Wetzel's comments the other day.

"White trash." She shook her head, the anger simmering like a flame in her dark eyes. "Only time anyone treated her well was when she dated my dad in high school."

"Daniel Abbott," he said. He didn't know much, but he knew that.

She nodded. "Golden boy quarterback. Parents owned half the town and couldn't abide that kind of mark on their family. Sent him away to college, and he came back with Lydia on his arm—someone they approved of."

Cole watched her expression change, watched the way she nibbled on her lip again, how she twisted her fingers together. The emotion was there, staring him in the face. Her upset about Lydia's words made sense.

It never occurred to him how much drama there was surrounding her life—aside from the blaze. He was a few years older, and their paths never crossed back then. The whispers about him around town made it easy to miss what they might've said about her. Made him realize how selfish he'd been as that angry teenager.

He leaned back, tongue in his cheek, trying to fit the pieces into the puzzle he only knew a small portion of. High school sweethearts, but Daniel had married someone else. He knew Daniel's other daughter well. Natasha was about the same age as Jocelyn, if he remembered correctly. Within a year or two, which meant...

Jocelyn raised a brow, knowing what he must've been realizing. Daniel had been a very busy man. So who was first?

The fact that he was married to Natasha's mom, Lydia, told the truth there.

Jocelyn waved her hands back and forth like she was trying to erase that part of the story. Maybe she wished she could.

"That's a therapy session for another day," she muttered.

His mouth quirked up, though she didn't smile at her own quip.

"Even if people's opinions of my mama weren't at play—and don't tell me it's not when they were quick enough to believe she was so drunk that she didn't wake up to a fire in her room—there's still one big thing not mentioned in any of the news stories."

He picked up his coffee for a sip. "And what's that?"

"There'd been a string of fires around town at that time. Suspected arson."

Cole froze, coffee halfway to his mouth.

NINE

*"Sometimes, what's dead must be burned away to make
room for new life." - Cristen Rodgers*

Nothing boosted Jocelyn's ego quite like landing
that line and watching Cole take the hit. His brows
slowly lowered over those pale blue eyes, his shoulders
pulling tight.

"Suspected arson," he repeated, setting his coffee down.

She'd already noticed his hands—long-fingered, calloused, more like a craftsman's than a restaurant owner's—and dragged her stare from the cup he'd set a little
too hard on the table. "Still unsolved."

He leaned forward, expression shrewd. "What do you
mean by 'a series'?"

A dark chuckle slipped from her, half frustration, half
thrill at making him work for it. "For the year before my
mama's death, there'd been several suspicious fires—hous-

es, businesses. Always accelerant, always strategic ignition points. No victims, no connections. Different methods each time."

He frowned and looked out the window, chewing on her words.

That burn ignited in her stomach again. Someone was finally listening. Other than her therapist—who didn't know the half of it—no one had cared enough to hear her out. Nan avoided the topic. Friends acted like it was some late-night crime show they hadn't subscribed to.

And so, Jocelyn licked her lips, eager to drop her next bomb. "The weirdest part?"

His head swung back, expression wary.

"They stopped after the fire that killed Mama. Look it up. How many fires since that night?"

"Hell if I know." His gravelly mutter sent a shiver down her spine that she ignored. "But judgin' by your face, not many."

Her grin broke before she could stop it. Their gazes locked for a beat or two before he allowed his own crooked smile.

"Next thing I know, you'll be stringin' up maps and red yarn on my restaurant wall."

She lifted her hands. "I just did research." And had a meticulously pieced-together journal dedicated to the whole thing, but he didn't need to know that.

"Just a regular Sherlock over here," he said, the corners of his mouth curving.

She raised a brow. "Don't tell me you want to be my Watson. I don't think you'd take orders very well."

He huffed a laugh. "Pegged me there." Shaking his head, he reached for his coffee again.

It felt to her like a distraction, a way to keep his smile from breaking wider. Whatever it was about this that amused or intrigued him didn't matter. She just appreciated the fact he'd let her lay it all out. It felt good to walk through it with someone.

"So, what's next?"

"Frank Leone."

He squinted one eye at her. "Explain."

So she did.

Even with Cole as backup this time, Jocelyn's palms grew clammy with anticipation as she waited. Two hours earlier, she'd explained Frank's connection to her family until Cole had to leave to open the restaurant. Afterward, she'd wandered over to the general store to get something for lunch and went back to her hotel room, forcing herself to concentrate on design work for a client in North Carolina. Normally, she would have finished the project quickly, but distraction dragged her under again and again.

Her thoughts kept circling back to her impending meeting with her mama's old boyfriend, making everything take twice as long.

That anxiety had spiked the moment she walked into the Nail—Cole's affectionate shorthand for the restaurant. The name had stuck, adopted by locals who treated it as their regular hangout. Rustic-industrial, classy and masculine without being overpowering, the place drew a clientele that ran the gamut of income and background.

On this side of the restaurant, the bar ran twice as long she was tall, the top a solid plank of cedar. Its epoxied surface gleamed under the copper pendant lights hanging above, drawing focus to its rich caramel color. Jocelyn twisted sideways on her stool so she could watch the door, the smooth coating beneath her palms the only thing keeping her steady.

Frank Leone worked as a mechanic in the next town over and often stopped at the Nail after work for a beer and burger a couple of times a week. As far as Cole knew, Frank had never settled down with anyone after her mama, though he admitted he made a habit of not sticking his nose where it didn't belong.

Jocelyn had been too young to fully understand her mother's relationship back then, but she'd known enough—Bonnie didn't make a habit of introducing boyfriends to her daughter. Frank had been different. Serious. A regular fixture in their home, talking about marriage more than once. Her mama had never outright said no, but looking back, Jocelyn wondered if she'd ever wanted to say yes.

Despite her mama's reluctance, Frank had seemed over the moon for her, which explained the way he'd reacted to Jocelyn the other day.

After Bonnie's death and before Nan decided to move them, Frank had come to see her a lot. But in those weeks after the fire, Jocelyn often felt she was consoling him more than the other way around. The day she and Nan had left, he'd given her a tight hug, told her he'd be in touch, and then she'd never heard from him again.

As a girl, the sting had been sharp, too many layers deep to heal quick. He'd been the closest thing to a father she'd known, and her world had been upended. But there were more important things now than chasing an apology from a man who'd clearly never moved on himself.

When she spotted Frank as he walked into the Nail, it seemed like he knew she was waiting for him. His gaze swept the room, posture hunched as if bracing for hurricane-force winds. The tension radiating off him mixed with her own, winding her tighter.

"Buy him a drink."

She stiffened, glancing backward.

Cole was busy pouring a beer behind the bar, his face tipped down to make it less obvious that the words had come from him.

Frank caught sight of her just as she turned forward again. He stood frozen for a moment, his expression making Jocelyn wonder if he'd turn and walk out. He surprised her by clenching his fists and squaring his shoulders, pushing through his reluctance.

With his compact build, black hair and wide-set dark eyes, his Italian heritage was apparent in both his features and his surname. In her memory, he'd moved with more of a swagger, but just then, he seemed a little brow-beaten.

"Hey, Jossie," he said stiffly, sliding onto the stool beside her.

"Hey, Frank." She faced the bar. "Can I buy you a drink?"

He shrugged without looking at her. "Sure."

Cole appeared, setting a beer in front of him. The two men exchanged a look Jocelyn couldn't read, leaving her with an inexplicable sense of exclusion that ran deeper than the moment. She rolled her shoulders to chase away the feeling.

Cole moved on, leaving the silence to stretch between her and Frank. What sat in that gap was heavy, and her heart strained under the weight of it.

"I'm sorry about the other day," she said, trying to ease the pressure. "I shouldn't have come at you like I did."

Frank shook his head, never looking away from the beer in his hand. "No, I'm sorry. I was off-kilter, and I didn't handle it well." He finally lifted his head, meeting her eye. "God, you're the spittin' image."

Heat rose in her cheeks. She wasn't sure if she was flattered or unsettled. Especially knowing how in love with her mama he'd been.

He turned away. "It just knocked me sideways."

A glass appeared in front of her—an old fashioned. Jocelyn blinked, then looked up in surprise. It was a good guess, but even if it hadn't been, it was a quiet gesture of support she wouldn't have expected, even from Cole.

She gave him a grateful smile then took a sip to steady herself. "How have you been, Frank?"

He lifted a shoulder and brought the beer to his lips, maybe to buy time—either to talk himself into being honest or to carefully craft a falsehood. The air felt heavy with both.

"Been alright," he said finally. "Plenty to complain about, but plenty to be grateful for."

Diplomatic. So neither. Or both.

She tapped on the sides of her glass, waiting for the liquid courage to kick in. "Well, I guess that's good."

Sighing, Frank folded both arms on the bar and turned to her. "Jossie, why are you here?"

She winced, taking a long stall sip. So much for easing in. The hurt and history between them had more of an impact than she'd care to admit. Why couldn't there be some part of her that wasn't bruised?

If anyone knew how the town had treated them, how badly her mama had wanted to leave Cedar Hollow, it was Frank. With his offers of marriage more than once came suggestions of moving, starting over somewhere people didn't know them. Frank would know there wasn't much reason for Jocelyn to come back now. The case was closed, even if none of them were healed.

She swallowed and almost told him the truth, but instinct held her back. His grief was still too obvious. She settled on a half-truth.

"I'm the same age Mama was," she said softly.

Frank went rigid, staring at her until he forced himself to take another drink of his beer. It would've looked normal but for his tension.

"I guess I just wanted some way to feel connected to her again. To understand her life as it was back then. My therapist encouraged me to... to find some closure."

Frank's jaw ticked.

"Anyway, John's award ceremony was an excuse to come. But she's the reason I'm staying for a little."

He rubbed a hand over his mouth, taking a long moment to digest that—or to hide what he didn't want her to see.

She let him have the time to process and glanced down the bar. Cole was pouring drinks at the other end, but his attention was angled toward them. He said something to someone, his gaze unwavering.

"So why talk to me?" Frank's tone held an edge she didn't understand, like he blamed her—the nine-year-old who left—for the silence that had followed.

She turned back to him, ignoring that new sting. "You were part of our lives," she said carefully. "You were important to her."

"Was I?" His fist tightened around his glass.

"She wouldn't have brought you around if you weren't." Jocelyn hesitated, thinking of how perceptive she'd been as a child, and how much she'd still missed.

Frank gave his head a small shake. "I loved your mama." The unspoken words echoed beneath what he said: *still do*.

Jocelyn had seen it the other day, the way his face lit at the sight of her, sending him to another time and place, before he realized she wasn't—couldn't be—Bonnie. It made her reluctant to ask the questions she truly wanted to. But one memory pressed forward, something she felt wouldn't tip her hand too far.

"Did you take Mama out that night?" she asked.

Frank drew a breath and looked upward, irritation edging his sigh. "I don't remember, Joss."

"Nan had me most of the evening," she pressed. "So I thought maybe you'd had a date."

"Probably. She was off that night, right?" His tone carried paternal exasperation, as if they were discussing something as trivial as her teenage spending habits.

From the other end of the bar, she felt Cole's focus settle on them again, the curiosity like a caress. Maybe the interaction wasn't as mundane-looking as she was hoping. It was just as well. She felt like her shoulders were tucked into her ears.

"Yeah," she said quietly, trying to concentrate on Frank. "How come you didn't stay after?"

His head snapped toward her. "What?"

"Why didn't you stay over like you usually did? You always made the best French toast."

Something like fear darted across his face for a moment. "I-I don't remember, Jossie. I'm sorry I wasn't there. I wish I had been. Maybe if—" His words broke off into an unsteady exhale.

Jocelyn bit her lip, feeling the weight of his grief. It was heavier than hers, unworked and raw. Pity filled her when the understanding settled more solidly that he truly hadn't moved on.

"It wasn't your fault, Frank." She placed her hand on his arm.

His eyes jerked away. He patted her hand once before pulling free. "That's about all I can handle tonight, Hon." He drained his glass and reached for his wallet.

"It's on me," she said quickly.

"No, it's not." He tossed cash on the bar and leaned down to press a kiss to the top of her head. "It was good to see you, baby girl."

She cupped her glass with both hands, blinking back tears as he walked away.

Several minutes passed as the Friday night rush pressed in, the room filling with chatter and movement. Jocelyn finished her drink, tasting none of it.

TEN

"Tradition is not the worship of ashes, but the preservation of fire." - Gustav Mahler

Cole's pencil scratched out an uneven rhythm as he scrawled measurements along the two-by-four he was about to cut. He stuck the pencil behind his ear, hefted the board to the table saw, and lined it up. The saw sat in the stale shade of the old house his granddad had grown up in—a Depression-era craftsman so small it made more sense as a shed than a home.

Sometimes Cole wondered how a family of seven had managed to cram inside it without killing each other.

Once his own house was finished, he figured he'd turn this place into a workshop. Sure, it could serve as a guesthouse, but who the hell would he ever host? He barely knew anyone outside Cedar Hollow, and the truth was, he didn't much care to.

The saw roared to life, drowning out the sound of a car crunching across gravel, but when Cole shut it off, the footsteps that followed rang out clear enough through the open windows. His sweat-soaked shirt clung to his back, proof of how useless his attempt at airflow had been. He ripped off his goggles, swiped a forearm across his brow, and waited.

A tall, lean figure filled the doorway, and Cole saw where Jocelyn got her height from.

His mood soured at once, his expression following quick behind. He'd already been trying—and failing—to shake Jocelyn Murphy from his head, but this unwelcome visitor did nothing to aid his efforts.

Daniel Abbott.

The older man smiled politely, pretending not to notice Cole's scowl. Abbott wasn't a fool. He was just annoying enough to make a man wish he was.

"Don't have the energy for you today," Cole grumbled, snatching up his water bottle. He nearly chucked it at the man but settled for an angry gulp instead.

Daniel's hands skimmed the stack of two-by-fours Cole had in the corner before stepping inside to lean against the wall, casual as a house cat. "You've been busy. Making good progress." He nodded toward the framed out first floor several yards out.

He looked too much like a proud father as he ignored Cole's dismissal completely.

Cole snapped the lid back onto his water. "Answer hasn't changed, so don't bother."

Abbott shrugged, unfazed. "Foundation's in the wrong place. You'd have a better view up on the hill."

Cole's jaw tightened. He set the bottle down too hard; the thunk was loud in the quiet. "Would've had to clear out trees and carve a new drive."

Daniel only nodded as he scanned the room, taking in every board, fixture, and antique Cole had piled up from auctions and shops. His gaze never landed on Cole, but that wasn't because of nerves. He was just being nosy as hell.

"I'll pay all the materials on top of the offer," Abbott said smoothly. "Got clearance to offer you more than anyone else can."

It was the same tired dance. Abbott had chased after the land for years before Cole inherited it, and now he was back at it again. Fifty acres that developers wanted to parcel into a subdivision. Cedar Hollow's "future."

Not if Cole had anything to say about it. The town did just fine without chain stores and traffic jams. Tourists came for the nostalgia, the waterfalls, the changing leaves. Growth was overrated.

"Stop wastin' my time." Cole's voice dropped to a growl.

Daniel's grin went from affable to shrewd. "You and Joe Murphy," he muttered. Then, pointing like they were sharing a private joke, he said, "I'll get you both somehow."

Cole had heard enough. He shoved his goggles back on and fired up the saw as answer. The machine screamed to life, drowning Abbott out until the other man sighed and slunk away.

Cole cut through two more boards, slow and deliberate, rounding edges that didn't need it. Anything to keep Abbott—and the name he'd dragged into Cole's head—from lingering.

Damn Abbott for planting her in his thoughts when she'd already taken root deeper than Cole cared to admit. He hadn't shaken the charge of her presence since she'd walked back into town, and it'd only gotten worse the more he'd interacted with her. Playing with fire.

When the saw finally went quiet again, another car crunched across the gravel. Cole's tension eased this time as he recognized the white sedan.

Just as his mama got out of her car, he stepped onto the sagging porch. He leaned a shoulder against the old post, ready to dump the rest of his water bottle over his head to cool off. The temptation to wait until his mama had walked up the stairs and was in the splash zone tugged strong. He'd been a respectable citizen for far too long, and it was high time she was reminded of the scoundrel she'd raised.

But her dress was mighty pretty, and the temptation passed quickly enough.

"Well, aren't you a picture," he said as she grinned up at him, her lips painted red.

"Oh." She tutted and waved him off, stopping a few feet from the steps.

"What, no hug for your boy?" he teased.

She gave him a shrewd look. "I saw that glint of mischief in your eye, Cole Hauser."

He laughed, the sound shaking loose the last of the bad mood Abbott had left on him.

"What are you doing all the way out here?" he asked, taking another swallow from his bottle.

"Checking in," she said lightly, but her eyes betrayed her. Watching him, weighing him.

Cole grunted his skepticism.

She winced, caught. "Still mad at your daddy?"

He shrugged, the move painfully dismissive. "Why would I be mad?"

"Cole." She started up the broken steps.

"I'm not mad, Ma."

She froze at the snap in his tone.

He vented a heavy sigh and worked some calm into his voice. "I'm not."

"Then why haven't you been by?"

"Busy."

"Your dad—"

"Oh, did Pop say somethin'?" Cole cut in, voice dry.

"No. It's like nothing's happened."

Cole snorted. "I'm sure."

"Cole." Her tone snapped this time, poking at that old rebellious streak in him.

He wrestled the feeling back.

"I'm not mad," he repeated, softer now that it wasn't a lie. Bothered, sure. But bothered and mad weren't the same thing. Not anymore. "Just got a lot going on. Abbott's been breathing down my neck, and with Jocelyn back in town, folks are panicking like she's fixing to ruin Harvest Festival or some shit."

"Watch your mouth," Ellen said automatically, though without heat. "Who's worried about Jocelyn ruinin' anything?"

"Everybody. Been stopped ten times easy by folks asking about her. Can't blame 'em—she's ruffling feathers."

His mama raised a brow. "Most notably yours."

Cole swiped a hand through the air. "I've been nice, like you asked." It came out a growl, childish at the edges.

She smirked. "Then what's really bothering you, baby?"

He dropped onto the one section of porch rail that wouldn't collapse under him, scowling at the tree line. "That Pop lied. That people keep actin' like I can influence Jocelyn. Like she's mine to handle." He stopped short of admitting the rest—that Jocelyn was under his skin, dug in deep.

Didn't matter. His mama's knowing look said she'd read it anyway.

"Come by for supper tonight," she said, brushing her hand down his arm. "Bring Jocelyn."

He groaned. "Ma…"

"I'll bake your favorite pie."

"What about Pop's diet?"

"Special occasion," she crooned, patting his cheek in triumph. She seemed awful sure when he hadn't agreed to any damn thing.

"I've got the restaurant. Sing-o night."

"Tomorrow, then."

Cole sighed, knowing he'd already lost. He'd never been able to say no to her. For all his grumbling, there wasn't a thing he wouldn't do for his mama.

Eleven

"Fire is the test of gold; adversity, of strong men." - Seneca

Clouds rolled overhead, thick and restless, but they offered no mercy from the heat. The only reprieve was the brusque wind that slapped at Jocelyn's linen pants—the new ones she'd bought from her sister's shop. She felt oddly self-conscious in them, as though the fabric itself might betray her, whispering where she'd gotten them, feeding small-town mouths with new fodder. She half-expected whispers to grow teeth, to attach meaning to a simple purchase, to paint intentions she never had.

She tried to push the thoughts away as she walked from the coffee shop toward the fire station. The woman who ran Southern Comfort had remembered her from when Cole brought her, even remembered her order. She'd been warm in a way that left Jocelyn momentarily light. That buoyancy held until she reached the fire station's front door, where the old dread came back and pooled in her stomach, a heaviness that pressed cold and uneasy.

Amber sat at the front desk again, and she smiled at the sight of Jocelyn, though her glance skittered nervously toward Chief Ward's closed office door. His voice was audible, low and curt, though Jocelyn couldn't make out the words. The tension was plain enough, though.

"Hi, Jocelyn." Amber looked toward the door again. "The chief is on the phone, so he might be a little bit."

"That's alright. I can wait." Jocelyn took one of the lobby chairs, folding herself neatly into it.

Fifteen minutes later, with Ward still shut away, she pulled out her laptop and buried herself in work for her Asheville client. The familiar rhythm of design notes kept her hands steady, if not her mind.

"I'm sorry," Amber said a while later, her tone a bit exasperated. "It was a call from his lawyer, so he wasn't prepared for that."

Jocelyn gave her a polite smile. "It's no problem at all."

It was another twenty minutes before Ward finally emerged, his face flushed. He caught sight of her sitting there, and a brief flash of anger burned in his eyes before he blinked and looked down at his watch, swearing under his breath.

"Jocelyn, I'm so sorry. Lost track of time."

"I don't mind." She tucked her laptop away, though anticipation rose sharp in her chest, like a match catching flame.

"I don't have as much time to offer you," he said, motioning her into his office.

Her face pinched despite the smile she tried to hold in place. "Whatever you can offer me would be incredibly helpful."

Ward busied himself straightening papers on his desk, releasing a long breath as if her presence itself wore on him. "Even if we had more time, I'm afraid I don't have much in the way of the information you'd asked for."

Her heart sank. "Nothing?"

He sat. She didn't.

"The report says more or less what we already talked about. The candle by the curtain in the master was the origin. Your mama was in that room, but she made no attempt to put it out."

"Where?" Jocelyn's voice came sharper than intended.

He blinked, unsettled. "Beg pardon?"

"Where was she found?"

A pause stretched, heavy with calculation. "On the floor."

"The floor," she repeated flatly. "Where on the floor? Near the window? The door?"

Ward's lips went flat and pale. "Between her bed and dresser."

The words sliced at her. For years, she'd pictured her mother asleep, swallowed in smoke and flame before she ever stirred. But between the bed and the dresser… That meant she had to have woken up, moved, tried to get out—tried and failed. And failed in a place farthest from escape.

"Can I see the report?" Jocelyn asked.

His hesitation was a physical presence. "It's public. You can request a copy through the usual legal channels."

Her brows drew together. She *had* requested it. The copy she'd received held none of this detail. So either he had access to a different version… or there were things he knew that weren't in the report.

She hated the thought, but suspicion rooted itself anyway.

Ward sighed. "I only suggest it because I'm not legally allowed to release it to you. It has to be through the legal route. For record integrity."

"I see," she said flatly.

He checked his watch, already rising. "I'm out of time today. If there's another day you'd like to come by, you can check with Amber about my schedule."

He shepherded her out despite her lack of response, and she gripped the strap of her bag tighter to keep the frustration in check. Without much more than a nod at Amber, he marched out the front door.

Amber stared after him, frowning, before she turned to Jocelyn. "I'm sorry about that. He, uh, is going through some stuff right now."

Jocelyn tilted her head. "Trouble at home." She let it fall as a statement, not a question.

Amber's sharp look confirmed it. "Yes."

The glimmer of success warmed her, inspiring her to press further. "The chief said I could ask you to make me a copy of the report from the fire."

Amber stiffened, uncertain. She looked to his office as if he were still there. "I suppose so. I'll have to see if I can find it."

She disappeared into the file room while Jocelyn's nerves crawled across her skin. Amber's uncertainty tainted her confidence. But minutes later, Amber returned with a stack of papers.

"There's a lot here to scan individually," she said. "Why don't I take care of that, and you can come on by a little later? That way I can take care of some of my other duties, too. There's a lot on the docket today."

Frustration threatened to unravel her politeness, but Jocelyn wrestled it back. Better this than refusal.

"Thank you," she said, quiet but sincere.

"You're welcome, Honey. You check on back in a couple of hours."

Outside, the air felt heavier. Her steps to the car dragged, as if she walked through water. Not a failure, she reminded herself. Just another waiting period.

Always waiting, she thought.

Inside the stifling car, she turned on the engine, letting the air cool her skin while her mind replayed Ward's words. Her mother, on the floor. Awake. Moving. Trying. Why hadn't she made it farther? Why stop there?

The questions gnawed at her as she drove, keeping her too occupied to realize where she was headed. It wasn't until she slowed the car in front of the empty lot where her childhood home once stood that she came back to herself. Only the foundation remained. A blank scar where her life had fractured.

Sometimes it felt like it had never existed. Like her mother had been a dream she'd told herself too many times.

This time she turned into the overgrown driveway, weeds brushing the tires. Green blanketed everything but that blank spot where the house should've been.

Those dream-like memories played in her head like an old movie, projecting faded and skipping scenes of a slight, dark-haired woman running through the sprinkler with her little girl on a hot July afternoon, squealing every time the cold water sprayed them.

Or those cooler autumn nights, when Jocelyn would sprawl across her mama's lap as she pushed them back and forth on the porch swing with one foot, humming her current favorite song. Bonnie's fingers would trace along the skin of Jocelyn's arms, sliding back and forth in time with the sway.

Her memory played other things. The buzz of cicadas, the slap of the screen door that hung crookedly against the frame, the creak of the porch step that always announced someone before they got a chance to knock.

Frustration leaked out of her like an old radiator, leaving behind a hollow ache as memory whistled through those echoey halls. Despite the southern heat that pressed against her body like a wool blanket, scratchy and uncomfortable, a chill rattled her on the inside.

"Can I help you?"

The voice was like that wool blanket—scratchy and warm—but Jocelyn turned more quickly than she meant to, and the woman halted, taking one step back. Gray-green eyes went wide, and the color leaked from her leathery cheeks as she took Jocelyn in.

"I'm sorry, Honey." She pressed a hand to her ample bosom. "But my word, it's like seein' a ghost."

Jocelyn inhaled slowly, bracing herself against the sting. It would always sting, being told she was her mama's shadow.

"Ms. Etta, right?" Jocelyn asked.

"That's right. I s'pose you weren't so little you wouldn't remember."

"I couldn't forget the chocolate milk and cookies you gave me." And the way flashing red and white lights had painted Etta's living room that night. And then Nan had arrived, whisking her away before the fire was even contained.

Etta sighed wistfully. "My bakin' days are behind me now. Diabetes." She gave Jocelyn a rueful look. "But I'm glad I made an impression."

Etta made no move to head back across the street, and Jocelyn glanced at the empty lot again. It sang to a loneliness she felt down to her bones.

"Why didn't anyone rebuild?" she wondered aloud.

Etta huffed a mirthless laugh. "That'd be on Ned Turner."

Electricity rippled along Jocelyn's body like there was a storm brewing. Ned Turner was their landlord back then. She remembered very little about him except that her mama was always complaining about him.

"What do you mean?"

With a frown and a shake of the head, Etta said, "The house was worth more gone than standing. Ned tried to sell the place out from under your mama, but he never could get anyone to bite. After the fire, insurance said he had to build and live there before he could sell it. He chose to keep the land and take the payout. The money's all he wanted anyway."

The breath stuck in Jocelyn's throat. Ned Turner. A name she'd skimmed past in every old file. He'd only ever been mentioned in passing, as if the town itself wanted to skip over him.

"I wouldn't be surprised if he'd set the fire for the insurance money," Etta added.

Jocelyn tapped her fingers against her thumbs. "He still live in town?"

Etta nodded, those eyes piercing Jocelyn with keen understanding. "You lookin' into this fire, baby girl?"

There was censure in her tone. Suspicion, too, and maybe even the edge of anger. But it was the *baby girl* that slammed Jocelyn back to that night. The way Etta's long, fake nails had tapped against the glass of chocolate milk before she'd handed it to Jocelyn. The shimmering pink lacquer had mesmerized her as it caught the light of the lamps around the older woman's living room, but it was that whispered "here ya go, baby girl" that stuck like a fly in sap. The sad drawl and the pitying looks became the standard in the weeks that followed.

But Etta had been the first, and it'd been a balm that night.

Jocelyn looked at Etta's hands now, nails bare and brittle-looking. "I don't know what I'm doing," she admitted.

And it was true. She wasn't an investigator. Just a daughter digging at an old grave.

"Ned ain't no gentleman," Etta warned, the edge softening. "He won't tell you a thing just 'cause you ask. He harassed your mama plenty."

Suspicion surged hotter. If Ned had anything to gain from that fire, then he was worth pressing. Cooperation or not, his response could be very telling.

"Thanks, Ms. Etta." Jocelyn touched her arm and dug a card from her purse. "Call me if you need anything. I can bring you a sugar-free treat—Nan's diabetic, too. I know the tricks."

Etta's smile warmed. "Aw, sure, Honey." She slipped the card into her pocket.

TWELVE

"The most powerful weapon on earth is the human soul on fire." - Ferdinand Foch

Cole figured it was about right that Jocelyn Murphy walked into the Nail the same day his mama ordered him to invite her to supper. And that was what she'd done—ordered him. Sat like a weight in his gut as he watched Jocelyn cut a line for the corner booth, folder in hand, jaw set hard enough to tell him she wasn't there for wings and a beer.

The room was quiet for now, but he knew what was coming. Thursdays meant sing-o night—families piling in, kids hollering, a DJ cranking music so loud it rattled the glasses. If Jocelyn planned on digging into that folder, she wasn't going to get far once the place filled up.

Didn't take a genius to know what she was carrying. Fire reports. Old ghosts. Her eyes gave her away—guilt slipping through before she shoved it down under all that determination.

He told himself not to care. He wasn't interested, not in her or her questions. Mama might've wrung a half-hearted promise out of him, but the more folks in town tried to push him toward Jocelyn Murphy, the more he wanted to dig his heels in. And the fact he couldn't stop noticing how damn good she looked sitting there? Just one more reason to keep his distance.

So he handed her section to Bea and steered clear. Safe plan.

Except he kept looking over anyway, catching every sigh, every shake of her head. His scowl deepened until Terra snorted on her way past.

"Better fix your face. You're scaring the kids," she said. "What's your problem?"

Cole shot her a look. "Thought you were off thirty minutes ago."

"Just stickin' around to watch you work at staying thirty feet from that Murphy girl like she slapped a restrainin' order on you." She hauled a tub of dishes toward the back, grinning.

"Shut the hell up and go home."

Her laughter trailed after her as she headed out through the back.

Soon after she left, Garrett Harrington pushed through the door, lugging his DJ-ing gear like a man dragging a corpse. Cole pulled the sing-o cards and markers from under the bar, and moved around the restaurant to pass them out across the tables. Which meant he had to head Jocelyn's way. No dodging it this time.

She looked up when he stopped. "What's this?"

"Sing-o."

Her brows rose.

"Bingo. With a DJ." He jerked his chin toward Garrett.

She pursed her lips, unimpressed.

"Come on. It's fun."

She shot him what could only be characterized as a scowl.

"You do have fun sometimes, don't you?" He rattled the bucket.

A grin stretched across her face as she raised a brow in challenge. "You playing?"

Well, hell. Hadn't planned to. But he couldn't walk away from a challenge. "I will if you will."

She pulled out two sets of cards and slid one across the table. Invitation made.

Cole sighed, muttering under his breath. "Be right back."

Turned out she was good. Better than good. She knew her music like she'd been raised on every station the dial had to offer. Her grin widened each time she beat him to a title, lips moving along with the words, shoulders bouncing. The game fired her up, and Cole found himself caught in it, leaning forward, pressing harder, until she finally slammed him with a sing-o win.

She practically danced her way back to the table after going up to match her card to the DJ's list to make sure she was right.

"What do I get for winning?" she asked gleefully, sliding into the booth. Her eyes glittered with triumph.

He leaned back, arms crossed. He tried to look stern, but his grin wouldn't quit. "Ain't winnin' enough?"

She placed her hands flat on the table, scoffing. "Come on. There's gotta be some reward. A free milkshake or something?"

He raised a brow. "That what you want?"

She shrugged, looking around the room, but that smug smile still curled the edge of her mouth. It gave him real pleasure to see it, and to find that she hadn't looked at the file she'd brought in with her since the game started.

Her attention touched on the families around the restaurant, maybe noting what he always did: there was not a phone or tablet to be seen. Folks usually distracted kids with screens to keep them quiet in restaurants, even this one.

But tonight, parents were interacting with their kids, only laughter and happy conversation filling the room, filling him with the rare buzz of contentment. He wondered if she felt it, too.

Her smile told him she did. "This is so great, Cole."

He shrugged. "It's not bad."

Her hand slid onto his arm. "Really, though. I love this."

He locked in on where her hand rested, something entirely different stirring inside him. Not just the electric reaction he'd had the second he'd seen her. Something entirely *other* that was just out of reach.

"I'll get your prize, then," he said, though he didn't—couldn't—move until she took her hand away.

But then she did, and he frowned, sliding out of his seat.

Air felt easier to get in and out of his lungs the farther he was from her, but he still felt the touch like she'd never removed her hand, even as he put in the order for the milkshake.

He made a point of checking in with the families closest to the bar until Jocelyn's prize was ready and while Garrett got set up for the next round of sing-o. Bea made sure new cards were handed out, but Cole didn't take new ones.

When he came back with the shake, Jocelyn was staring out the window, folder still tucked to the side, but it was only a matter of time.

"Thank you," she murmured, smiling only briefly.

The easy banter from the game had burned out quick, smothered under whatever was clawing at Jocelyn now. Cole glanced at the folder she'd shoved to the side, neat and tidy, like hiding it made it less dangerous.

"What's that?" he asked, deciding to quit circling. So much for him not being interested.

Her mouth twisted like she wasn't going to let the explanation loose. But she'd already laid her suspicions bare once.

"It's a report about the day my mama died."

As he'd figured. "So what's got you twisted up about it?"

She didn't answer right then, just stirred her milkshake, spoon clinking against the glass.

"I got all night, Darlin'," Cole drawled, keeping his tone lazy even while the words knotted his gut because that was an image. "You wanna talk it out, I'll listen."

Her lips pressed together, then she flipped the folder open, ruffled a few pages, shut it again. "I was comparing it to the other one I'd gotten. This copy came from the fire station. I thought maybe it'd have something new."

The disappointment weighed heavy in her words, thick and hard to shake.

"But it didn't," he guessed.

She shook her head. "Chief Ward mentioned something this morning. Said Mama was found on the floor between her bed and dresser."

Cole grimaced. He didn't have to guess what kind of picture that put in her head. "But?"

Her eyes found his, dark and sharp. "That detail wasn't in the report I had."

He jerked his chin toward the folder. "In this one?"

Her lips flattened. "No. It's the same. Word for word. I don't even know why I bothered."

Anger edged her voice, but she didn't slam the table like he might've. She held it in, all that heat just simmering under the surface. She jabbed the spoon into her milkshake.

"I'm sorry," he said, quieter. "Hell of a setback."

"It is what it is." She shrugged, gaze slipping away as she let it sit.

But he could tell she wasn't done, and he waited her out.

"It just bugs me," she finally said. "Her wine glass was there, by the window. That was always weird enough. But after what Ward said…" Her jaw clenched. "Why was it there if she was drunk and passed out over by the bed?"

"Don't add up," he agreed.

His sincerity pulled her focus back to him, and then she dropped her eyes to her hands. "Thanks for listening, Cole."

Well, damn. His stomach dropped, then something else flared hot through his chest, moving all the way to his fingertips. He curled his hands into fists slow, steady.

"My pleasure, Darlin'."

Her head lifted, a faint smile tugging at her mouth. "Why do you call me that?"

"What? 'Darlin'?" He shrugged. "Just instinct, I guess." He couldn't explain it, not even to himself. Some part of her pulled it out of him.

"My mama called me 'honeybee' when I was little."

The sound of it made him picture her that way—small, tender, untouched by all the hard years between then and now. It was rage that had burned that image into his memory back then, but it wasn't anger pulling it up now.

"My mama called me 'Tug,'" he said, mouth twisting.

Jocelyn tilted her head. "Why?"

He gave a short laugh. "Like tug-o-war. I was always pulling against her. Never made it easy."

"She did say you were hard to reel in." Jocelyn folded her arms, studying him. "But she's proud of what you built." Her hand swept toward the restaurant. "Maybe pulling against the current isn't always wrong."

The words sank deeper than they should've. Pride, clear in her voice. Like she had some kind of claim in the life he'd built. Truth was, she probably did. She'd known his mama most of her life now—long enough to understand more than most.

He had to look away, heat crawling through his blood. "Speaking of Ma," he muttered, shifting gears. "She wants you to come for supper tomorrow night."

Color bloomed in her cheeks. "Is that wise? Isn't your dad mad at me?"

Cole snorted. "Pop doesn't get mad at anybody but me."

She gave him a look—half doubt, half pity.

"If Ma invited you, there's no bad blood."

"Alright," Jocelyn said, voice quiet. "I'll come."

Relief cut through him, easing tension he hadn't realized was wound so tight. If she'd said no, it would've felt too much like she was turning him down, not his mama.

"I'll pick you up at the hotel on my way. Six-thirty?"

"Sounds fine."

Mercy, the look she gave him curled in his belly.

But the moment broke sharp when Jocelyn went stiff, attention going to the door. He turned to see that Natasha Abbott had walked in. Her steps faltered when she spotted Jocelyn in the booth with him.

When he turned back, Jocelyn's eyes were wide, searching the room like she was trapped. He knew that look too well—the need to escape before the past cornered you.

"There's a door to the alley back there," he said low, nodding toward the bar.

Thirteen

"Some women fear the fire. Some women simply become it." - R.H. Sin

Jocelyn's whole body tensed at Cole's words. He tipped his head toward the swinging door she'd seen him and other servers disappear through. Apparently, it led to more than just the kitchen.

"Natasha isn't like her family." He leaned forward, pushing out of his seat. "Might want to give her a shot."

She watched him stand. He didn't act like he was going to sit again, and panic clawed at her belly that he was about to abandon her to her sister. Natasha had been pleasant the day before, but Jocelyn's interaction with Lydia left a stamp of fear that she'd read her wrong—that she was about to experience a betrayal of memory. The familiar ache of being misunderstood settled in her chest like an old companion.

"Didn't ask for my two cents, I know." Leaning down, Cole placed his hands on the table. "But I think you'll be surprised."

"Wait," she said, grabbing his wrist as he pushed away before she could think better of it.

He pried her hand off but held it warm and tight, and in a move that shocked her out of her panic, pressed it to his lips. "You'll be fine, Darlin'. Promise."

Her mouth fell open for a moment before Natasha reached them, like some unseen tether had pulled her across the restaurant. Jocelyn's attempt at a smile didn't feel successful—probably because she was still reeling from Cole's gesture, analyzing every nuance of what it might mean.

"Hey there, Cole," Natasha said warmly.

"Hey, Tash," he replied with a gentle smile. "Get you something?"

Natasha glanced at Jocelyn, uncertain. The panic in her face matched what raged in Jocelyn's gut. Then she looked at the sing-o card left where he'd been. "Am I takin' your seat?"

"Gotta make the rounds. Help yourself."

Natasha looked again at Jocelyn, who only shrugged and scooted her empty milkshake to the side. Even that small movement made her feel like she was giving up more ground than she wanted to.

"Can I get the hangover burger?" Natasha asked as she sat.

Cole nodded then looked at Jocelyn for her order.

Jocelyn couldn't imagine stomaching much. "Fries."

He nodded and left, but Jocelyn's nerves remained, buzzing under her skin. She rubbed her palms against her thighs as if she could erase the tension. This was a mistake. A horrible idea. Right?

Across the room, a few curious glances lingered on them. Jocelyn told herself not to care, but heat still climbed her neck, spreading up to paint her cheeks. Natasha seemed unaffected, her discomfort rooted not in the crowd but in Jocelyn's presence.

"Is sing-o night your usual activity of choice?" Jocelyn asked, trying to fill the silence that stretched between them.

Natasha gave a soft laugh. "Not usually, but I don't mind it. It's kinda fun."

Jocelyn glanced around the room again. All of the gawkers had moved on with their meals. "It is, isn't it?"

"You played against Cole," Natasha said, spinning his used sing-o sheet under her pointer finger.

"I issued a challenge. He accepted."

Natasha let out a low whistle. "Lord, he does like a challenge."

A weird twinge of jealousy stole through her at the thought that Natasha knew him—and he knew her—in ways Jocelyn didn't. She scolded herself for caring on either front.

"Glad you got him to cut loose a little. He stays wound up tight most of the time."

"Does he?" Jocelyn mused. Wound up wasn't exactly the phrase she'd use. Intense was more in line with her experience. Even now, she felt his gaze burning across the room, charged with energy.

"A lot of it has to do with John," Natasha continued, her neatly manicured fingers tearing tiny pieces off the corner of the sing-o sheet. "He figures—and folks around here don't let him forget it—that he's gotta prove he belongs in this town, live up to his daddy's name."

Jocelyn's brows knit low as she glanced toward Cole again. He was talking to someone at the bar now, his fingers drumming lightly over the surface like he needed to burn some of that pent-up energy.

"His daddy's name," Jocelyn repeated dryly, giving her half-sister a wry smile.

Natasha returned it. "The hero who saved a little girl."

Jocelyn clicked her tongue, looking down at her hands on the table. It was still strange to hear it put that way, like she was a newspaper headline, a human interest story. But it was her childhood that had gone up in smoke.

"I remember driving by your house," Natasha said softly, expression cautious. "We drove by that way a lot. One day the house was there. The next day, it was gone."

Oh, how those words smarted. Jocelyn took one long toke of oxygen, desperate to keep the conversation moving. "I stopped over there a couple times. It's still weird that there's nothing there."

Her sister's expression softened. "I've seen it so many times now, just empty like that. It's sad. But it's become almost normal."

Another zing of pain pin-balled through Jocelyn's heart. There was nothing normal about it, but she knew that wasn't what Natasha meant. She redirected the pain—and the anger—and when she looked away, she caught Cole's appraising eye for a moment, like he knew they were talking about tough things.

Wouldn't have been a stretch, no matter the topic.

"Why does Cole think he has to prove anything to anyone?" she asked, turning back.

She'd heard enough of his history to know he'd floundered, but why that had any bearing on his life now, or his reputation in this town, she couldn't fathom. But she wasn't a stranger to the label a parent's name placed on their child.

Natasha's smile was grim. "He was the town hell-raiser for a long while."

Jocelyn snorted. Ellen Hauser had said as much plenty of times in her letters, though she never did go into detail.

"What kind of hell? We talking tee-peeing the principal's house? Or selling drugs to elementary school kids?"

Natasha laughed at the wide spectrum of options. "Somewhere in between? I was too young to catch the details, but I remember he got himself arrested more than once."

Jocelyn's jaw dropped. That was definitely not anything Ellen had shared with her, though it made sense the woman's kind heart wouldn't want to paint her son in such a negative light.

"For what?"

"Petty theft, far as I remember. Don't think he ever sold drugs, though folks like to talk about how he dabbled in tryin' some. But that's mostly just the mothers—you know how they are."

"The mothers," Jocelyn repeated, leaning back in her seat. "Sounds like the name of a horror movie."

Natasha huffed a laugh. "They can be downright awful." She rolled some of the paper scraps between her finger and thumb, back and forth. "Mama and her little pack of high-and-mighty friends."

"Ah, yes," Jocelyn murmured.

"Anyway, they embellish."

"Who doesn't?" There was a bitter edge to Jocelyn's words she couldn't block. The things they'd said about her mama...

Natasha winced. "Anyhow, he was the wild one, and him and his daddy never did have an easy go of it."

Based on Cole's words a few moments before, that wasn't surprising. Ellen had hinted that there was fault on both sides. But Jocelyn's experience at their house the other day hadn't seemed as strained as she'd been led to believe. And the way Cole jumped to John's defense...

"He looks at you a fair bit," Natasha noted.

Jocelyn didn't have to ask who. She was all too aware of how often Cole's attention lingered on her—or the way he seemed to reluctantly seek her out whenever she was around. The flutter in her stomach and the easy way they seemed to fall into flirting banter told her it was *not* a good idea. It was best she added the distance while she could.

"I'm not here to stay," Jocelyn said, though Natasha hadn't asked the question. The implication had been there clear enough.

Her half-sister cocked her head. "What're you here for, then?"

Jocelyn hesitated. As much as she felt she owed this town nothing, Natasha was different. *Seemed* to be different. And they were sisters. Yet her mouth remained closed.

"It's okay. You don't have to tell me," Natasha said as Jocelyn's hesitation stretched.

Jocelyn took a bracing breath, but Cole's reappearance interrupted her.

He slid their food onto the table, then shifted closer. "Brian's here. Want me to get rid of him?"

Natasha started to sink lower before she thought better of it and straightened. "No, it's fine. Thanks, Cole."

He nodded, his eyes flashing to Jocelyn before moving on. But his steps carried him toward the man she assumed was Brian, his movement belying a predatory grace. A story there, certainly.

"Who's Brian?" Jocelyn asked.

Natasha's lips twisted against an answer. But as she spun her basket and pulled out the ketchup, she sighed. "That'd be my ex."

Must've been a bad break-up if Cole was willing to toss him out over it.

"He's an asshole," Natasha muttered.

"That asshole is coming over here." Jocelyn tracked the dark-eyed, dark-haired swaggering cowboy whose gaze had locked on her sister.

Natasha rolled her shoulders back like she was about to enter a boxing ring.

"Hey, Tash," the cowboy drawled, appraising Jocelyn with an interested slant to his expression.

She nodded. "Brian."

"Who's your friend?" he asked, winking as he stuffed his hands into his pockets. A wedding ring caught the light before it disappeared into the denim, and suspicion stirred hot in Jocelyn's chest.

"She's..." Natasha faltered, looking at Jocelyn.

Might as well dive right in. It wasn't a step Jocelyn wanted to gloss over.

"I'm her sister," she said, not offering to shake his hand.

Natasha gave her a grateful smile, tentative and brief.

His brows shot up. "Sister? Well, I'll be."

"Damned?" Jocelyn offered.

Natasha's surprised snicker had Brian shifting his weight.

He gave Jocelyn a tight once-over before turning his attention fully on Natasha. "I'm in town for tonight, Tash. Would love to catch up."

Her cheeks flushed. "That's not a good idea, Brian."

"Aw, just old friends talkin' and stuff." He flashed her a solicitous smile, used to that working.

No doubt "and stuff" meant a hell of a lot more than just chitchat.

Natasha's fingers fluttered on the table, her gaze fixed on the food before her. Jocelyn could practically feel her sister's resolve wavering.

But she gave a firm shake of her head. "No, thanks."

He opened his mouth to protest again, wearing the look of a man certain this was some kind of game.

"We already have plans," Jocelyn cut in before he could get another word out. "And family trumps... whatever you are." She waved her hand up and down his body like he was a weird and disgusting abstract sculpture.

A sneer threatened to mar his obnoxiously pretty face, but before he could say whatever he was gearing up for, Cole interrupted.

"How's everything look, ladies?" His tone was pleasant, but his eyes were hard, his expression anything but friendly as he regarded the cowboy.

"Looks great, Cole, thank you," Jocelyn replied when Natasha said nothing. The red that had bloomed on her sister's face had only deepened.

"You gonna order somethin'?" Cole's question sounded more like a threat than an invitation.

Brian looked at Natasha, who refused to meet his gaze. "Tash?"

Natasha looked at Jocelyn and lifted her chin a little higher. "As she said, we already have plans."

Brian sputtered, then glared at Jocelyn before grunting in frustration and storming toward the door.

Cole gave the sisters a nod and moved on, though he tracked Brian's progress until the man was out the door.

Jocelyn found herself a bit amped even after he was gone, and she looked at her half-sister, whose food sat untouched. She wanted to ask for the story but fear of breaking what little bridge they had built kept her mouth shut.

The seconds ticked, and Jocelyn was about ready to throw caution to the wind when the words burst from Natasha like a dam breaking.

"He was engaged." Her blue eyes flashed up, full of regret, before dropping again. "I didn't know. Not at first, anyway."

Jocelyn worked hard to slow her intake of breath. This new connection felt too fragile for her to react, though every part of her wanted to.

"He's with the rodeo circuit. Breezes into town, then is gone for months. So it was a fling. Supposed to be a fling. But by the time I figured it out, I was in too deep. Took me a long while to let go." Natasha pulled a lock of ashy blonde hair forward, winding it around her finger. "Then he up and brought her through town, and I saw her. Saw him *with* her. And that's when it hit me—he was never gonna leave her for me."

The parallels were cruel. Jocelyn's mama, too, had once been trapped in the orbit of a man who would never choose her. Jocelyn had lived her whole life with the fallout of that truth, and now she saw it mirrored in Natasha's regret.

"Problem is," Natasha whispered, "my fool heart still wants him, even though my head knows better."

Jocelyn swallowed hard. She understood, too well, the ache of wanting what you knew you could never truly have.

Then, on instinct, she reached across the table and closed her hand over Natasha's. For once, she didn't analyze it or pull back. She simply held on, silently wondering if maybe all the brokenness in their pasts had been leading to this—two half-sisters finding a sliver of connection.

Because if she had come back to Cedar Hollow a year or two earlier, Natasha might never have let her close at all.

Their decisions might have defined them, but the consequences had changed them, and now a door existed where it hadn't been before.

FOURTEEN

"A spark neglected makes a mighty fire." - Robert Herrick

Heath had headphones tucked in his ears, his lined face locked in focus. Cole appreciated that about him. Heath didn't pry, didn't talk much, didn't expect anything. Just worked. He was one of the few people Cole could spend time with and not feel the need to fill silence.

Heath had come to Cedar Hollow nearly twenty years ago with little fanfare, quietly buying the old Hollow Inn and fixing it up piece by piece until it thrived again. Sally Anne Marsden had been at his side soon after, bright where Heath was steady, and the two of them had run the inn together ever since.

For Cole, Heath was the kind of friend you didn't have to explain yourself to, someone who offered space without judgment. It made the grunt work of building booths for the Harvest Festival tolerable, even pleasant.

The rhythm of hammering and sawing was almost musical, a steady counterpoint to the distant thrum of Boston bleeding from Heath's earbuds. It soothed the restless energy always burning through Cole's veins, the kind of static he usually outran on long stretches of pavement.

When Cole shifted the booth into place and caught Heath's raised brows, he mouthed, "Lunch?"

Heath nodded. "Sally made sandwiches."

Cole gave him a quick salute and headed up the grassy hill toward the inn. The place always stole his breath in autumn, the rolling grounds and trees waiting to burst into color. It was worth slowing his pace just to take in the pleasant breeze—the weather cooler after the storm that had rolled in the day before.

He'd just made it through the back door when a voice snagged his attention.

"Why are you asking me about Ned Turner?"

Sally Anne.

"He was our landlord," came Jocelyn's reply.

Cole froze, one hand still on the fridge handle. The sound of her voice cut sharper than it should have, his chest going tight as he let the fridge door close with a dull thud.

"I know that, Jossie." Sally's tone had softened. "But why're you asking about him?"

"He wanted me and Mama out of that house."

Cole's brows shot up. Jocelyn hadn't mentioned that when she'd laid out her suspicions about her mama's fire. A strange offense pricked at him, sharp and unwelcome. She'd trusted him with part of the truth but not all of it.

"Do you think he might've started the fire?" Jocelyn's voice dropped lower, almost secretive.

Cole's pulse kicked hard. Could he see Ned Turner torching his own property to get his way? Sure could. But Jocelyn had mentioned other fires, and it didn't make sense for Turner to have started those, too. Possible they weren't related at all, and the tragedy that had haunted Cedar Hollow for twenty years was just a one time bit of malice.

Cole drifted down the hallway without deciding to, straining to catch more until Sally Anne's office door clicked shut. The muffled voices only stoked the fire under his ribs.

When the door opened again, Sally Anne's voice drifted out, heavy with bother. "... what you're diggin' through'll just stir up dirt and nothing more."

She nearly stumbled into him as she turned. When she saw him standing there, relief rolled over her face. "Oh, Cole. You boys need somethin'?"

"Sandwiches," he said evenly.

Jocelyn slipped out of the office behind Sally, her dark eyes cutting sharp into his. Suspicion. Challenge. Maybe even guilt.

"They're right in here." Sally moved toward the kitchen, but Cole didn't follow. His gaze stayed locked on Jocelyn.

She didn't flinch, but her jaw ticked like she was chewing on words she wouldn't give him.

Sally Anne passed him the food, her brows drawing together at the thick silence between them. Jocelyn was the first to break it, turning on her heel and striding away.

Cole followed.

"Jocelyn," he called, pushing into a jog.

Her shoulders climbed higher, but she didn't turn. The dismissal set his teeth on edge. What had shifted between them since last night, when their banter had been easy and damn near dangerous in how much he'd enjoyed it?

She and Natasha had seemed alright during their supper together, but then they both cleared out without a word. Had him wondering if something happened between them that lingered through to this morning and had her freezing him out.

He caught her just outside the inn's front doors, the humid air pressing down like a weight. She wouldn't look at him, her chin set at a stubborn tilt, and he was searching for something—anything—that would make her stop running from him when a syrupy voice cut through the thick air.

"Well, now. Here's an interestin' sight."

Both of them turned.

Kiki Womack stood on the gravel path, one manicured hand perched on her hip, the other clutching a shopping bag from the corner market. Her smile glinted with the satisfaction of catching something she shouldn't.

"Jocelyn Murphy and Cole Hauser, thick as thieves," Kiki drawled, shooting fire at Cole like he was the only one responsible.

Jocelyn stiffened beside him as the heat crawled up his neck, a growl threatening in his chest, but she got bolder the more they bristled, like she fed off it.

"'Course, I can't blame you for wanting company," she said to Jocelyn, her smile turning sharp. "Your mama never liked being alone, either. Always had someone hanging around her, even if they weren't the kind you'd call good company."

The words landed like a stone between them, heavy and cold, drawing a sharp breath from Jocelyn.

"Now, Miz Kiki," Cole warned, voice low, and it pulled her venomous gaze in his direction.

"Funny, isn't it?" she went on. "Even though some folks walk around like they're carrying a hero's name, the world don't always see it the same way."

She let the pause hang, her lips curving into a sly, almost triumphant smile. "Your daddy... he's done a lot for this town, no question. Seems the apple fell a little far from the tree, though. Might wanna watch who you spend time with, Jocelyn. Don't want your mama's reputation confirmed."

Cole took a hard step toward her, his jaw flexing. "That's enough, Kiki."

"I'm afraid it's not enough." The older woman took that as her exit line, and silence settled like ash in her wake.

Fury tore through him, but the sight of Jocelyn with her arms wrapped tight around her middle, gaze fixed on the ground, held him rooted. He fought the burn of the rage—at Kiki, at the town, at the way the past refused to stay buried—because he had to make sure she was alright.

"Don't listen to her," he said, his voice rougher than he meant. "Kiki's got a mean streak wide as the Mississippi, but she doesn't know a damn thing."

Jocelyn's head snapped up, anger flashing across her face. "She knows enough to drag my mama's name through the dirt like it's some kind of entertainment."

He clenched his jaw, wanting to put his fist through something. "And I should've shut her down harder."

"You think that would've stopped her?" Jocelyn shot back, her voice low but sharp. "People like Kiki don't stop. They feed on this. On me. On you." Her breath hitched, and she pressed her lips together like she hated herself for showing even that much.

Cole's hand flexed at his side, aching to reach for her, to pull her out from under the weight of it all. But the steel in her posture warned him off.

"She had no right swingin' at your mama or bringin' Pop into it," he muttered.

That made Jocelyn's gaze soften for a beat then shutter again. "Everybody's fair game in this town, Cole. You know as well as I do. Maybe better these days."

The sting of it cut deep. He hated that she was right. Hated more that he let those opinions get under his skin, let them feel true even if they weren't.

"Jocelyn." He stepped closer, enough that the summer heat between them carried her scent, clean and citrusy. His voice dropped. "If you keep diggin' into this, that—" he gestured toward the road where Kiki had disappeared, "—becomes more than talk. People might get hurt. Reputations might get ruined."

Her eyes lifted to his, dark and shining with a mix of fire and hurt. "And what if the truth ruins more than that?"

The words landed hard, heavier than Kiki's gossip had. Cole's chest went tight, and he saw the fear beneath her stubbornness—the risk she was carrying alone.

He wanted to promise her he could handle it. That he wouldn't let the town tear her apart. But there was a chance he'd get ripped up, too.

The way she was looking at him, daring him to promise something he wasn't ready to offer, told him she might not have been ready for it, either.

"Does it matter to you if it does?" he asked.

Her jaw worked, like she was biting down on a thousand things she couldn't say, before she turned sharply and started walking.

Cole let her go this time, the wrapped sandwiches still tucked under his arm, the weight of Kiki's words settling over him like smoke that wouldn't clear.

Fifteen

"It is a fire that consumes me, but I am the fire." - Jorge Luis Borges

The heat of Cole's gaze chased her to her car, but it was Kiki Womack's words that rolled over and over in her mind. Because the woman had hit the right buttons for both of them. It might've been twenty years, but Jocelyn remembered *her* just fine.

Kiki was one of the girls who'd had it out for her mama from grade school, and when Bonnie had made her way back to town with her illegitimate child in tow, Kiki and her friends had made it their mission to snub her whenever possible. It didn't help that they'd been cozy with Lydia Abbott by that time, either.

Jocelyn could've dismissed everything she said, the words nothin' more than a sliver of truth edged with mean. But it was the stuff about Cole that had her circling.

The things about John—said mostly to get Cole's back up—reminded her of the disappointment she'd felt about whatever secret he'd been keeping.

She hadn't dug into that yet. Not when the memory of Cole's anger that night still rolled fresh in her mind. He was worried about reputations getting ruined. Maybe he was worried about hers, but it felt a little like he wanted to save his own.

There wasn't anything wrong with that. At least, there shouldn't have been. But it made a painful little twist in her heart anyway.

And that almost made her stumble, but she didn't stop. Not until she spotted the folded up piece of paper tucked under her windshield wiper.

Her fingers tightened around the strap of her bag as she stared at it, and then she let her feet carry her the last few steps to the vehicle. Her hand was like a foreign object before her as she reached for the piece of paper, the knowing that this wouldn't be a ticket for a traffic violation settling heavily in her chest. It wasn't official-looking enough for that.

She snatched it from under the wiper, the thick card stock abrasive against her skin, and flipped it open.

some questions are better left unanswered

Her head snapped up, and she scanned the street for anyone acting suspicious. Not that the person who'd written it would hang around to see her reaction—or if they did, they certainly wouldn't be visible.

Still, she couldn't help willing herself to see through walls and into shadows. A better superpower would've been to read fingerprints.

After stuffing the note into her purse and searching the area one more time, she got into her car and drove, flying along the winding hills and tunnels of trees until there was nothing but open hills dotted with livestock and thick stands of trees.

Her next step wasn't clear yet, and she was too worked up to think anyway. Sure, Ned Turner had climbed up her list, but she didn't have a clue of where to find him. Probably should've asked Cole, but they'd been distracted.

Kiki Womack.

Jocelyn cursed and looked at her purse where she'd tucked the note away. It only took a second for her to consider and then dismiss the possibility of Kiki being the culprit for the note. It was certainly a sentiment that matched the attitude, though part of her felt Kiki was punishing Cole more than herself with her words.

Besides, Kiki had looked like she'd come from a store when she'd run into them. A woman that intent on getting someone's back up wouldn't try to do it anonymously. She wanted them to see exactly who was spitting the mean.

And did it really matter who had left it? Plenty of people didn't like what she was doing. She was tired of giving a damn.

Justice and the truth were her aim.

So, next steps.

She couldn't explain what had led her where she found herself, but, heavens, the Abbott mansion was a sight to behold. Surrounded by sweeping hills and still carpeted in green despite it being officially autumn, the house rose majestically. Trees stretched their limbs lazily toward the house like they were holding it back rather than protecting it.

She didn't cross the property line. She simply slowed to stare at the sweeping porch that shaded the antebellum edifice as she drove past on her way back toward town. It had once been a plantation house, the center of a vast network of fields worked by hands that were claimed as property. The Abbotts didn't deny their history, but they made a point of serving Cedar Hollow from on high like it was their penance.

She supposed it was her history, too, on some level.

Just looking at it made it clear her heart wasn't quite ready to face her father. Jocelyn had hardly spoken to him even before her mama's death, and she wasn't quite sure what her approach would be now. It certainly wouldn't be to change their previously established dynamic of practical strangers.

She wanted to pretend it was just happenstance because she needed to blow off steam, but it was more than that. Some part of her had known she'd end up there, driving past the Abbott mansion like some sort of punishment.

Her mama had rarely taken her by, no doubt avoiding the reminder of the life she might've had if fate had twisted differently. If the family on the hill hadn't turned their noses up at the girl from the wrong side of town and pushed their son into a more respectable direction.

They'd all paid the price for that, though her mama's had been the most costly.

Yes, some questions were better left unanswered, but it didn't mean she would stop searching for the ones she needed.

And so she headed back to town. Her goal before she'd asked Sally about Ned Turner had been to search the newspaper archives for their reports both on her mother's fire and the suspected arson cases from that same time frame.

What she'd found online had been national reports only, vague sensationalist overviews of a shocking tragedy in a small southern town. Cedar Hollow was slow to digitize their archives, so her best bet was to look through hard copies.

But now that Ned was on her radar, she had a specific track to take in her investigating. If he was responsible for her house fire, was he responsible for the others? The only way to find out was to look for any connections to him.

And since talking to Eric Ward about where her mama had been found, that itch to find confirmation somewhere else weighed on her mind. Maybe she would strike gold and find something that mentioned why Bonnie was on the floor that night.

She frowned. And maybe she could time travel and stop the whole thing from happening at all.

One could hope for miracles. Didn't mean you'd get them.

The newspaper office of the Hollow Gazette was a small brick building tucked between an antique shop and the bank. If she hadn't been looking for it, she might've missed it altogether.

The woman inside eyed her with a knowing glint when she walked in. Old enough to know who Jocelyn was and apparently connected enough to hold a ready opinion of her, the woman offered no greeting. The curse of a small town.

"Hi, there," Jocelyn said, working up her smile anyway. "I was wondering if I might have a look around your archives?"

The woman's flat expression didn't waver, though she gave Jocelyn a once over. "Archives older than ten years got moved to the library."

At least she didn't have to go through the explanation of what she was looking for. Could've done without the attitude, but she would take what she could get. "Thank you."

She pushed out into the bright sunlight, briefly wished small towns didn't work the way they did, and set her mind on walking the two blocks to the library. It was a squat brick building with little to recommend it—ugly, rundown, and smelling faintly like wet laundry left out too long.

A younger woman sat behind the desk, looking very little like the stereotypical librarian. She had bright blue eyes set in a luminous and youthful face free of glasses or a lined scowl.

"Hey, there," she said with a smile.

Jocelyn tried not to be wary, but a returning smile was hard to drag up after her most recent interaction. "Hello."

"You look like you need some direction."

Jocelyn waited, thinking the recognition would settle soon, and the woman would snub her like the rest of them did.

When the pleasant expression on her face didn't change, Jocelyn stumbled through her request. "I'm looking for the old newspaper archives."

Both brows rose, setting wrinkles into the smooth forehead. "Don't hear that every day. Well, come on back with me. I'll show you where they are."

She breezed out from behind the desk, a flowing gauzy skirt swirling around her. "I'm Bethany, by the way."

"Jocelyn," she said carefully.

Bethany waved her off. "Oh, I know."

That was a surprise. "You do?"

"Sure. We were in school together, though you might not remember. I was a year behind."

Her light tone made Jocelyn's walls shoot up. Surely this was a ploy? "I'm sorry. I don't remember."

Bethany turned to smile at her. "It's alright. It was a long time ago, and you've got plenty of reasons to want to forget."

She slowed to a stop in the back corner of the building where a wide doorway opened into a darkened room. The jewel eyes settled on Jocelyn again. "I suppose you're not wanting to forget anymore, though. That why you need the archives?"

She didn't want to believe Bethany's friendliness had more to do with pumping Jocelyn for information than genuine kindness. She hadn't made it a secret why she was back, but it wasn't like she was advertising, either. It was just hard not to think the worst of people.

"Something like that," she finally said.

Bethany's mouth tipped down a little. "I'm real sorry about what happened to your mama. Grammy always said she was the sweetest."

Another surprise there.

Bethany caught on, offering a soft smile. "My grammy's opinion matters more than most in my world."

Jocelyn took a breath, hesitating for a moment. But she let herself soften just a smidge. "I appreciate it. Your condolences and your help."

Bethany beamed. "Anytime. Let me know if you need anything else."

"Thank you," she said as Bethany headed back toward the front desk.

Jocelyn turned to the tables filled with plastic bins and hanging folders. Moving to the first, she checked the dates to get her bearings. She'd scoured the internet for national coverage of the fire, but local reports had been scarce. Digitizing clearly wasn't a high priority in a town this size, where not much usually happened.

When she found the right time frame, flipping through the dates, anger stirred low in her gut at the lack of outcry for investigation in what was reported. Most of the coverage fixated on John Hauser's heroics that night—and the tragic story of the little girl he'd saved, abandoned by a neglectful mother who'd drunk too much wine and left a candle burning by a gauzy curtain.

It shouldn't have been a surprise, nor should the rage have clawed so violently through her. That had been the narrative her whole life, and she'd been told to move forward time and time again.

But how could she when her search so far had just brought more questions? And though that gave her a dose of frustration, it came with the sense that she was on the right track. All the preconceived notions were slowly crumbling, even if she was the only one chipping away at them.

All this time wondering if there was more to it had led her to take the first step. And now the little fissures in the accepted version of events proved that her lack of peace came from the truth being intentionally buried.

And so she dug through copies of newspapers, ink marking her skin as evidence of her effort as she skimmed article after article for mentions of the other fires. As she'd told Cole, arson had been labeled likely even back then, though there'd been no defining feature linking them beyond geography. All in Cedar Hollow or nearby towns. And Cedar Hollow, small as it was, served as the county seat and the home base for the investigations.

Now she had the possible link of Ned Turner.

The problem was that none of the articles she came across mentioned anything about Ned Turner. Not even once did he come up in the reports about the fire in the house he owned.

Anger stirred again, and she flipped through the papers with more aggression as the articles on the fires moved farther and farther from the front page. Slamming her hand against the bin didn't change the facts, but it made her feel marginally better.

Then a name caught her eye, drawing her to read the quote she'd already skimmed.

"We did everything we could," said firefighter Eric Ward, one of the first responders. "It's a tragedy. Fires move fast, especially when accelerant is involved. There was nothing anyone could've done. Even John Hauser barely made it to the scene in time."

She had read it already, but this time, the words landed in her gut like stones.

Accelerant.

Her mind spun back to what she knew. She didn't remember the fire report she'd gotten from Amber mentioning it? Or had Ward been speculating because of the wine glass in the window sill, and as a low-level crew member, he was repeating guesses? Or had there been suspicions initially that were discarded later?

Or worse, covered up?

In light of the other suspected arson cases, she couldn't rule anything out.

The rest of the article was more of the same of what she already knew, that John Hauser was off-duty that night and happened to be walking by, that he'd seen the smoke, heard the pop and crackle of flame, and had come running.

That one quote from Eric Ward was the only mention of possible accelerants in the whole article, and she flipped through some of the stories run after, just to see if it came up again. Nothing that she could find, and she huffed in frustration.

Maybe she needed to comb through what she had again to compare what she'd found here. At least she had that line to pursue for now. Once she finished, she would see how far Bethany's goodwill stretched by asking if she might know where to find Ned Turner and make that tomorrow's priority.

For now, she lugged the box with the relevant articles to an open table and sat. Pulling out the folder she'd been putting together for the last year, she settled in with her notebook open and pen poised.

Sixteen

"In the heart of the blaze, truth reveals itself naked and without mercy." - Unknown

The nerves bounced around inside Cole, sparking up all the energy he'd worked out of his body earlier that day. After the unresolved exchange with Jocelyn, he'd spent several hours out at his property getting two new walls framed on the house. Once he'd cooled down with an icy shower, he'd stopped by the Nail to check in—earning Terra's wrath for showing up on his night off.

None of it had burned off the jitters in his gut anyway, and he walked the second-floor hallway of the Hollow Inn toward Jocelyn's door feeling like that damn woodpecker out on his land had taken up residence in his stomach, hammering at his insides.

For all he knew, their interaction earlier had turned her opinion of him and his folks, and she had no intention of going to supper at all. He'd have to face his mama's disappointment for screwing that one up.

He hesitated before knocking, the metallic numbers on her door glinting like they knew exactly how foolish he felt. His palm scraped along his jaw, then he forced his knuckles to the wood. His gut clenched, braced for whatever came next.

Her footsteps were soft, but he heard them. He was strung so tight he probably could've caught the sound of her breath. The lock clicked; the door swung open.

Well, shit. No smile. Not even the ghost of one. Surprise, maybe, that he was standing there.

"Cole." She sighed, shutting her eyes for half a second. "Right. Dinner. I'm sorry; I lost track of time. Come in."

She turned, leaving the door wide for him, and he stepped inside. Small room, but it carried a farmhouse charm no chain hotel could imitate. Gingham curtains framed the window, a wrought-iron headboard stood against a ship-lapped wall, and a picture of a hen presided over a bed littered with papers spread like lost feathers.

The closet door hung open, suitcase tucked in the corner, half-empty hangers on the rack. If it were him staying there, the floor would be buried in clothes spilling out of the bag like it had puked them up.

Except for the chaos of whatever she'd been working on, everything else was neat.

He nodded toward the papers spread all over the bed. "Looks like somebody lost a fight with a paper mill."

She gave him a wry look. "Don't tell me you're one of those neat freaks who folds their socks in pairs. I'll have to rethink dinner."

He laughed, the tension loosening just a bit. "Helps to have socks that all look the same."

The flash of a smile was brief. "Sorry about the mess," she said, scrambling to collect the papers.

She shoved them into a folder then into the oversized purse in the corner. Her hair—undone for once, dark waves falling down her back—slipped forward, sliding over her shoulder. With it loose, she looked freer, almost earthy, and he felt that deep. He shouldn't have, but he did.

She bent for her sandals then grabbed a flimsy cover-up that draped over her tank top. The regret hit hard when she twisted her hair back up into a bun. Consolation came in the stray tendrils she didn't catch and left loose.

Almost against his will, he murmured, "Should've left it like that."

She looked over at him, puzzled. Then she caught his line of sight and touched her hair. "What, messy?"

He grinned. "Nah. Free."

A smile tugged at her mouth, but she dipped her chin to hide the color in her cheeks. "Maybe next time."

He jammed his hands into his pockets with a shrug, held tight enough by that blush that he didn't even mind she wasn't taking his suggestion.

The drive to his parents' place was quiet. Something sat on Jocelyn's mind, plain as the finger moving back and forth along her bottom lip. It took all of seven minutes to get there, but the weight of her silence made it feel harder than an hour would've. Whatever storm brewed in her head, she wasn't voicing it, and he couldn't let it stand.

"You're awful quiet over there," he commented. "That bad of company?"

She smirked but didn't glance over. "I figure you need the practice."

"Practice?"

She raised a brow, finally looking at him. "Being around somebody without arguing."

Cole let out a surprised chuckle, planting his hand on his chest. "Oh, Darlin', you wound me."

Her laugh was soft and quick, but it hit him like a shot of whiskey—smooth and warm going down. Then she faced forward again, and little by little, that silence slipped back in. It didn't feel as heavy as before, and considering the way they'd left things earlier, Cole let the silence stand. His mother's relentless social streak would drag Jocelyn into conversation soon enough.

Still, his humor didn't fully shake her tension, and it stirred in his mind. Might've been about the dinner, since the last time they'd been to his folks' place, it hadn't ended well. Might've been something else entirely, but he had to tamp down the urge to reach for her hand, to anchor her to the moment. Most innocent impulse he'd had toward her, but even that wasn't his right. He wasn't her comfort. Not yet, anyway.

It should've shocked him to know he wanted to be, but he'd already started the descent into surrender. About time he stopped fighting it.

When they drove up, his mama was on the porch with her watering can in hand, the one with the daisies painted on its side. Like clockwork, she came out when the sun slid past the front of the house to water her plants. She waved as soon as she saw them.

Jocelyn's smile didn't smooth the little crease between her brows as they climbed out of the truck. At first Cole pegged it for nerves, but she wasn't fidgeting. No, the set of her shoulders, the line between her brows looked more like she was turning something over in her head.

So maybe whatever weighed on her had nothing to do with his folks. Maybe not even him, though they'd chewed each other up plenty of times already.

His mama's smile bloomed as they came up the walk. "My, you two look like a dream." The watering can swung low in her hand, and her expression was soft and wistful. There was that look in her eye—the one southern mothers in their twilight years got when their only child was past thirty and still hadn't given them grand babies.

"That's only 'cause Jocelyn's prettier than a picture," Cole drawled, letting his gaze flick her way.

Jocelyn's mouth curved, half humor, half suspicion. "Smooth, Hauser. You use that line often?"

He winked. "Only when it's true."

"And it is true," Ellen agreed with a smile, tugging Jocelyn into a hug.

Cole got the quick version of the embrace—Ma saw him near every day—and then she was already ushering them toward the house. The scent of meatloaf hit him as soon as the door opened, cinnamon riding the air, too. Must've been the pie she'd promised.

"Hey, there, kids." John lumbered out from the back den, yanking his cheaters off and stuffing them into his pocket.

Jocelyn gave a shy wave.

"None of that, here, Jossie." John wrapped her up against his barrel chest, and Cole leaned against the wall, watching. "You're family."

"Proof would be that we got into a disagreement in the living room," Cole said when Jocelyn was freed.

"Just one in a long line," Ellen added with a pat on his cheek.

Jocelyn glanced his way, wry understanding in the twist of her lips.

"Yes, Darlin'," Cole said with a smirk. "It was mostly me doing the disagreein'."

"To put it mildly," John put in.

The spike of irritation hit Cole fast, and his jaw tightened before he tamped it down. His daddy missed it, of course. No one else did. Story of his life.

"That was just a warm-up," Jocelyn said, attempting to lighten the mood again. "I'll win the next round."

Cole's laugh was low and only a little forced. "You are welcome to try."

Her half-smile kicked the rest of his mood, and he let himself relax again.

Ellen beamed at the exchange, then gestured for them to file into the dining room while she went to the kitchen. The table was set with her good china, a vase of flowers in the center—the whole spread. Felt unnecessarily fussy when the standard fare had sufficed last time.

But Jocelyn noticed the effort, her soft gasp pulling his attention to her. He saw how it affected her in the delighted smile that slid across her face as she took it in. Made the whole production worth it, and he filed the image away like a squirrel hoarding acorns for the long winter.

He pulled her chair out, and she smiled at him for it—genuine, easy—and that was another thing he stored up. Could live off one of those smiles a week if he had to. Maybe they'd be alright after their talk earlier. Things felt lighter just then, anyway.

Cole took the spot opposite Jocelyn, leaving the ends for his folks, as was standard.

"Sweet tea!" Ellen sang as she swept in with a pitcher.

John followed with the meatloaf and a salad bowl.

"So much for sugar intake," Cole said with a look at his mama.

"Special occasions, remember?"

He turned to his daddy. "How many of those this week, Pop?"

John made a show of counting on his fingers. "Three or four."

"Uh-huh."

Ellen spun on her husband as he moved to sit. "John Hauser! You said you'd watch it so I wouldn't have to worry about this dinner."

"El." He let out a sigh, and that was the whole of his defense.

Her glare stayed sharp, her chair angled at Cole's right like she was ready to pounce.

Cole slid a glance at Jocelyn, sharing the joke in the middle of it, and damn if her sly grin didn't almost undo him. Too much flirting that evening getting to his head. In mixed company, he kept his reaction locked down, but inside he was groaning under the weight of what that smile—and everything before it—did to him.

"Dish us up, Pop," Cole cut in, needing the conversation to shift—mostly for his own sake. "Diet starts tomorrow, like we all tell ourselves after fallin' off the wagon."

"Have to be on the wagon to fall off it," Ellen muttered, still pinning John with that look.

He just chuckled and stretched a hand toward Jocelyn. "Help me out here, Jossie. Change the subject and save me."

Her smile flashed as she passed him her plate. "I do owe you one." She gave the portion he scooped a quick glance then nodded.

He barked out a laugh, sliding the plate back to her. "You definitely do not."

Ellen pounced on the opening, her focus shifting to Jocelyn. "Tell us about your work, Jocelyn. Did you take time off to visit?"

Jocelyn smiled, the brightness again catching Cole in the chest like a fist. "Most of it can be done remotely. I made sure to get my major projects done before coming here, but I have ongoing work with certain clients. I've been balancing that between..."

Her words faltered, smile shrinking.

"It's alright, Jossie," John said. "Don't need to dance around it. We know why you're here, and you deserve those answers."

Ellen's nod was quick and certain. Pride nudged at Cole's ribs. Jocelyn still looked stricken, but she gave a slow nod.

Still killed the conversation and that smile Cole couldn't get enough of.

"Let's say Grace, so we can dig in." Ellen lifted her brows at her husband. "John?"

His daddy's old prayer rolled over Cole like a familiar song. He peeked one eye open. Jocelyn's head was bowed, but she was staring down at the food, her mind miles away.

The meal carried on. Jocelyn came alive again when she talked more about her work—graphic design, marketing, building other people's visions. He watched her light up and felt that squeeze in his chest again, like she belonged here, at this table.

Then Ellen asked about Cole's progress on the house. He kept it short—"slow and steady." But his mama went right on filling Jocelyn in about her daddy passing the family land on to Cole.

"Fifty acres," Jocelyn repeated, her mouth dropping open. "You're building it yourself?"

"Two walls framed up today." He shrugged like it was nothing.

"That's amazing."

Her words made his skin itch. Praise never sat right, not on him. John barely grunted whenever Cole mentioned the project. Only his mama ever bragged on him.

And she sure puffed up like a hen showing off her best feathers. "You'll have to take her over while she's in town."

"Ellen," John warned.

"I'd love to see it," Jocelyn said, and it didn't sound like politeness.

Cole tried for casual, gave another shrug. "Happy to show you sometime."

Silence followed while John stared at his wife. She ignored him, all triumph and smiles. Cole caught Jocelyn's eye, enjoying another shared joke at his mama's not-so-subtle matchmaking. Maybe Jocelyn didn't mind. He sure as hell didn't.

The moment broke when Ellen shoved her chair back. "Why don't y'all go into the living room while I get the pie ready?"

His daddy's stare didn't waver, but he got up, too, stacking dishes.

"Don't you dare touch that plate, Jocelyn Murphy," Ellen snapped when Jocelyn made to help.

Her hands shot up in surrender, and Cole couldn't help the laugh that cracked out at the shock on Jocelyn's face. The full-name *Mom Voice* could rattle anybody.

"I got her, Ma," Cole said, brushing his hand against Jocelyn's back to steer her toward the living room.

"Your mother is such a sweetheart, but wow," Jocelyn murmured, a smile lacing through the words.

"She's a spitfire when she needs to be," he agreed. "The full-name treatment'll knock the fight right out of anybody."

"Including you?"

He tipped his head. "Especially me. But don't go spreadin' that around."

She laughed as they moved across the hall to the living room. No doubt John was back there giving Cole's mama an earful about her scheming, but Cole shoved that out of his head and watched Jocelyn instead—watched her cross the room and perch on the far end of the couch like it was neutral ground.

"I think it's amazing that you're building your own house." Her voice carried that warm ease, her expression soft.

"We'll see if it turns out."

She tilted her head at his deflection. "I think it says a lot about you."

His brows ticked up as he resisted the urge to rub at the heat crawling up his neck. "What's it say?"

She studied his reaction. "That you know how to stick with something. Most people don't."

His mouth curved. "That's a nice way of callin' me stubborn."

She pursed her lips, looking like she wanted to press, but before she could, Ellen swept in with two plates of peach pie.

"Here you go, baby," she said, handing the first to him.

She crossed to Jocelyn, leaning over the coffee table to give her the other plate. The fork slid off, bouncing off Jocelyn's knee to clatter onto the floor.

"Oh!" they both said at once.

Jocelyn bent to grab it and came up with a slip of paper, too.

"That must be from my scrapbooking the other day," Ellen said, taking the fork from her. "I'll get you a new fork. Just set the paper on the table—I save all my scraps." She breezed out without a second glance.

But Jocelyn didn't just toss the scrap aside. She stared at it, studying the ripped edge like it held some secret she'd been searching for.

"Problem?" Cole asked, watching her closely.

"Scrapbooking," she repeated, distracted.

"Yeah. The old lady hobby she picked up a while back," Cole said, his tone edged with humor. "Don't let her rope you in, or you'll be stuck here all night flipping through the hundreds of albums she's got stashed upstairs."

"Oh, Cole." Ellen swatted his arm like he'd insulted her honor as she walked back in.

She handed a fresh fork to Jocelyn, then took her own plate from John, who'd trailed in behind her. Jocelyn didn't even crack a smile, just dug into the pie like it was duty instead of dessert.

Something had been knocked sideways, and he wasn't the only one who noticed.

"You alright, Jocelyn, Honey?" Ellen asked, sharp as always when it came to sniffing out moods.

"Just a sudden headache," Jocelyn murmured.

His folks traded looks, then sent the same questioning glance Cole's way. Pop's was more accusatory than his mama's. But he just shrugged, not knowing what to make of it, then offered to take Jocelyn home once the plates were cleared.

"We'd love to have you again," Ellen said as she walked them to the door, her attention locked on the way Jocelyn's shoulders crept up toward her ears.

"Thank you so much for your hospitality," Jocelyn said, voice too polite, too thin. "I'm sorry to cut out early."

"No need for sorry, Honey." Ellen gave her one of those soft, mothering smiles, though the worry never left her eyes. "You holler if you need something."

Jocelyn tried to return the smile, but it died out quick. "Thank you, Ellen. John." She gave them both a nod.

"Night, Jossie," John said, bushy brows pulled low.

In the truck, Jocelyn waved off Cole's offer of pain meds. When she clicked her buckle into place, her movements held the barely contained aggression of anger, her hands shaking.

"What's going on here, Jocelyn?" It wasn't quite a demand, but there was no softness in his tone.

A sigh cut through her lips, but she refused to look at him. "Please, just take me to the hotel."

His grip tightened on the wheel as he backed out, frustration and confusion twisting in his gut.

It only took a few minutes for the silence to crack.

"Tell me, Cole. Did your dad confess something to you last week? After our... disagreement?"

Rage lit him up from the inside like a shot of tequila. "The hell does that matter?"

He expected her to yell, but her chin trembled. "Why was he there the night of the fire? He wasn't on shift. Why was he at my house so fast—before the fire station had even been alerted?"

The question hung there between them, sharp enough to cut him open.

SEVENTEEN

*"Only in the fire do we forge the unbreakable." -
Unkown*

Cole's head jerked toward her, the anger he'd carried a moment ago gone as quick as it came. Jocelyn had heard it in his voice, felt it crackle in the air, but now something else danced in his pale blue gaze—something sharper, questioning.

"When I talked to Chief Ward, he mentioned how your dad just happened to be nearby that night. And then I got this note telling me to back off my digging. Same kind of paper I found on the floor of your parents' living room just now. Makes me wonder if all that kindness of theirs is just a mask. Like maybe your dad's got something to hide." Her words poured out too fast, tumbling over each other until her lungs ached for air. "But God, I'm terrified of that being true, Cole. I love your parents. I don't want to lose them."

It took him a beat to process, then his brows sank low and his voice came out rough. "You got a note threatenin' you?"

Jocelyn twisted her fingers together. "Not exactly threatening."

"What the hell did it say?" The growl in his throat made her heart knock against her ribs. It was protective, primal, the kind of sound a man made when danger circled close to something or someone important.

That realization held her captive for a moment. She kept her silence one second more—not because she couldn't remember. No, those words were burned into her mind, just one more piece of paper she'd committed to memory.

But because she wanted to cherish the thought that someone cared that much, even if it wasn't truly a threat.

Finally, she forced the words out, flat and cold: "'Some questions are better left unanswered.'"

Cole sucked in a breath, his jaw ticking as he stared out the windshield. The truck rumbled on down the road, but his thoughts were somewhere else entirely.

He turned into the alley, parked, then smacked his palms against the steering wheel with a muttered curse. "Forgot to take you back to the hotel."

"It's fine. I think I need a minute, anyway," she admitted, though she wasn't sure what good a minute would do.

His head tipped toward the back door of the building. "You wanna come up? My place is on the second floor." He killed the engine, already shoving his door open before she could answer.

Jocelyn slid out, too, more to clear her head than follow him. Her feet kept her near the truck while he strode toward the entrance, only stopping when he noticed she wasn't behind him. He turned and something in her stuttered.

She remembered John all those years ago—a bit thicker than Cole, not quite as tall—turning to look at her when she'd called for him. He'd handed her off to paramedics, and she'd fallen into full hysterics. He'd turned back, gone to comfort her so they could do a thorough check.

She pushed the memory back and stared hard at Cole. "What do you know about why your dad was there that night?"

Cole's nostrils flared as he shoved a hand through his hair. "You asking me if my old man started that fire, Jocelyn?"

Anger again.

It didn't stir any in her. In fact, pressure built against her eyeballs, the threatening fear and sadness at the possibility flipping her calm upside-down.

"No." She had to pause, swallow back her tears. "I'm asking what you know. What he told you."

Cole came toward her, hard-edged. "Why the hell didn't you ask him at dinner?"

Finally, her own fury surfaced, and she thought, *Thank God*. She wasn't sure she could handle it if she broke down right then and there, let her grief and heartbreak spill out in the face of his anger.

"Because I wasn't questioning a damn thing until I found that paper. And then I couldn't stop wondering if the man who saved my life also betrayed me. Or if your mama's kindness was just an act to cover a scheme to run me out of town." Her chest heaved, the pressure of the anger and grief a band around her ribs, getting tighter and tighter. "I don't want to believe it. I don't want to hurt them by asking the question. But—"

Cole's voice sliced through hers, sharp as barbed wire: "You sure don't mind cutting me open with the question, do you?"

Her silence only seemed to wound him further.

"Got it," he said bitterly. "They matter more to you than I do. I'm nothing, so why not shove the hard questions on me instead of them?"

"No," she said softly. "You're not..."

His chin shifted forward when she didn't continue. "Not what?"

"Not nothing." It was all she could offer just then. Because he *wasn't* nothing, but he wasn't *something* yet, either. She wasn't sure if she could handle it if he ever became something. "I don't want to hurt you."

He interrupted her with a humorless laugh, low and ragged. Turning away, he dragged a hand through his hair again, ruffling curls loose.

"I don't, Cole," she insisted. "But I need answers."

Answers had become as precious to her in that moment as the air she dragged in and out. And because he'd turned away from her, he couldn't see that, even if she *hated* asking the question, it might alleviate the pain that had slowly been building the moment her fingers touched that piece of card stock, torn on the edge just like the note she'd found.

She was burning up with it, this heartbreak that was waiting to happen.

He spun back, face carved in fury. "Well, here's one for you. Pop didn't set that fire. He was walking off a high."

She blinked. "What?"

Cole's jaw worked, and those eyes, those serene pools, shifted from her face. It was shame that made him turn away, she realized.

"He was addicted to pain killers—Oxy. Been clean since that night." The words came raw like they'd been dragged against jagged rocks.

She heard more in his voice than the shame. There was betrayal there, and the complicated history of a man who'd had a difficult relationship with his father.

Now that was something she could empathize with.

Cole put his hands on the hood of his truck like he needed the anchor. Despite his stillness, the buzz of energy pulsed in the air. "Always had this image of him in my head, you know? The guy who put his life on the line for everyone but us. And then he was the hero. Even if he wasn't there for his family, at least he was the picture of what a man's supposed to be." His laugh was short and bitter. "Turns out that picture was crooked as hell."

Sadness nudged at her heart, softened her voice. "Doesn't knowing he's human make him... more real? More like the rest of us?"

Cole muttered a curse. "Ain't that the funny part? It just pisses me off more."

Silence grew heavy between them until she spoke again, quiet and careful. "Nobody else knows, do they?"

His lips pressed thin.

"And if they did... it'd ruin him."

"It's not exactly rare. Lot of guys on the crew wrestle with one demon or another. You live in fire every damn day, you start lookin' for a way to take the edge off. High-risk job, high-risk stress relief."

Her heart squeezed. High-risk stress relief... like arson? She almost flinched at the thought. She wanted to believe the best about John, if not for his own sake, for Ellen's and Cole's. But she couldn't deny that walking off a high wasn't exactly an alibi. If anything, it pointed to the greater possibility of him having started the fire, even if accidentally. Who better to set a fire and make it look like an accident than a firefighter?

Her chest ached at the truth of it, how much it threw into question for her, how it had thrown them both off. She tried to steady herself, but her thumb rubbed unconsciously at the ache beneath her sternum. He caught the gesture, made her aware of it.

"Been quite the day. For both of us," he said, voice softening for the first time. "You okay?"

Her response came automatic: "I'm fine."

He studied her, unconvinced. "Fine? Now, really, Darlin'?" A smirk tugged at his mouth, humorless and knowing. "Don't sound like fine to me."

Her gaze lifted skyward. She hated the naked feeling and the contradiction of terror that he could see past the mask, see the sadness at the possibility of him walking away if she was honest. It was dizzying.

"I expected the emotions," she admitted. "The grief. Even some push back from people in town. But..."

"But what?" There was a tightness to his voice that drew her eyes to his face.

Did he know what was coming? Could he sense the doubt that threatened to drown her?

A vine of fear snaked through her stomach, winding its way up her throat to choke out the real answer. What came out was: "I just didn't realize it would be this hard."

His shoulders hunched for a moment. Could he hear the lie in her voice or did he believe her words? The last thing she wanted was to hurt him, to damage whatever this was between them, even if it was ridiculous to consider that it could be anything.

She was well-versed in the hazards of a woman who followed her feelings for a man into disaster. She was a Murphy, after all.

Neither of them spoke for a moment, the silence heavy as autumn fog.

Then a siren split the air like an ax through a log. They both flinched, but she started moving first because something about it rattled in her bones with a foreboding she couldn't shake.

Working their way through the alley, they made it to the sidewalk in time to catch the engine that barreled out of the station and cut right in front of them on its way down First Street.

It was an odd sixth sense, maybe because of heightened emotions, maybe because she had an intimate knowledge of fire. But the foreboding turned into leaden dread when she spotted the smoke snaking into the dusky blue sky—thick, black, toxic.

Cole looked at her, a silent question in his eyes.

And then they ran.

Eighteen

"I survived because the fire inside burned brighter than the fire around me." - Joshua Graham

They slowed at the corner where First met Walnut, but Cole felt the way Jocelyn internalized the sight before them. The Hollow Inn—the only hotel in town—wasn't completely swallowed by fire. Yet. But the right wing was coughing out heavy smoke, the kind that meant the blaze was still chewing its way through the old bones of the place.

Being a firefighter's son, he knew the crew had gotten there quick enough to save most of the structure. Odds were good the left side would stand, patched up and still workable for Heath and Sally Anne to limp their business along. But that depended on how fast they could get the flames wrangled.

He cut a glance at Jocelyn. Her face had gone pale as ash, and she hugged her arms tight around her middle, bracing like she could hold herself together by sheer force of will.

"My room's on that side," she whispered.

Cole's chest pulled tight. "Hopefully the fire hasn't touched it."

She only nodded, jaw flexing as she watched the parking lot crowd. Barely contained panic rolled through the folks who'd been caught in the chaos.

Their talk before about the arsonist from twenty years back rose up in his mind like smoke curling out of an old chimney. Logic said it could be coincidence. The Hollow Inn was a turn-of-the-century relic, full of bad wiring and outdated guts. But the idea of coincidence didn't sit with any measure of rightness, especially knowing how thorough Heath was about that kind of thing. That, with Jocelyn's note, her digging, her history with this town and fire itself—it all added up to more than happenstance.

"My clothes will be ruined," she murmured.

Her words yanked his attention back to her. Her color still wasn't promising, but there was a hardness to her expression and a set to her chin like she was ready to go to war with whoever had done this.

"Even if they aren't burned, the smoke'll stain everything—" She cut herself off, the anger in her throat choking out the rest.

Before Cole could say a thing, she spun on her heel and stalked down the sidewalk. Took him a few beats to shake off the whiplash and catch up.

"Where you goin'?"

"Getting my car." She didn't even look at him, but her face carried a hard edge that put a chill down his spine.

"Then what?" he asked, picking up his pace.

She wheeled around so fast he almost plowed into her. "Why? Why do you need to know, Cole?"

Her gaze cut him open. His mouth went dry. "Because I wanna make sure you're alright."

"I'm fine."

The way she said it lit him up inside, sharp and hot, like a slap. He could see the wall going up between them, stone by stone. Maybe it'd been there all along, and he'd just been fool enough to think he could slip past it.

His fingers curled in tight. "Alright, then."

He brushed by her, stalking back toward the Nail, every step clipped and hard. Stupid, probably, but that old itch was riding him—the one that said he had to be like his daddy, had to measure up to the hero everybody else remembered. Maybe even prove to Jocelyn that he was cut from the same cloth, no matter how tarnished his father's image was now.

Couldn't prove a damn thing if she didn't give him the chance to, if she didn't let someone help her with that burden.

Inside the Nail, Terra gave him a sharp stare as he blew past her. He ignored it, heading for the back stairs. Up, down, up again—three times he pounded them out, burning off the mad coursing through his veins.

When he finally shoved into his apartment, he paced the floor like a caged animal. The window showed thinning smoke rising over the Inn now, which meant the fire was nearly out, thank God. Heath and Sally Anne would be buried under mess enough without losing the whole place. He'd check on them soon, once the crowd cleared.

But even as he tried to settle, Jocelyn's face kept flashing in his mind—her suspicion, her fear, her anger so sharp it had teeth. She'd stormed off mad, but he knew better. There was more under it: frustration, maybe loss, maybe that same shadow of fear that chased his own thoughts.

That stirred something in his gut—the idea that she would be scared, this woman he really barely knew but had heard about his whole life. His mama had talked about her plenty. And so he did know. He knew her history without ever asking. Varsity soccer, full ride scholarship, the serious boyfriend, the first job. He knew her like family, but the pull under his skin told him she was anything but.

He rubbed his hands together, heat sparking in his palms, needing something to do. The need to move, to work, was bred in him same as breathing. His granddad used to say he had ants in his pants. His mama knew better—it was a body that couldn't sit still, a man that had to put his hands to use.

And now he had something worth that restless energy. Jocelyn needed help—even if she didn't know it, even if she didn't want it. He could give her that. He wanted to give her that. And not because of who his daddy was.

It was that fire. The note. No, not coincidence at all. Deliberate.

Purpose lit him up, quick and sure.

Cole jogged for the stairs again, already knowing he wouldn't keep his distance anymore. She could shut him out if she wanted, but he wasn't backing down. Not this time.

Cole breezed down to the restaurant, and the wall of sound struck him like a freight train.

"What the hell?" he muttered as he rounded in behind the bar.

"Fire is good for business," Terra said with a raised brow. She was almost yelling over the din.

"Good for business, bad for my ears. What're they sayin'?"

"All kinds. Saw Jocelyn runnin' away like maybe she'd lit it." Cole cut her a razor look, but she kept on. "There was an explosion before it went up. It was just a small blaze—started by some kids. It came from the kitchen. A smoker leaving cigarettes unattended in a room. Take your pick."

The growl rumbled in his chest, and he scowled out at the chaos of the dining room. No one was eating a quiet dinner tonight. Not that the Nail was the place for quiet, but it usually was calm enough for a conversation at least.

No one wanted conversation now. This was a trading room for theories and speculation.

"Cole, Edith saw you there at the hotel." Henry Wetzel shoved his way to the bar.

"Yeah, I was there. Gonna check in on Heath and Sally when all's said and done. Offer my help."

Henry's lips flattened at the veiled admonishment. Cole made sure the edge was in his voice so there'd be no doubt about it.

"Any ideas what caused it?" Henry ventured.

"No." Cole moved along the bar, grabbing a glass to fill with Henry's beer of choice.

"Edith said Jocelyn was with you."

Cole's gaze sliced up to meet Henry's. "Yep."

The other man opened his mouth, shut it. Tried again. "Do you think the fire'll affect the Fest?"

"Doubt it. Look around you. Intrigue is good for business." Cole set the glass before Henry and gave him a hard stare.

The man took the hint, gave a curt nod, and squeezed back out through the crowd, pulling Cole's gaze with him.

It's how he managed to spot Lydia Abbott in a booth across the room. Natasha was with her, face creased into worry. Bodies slid back together, blocking his view. But not his determination.

He slapped his hand on the bar and pushed away, ignoring Terra's questioning look.

It was hell trying to make it through the throng, but he pushed his way through soon enough. Natasha was missing by the time he made it over.

"Sorry about this noise, Miz Abbott. Anything I can get you?"

Her perfectly painted mouth was tipped down. "It's not your fault, Cole, but thank you for asking. Natasha went to take care of the drinks since we've been waiting to even order food."

"Sorry about that." The freshness of the fire, the frustration from his interactions with Jocelyn, and the suspicion she'd planted in his mind brought the topic to his tongue. "Sad business, this fire."

Lydia's expression didn't budge. "Yes. I've heard they've got it out by now, though."

"Some speculation's goin' around that it wasn't an accident."

Her eyes tightened. "It's worth investigating every possibility, just to be sure."

He squared his stance, folding his arms. "Sure. Probably just talk anyhow."

The smile she gave him was almost painful. "It's a favorite pastime around here. There's always someone stirring things up, someone knocking on doors that ought to stay shut."

That felt a bit like a dig. "I'll hear facts myself when I check in with Heath," he said, measuring her. "Figure I can help him and Sally Anne when things clear out."

"Mercy, Cole, I don't know how you keep up," Lydia said, the first sign of a bite in her voice. "Stepping in to help, just like your daddy. But then y'all have always been known for taking on… strays."

He stiffened. Definitely a dig. When she scooted out of her seat, it forced him to step back.

"Taken care of, Mama," Natasha said breezily as she joined them. "Hey, Cole. Sorry, but we paid for our drinks and will try another day for a meal. This is… madness."

He nodded in her direction, but his eyes didn't leave Lydia. "Next one's on me, ladies."

"Mighty kind of you, Cole," Natasha said, her tone uncertain as she looked between them. Wasn't the first time her mama had ruffled feathers, though she tended to be more subtle about it.

"You take care, now," he said, tearing his gaze from the mother to give her daughter a quick smile.

The women made it to the door, and he tracked their progress until they were gone, something sitting in his belly he couldn't quite name. No surprise Lydia'd be bothered by Jocelyn's presence. Probably even felt betrayed by anyone who offered her kindness.

Everything about this new fire sat wrong, stirred the suspicion that wasn't too far from the surface. And with his mind already made up to help Jocelyn, it sure put every interaction he had in a new, harsh light.

And that just pissed him off.

Nineteen

"What fire does not destroy, it hardens." - Oscar Wilde

With no real plan, Jocelyn drove the weaving country roads until her anger cooled and her thoughts steadied. After spinning through the few options she had, the wild card she decided to play was one she'd almost forgotten about, which teased the guilt forward.

By the time the sun dipped behind the hills, she was turning into the drive up to her uncle's house. It wasn't as far gone as she'd expected, even as the images of what she remembered rolled through her mind. The paint was still peeling, the windows just as grimy, but the structure looked more solid than what was in her memory.

Her arrival kicked up dust, luring Joe Murphy out to the porch. He wore work coveralls and a scowl, both broken in from years of use. He didn't walk down the porch steps or greet her as she got out of the car, and uncertainty settled over her like a blanket.

Nan hadn't spoken with her younger brother in several years, cutting him off because of the number of times he'd called or come around asking for money when he'd blown all of what he had on booze and gambling.

Despite the lack of welcome, Jocelyn walked the few feet toward the porch, desperate more than hopeful.

"Well, ain't this a surprise," he said, eyeing her. "Bonnie's little mini finally come to see me. Heard you were in town."

Jocelyn shoved her hands into her pockets. "Hey, Uncle Joe."

"Well, come on in." His movements weren't sloppy as he led the way, but hard living more than age had slowed him.

She mounted the porch carefully, surprised to find it sturdy—and new. Inside, she stopped cold. Last they'd visited, years ago, the place had been filthy, cluttered, and nearly collapsing. These walls were patched and painted with new light fixtures in place, and fresh trim had been nailed along the edges of floors, ceilings, and around windows and doors.

Joe's mouth hitched at her stunned expression. "Welcome to my sobriety project."

She couldn't believe it. This hundred-year-old house had barely been hanging on when she was a kid. Nan would lament that her childhood home was being destroyed by her lush of a younger brother. Not that her grandmother's memories of her upbringing were positive with the history of their family. It was honestly no wonder her brother had walked the path of alcoholism and degeneracy.

But Nan had always said how much she loved the house and the history of it—built by her grandfather at the turn of the century.

Jocelyn peeked into the small bathroom—the only one in the house—to find a new vanity, an ornate mirror hanging above, and a checked floor tile design.

When she turned around, Joe was waiting in the archway between the living room and the kitchen, holding two glasses of sweet tea. A strangely sheepish expression cradled his prematurely weathered face—the result of a lifetime of heavy smoking and drinking.

"You did all this yourself?"

He shrugged a boney shoulder. "'Fraid so. Not the best work, but it beats the bottle."

A laugh escaped her. "It looks amazing, Uncle Joe. Nan should see it."

"Maybe when it's finished," he muttered, handing her a glass. He settled into one of two recliners, gesturing for her to sit. "Now tell me, Jossie, what brings you by?"

"That award they gave to John Hauser," she said. "I owed it to him to come."

Joe nodded slowly. "Heard it was a big deal."

There was something in his expression she couldn't quite put her finger on, but he said nothing more, his attention drifting to the TV across the room.

"Where you staying?" he asked, taking a sip of his tea.

Jocelyn released all the air in her lungs in a whoosh, sinking deeper into the chair. "I was at the Hollow Inn."

Her tone pulled his focus from the TV. "Was?"

The light from the lamp caught in the crystal of her glass, and she stared at it a moment to steady herself.

"Well, there was a fire there tonight."

He lurched forward, nearly spilling his tea. "What?"

"I wasn't there. Lost my stuff, though."

He eyed her with some level of suspicion that was all too familiar. "A fire where you're staying. Don't sound like coincidence."

She gave him a grim smile. "I don't think so either."

That shrewd look remained on her. "You don't suppose your mama's was, either."

"Nan never did."

He snorted. "Fat lot of good it did her."

The bitterness filled the air like an aroma, though it was true enough. Nan had raged about it. Always said it wasn't right, that they closed the investigation too quickly, that they all did her and Mama wrong. But she sure didn't like the idea of Jocelyn coming back, asking the questions she'd always wondered about. Too much like stirring the pot, and that was something Nan never did.

"That why you're really here?" Joe asked.

The look she slanted in his direction pulled a chuckle out of him.

He shook his head. "You sure are your mother's daughter. Where your nan let life happen to her, your mama made damn sure she happened to life."

It was strange hearing her mother described that way, knowing the life they'd led. A bit of scraping by that didn't equate to much. But Mama sure did have that winning smile, and she loved to laugh. She'd sought out reasons to as often as she could. Maybe Jocelyn did remember a bit of a spark.

She wanted some of that. She wanted to happen to life.

"Stay here 'til you sort things out," Joe said, turning back to the TV. "Got a room upstairs finished that needs a test-run."

Relief softened her face. "Thanks, Uncle Joe."

He nodded, seeming distracted. But then his flinty words hit her squarely. "And then you give those responsible for your mama the hell they deserve."

Sunrise painted the old barn with warmth. What once had looked rickety and decrepit seemed stubborn and rugged in the new dawn.

Admittedly, it was probably just Jocelyn's own mindset shift. She'd slept well despite the circumstances that had brought her to the house. But seeing what Uncle Joe had managed to do, a new determination shored up her bones.

Even something seeming too far gone could be rebuilt.

Joe stepped out onto the porch, and she turned.

"Made some waffles."

She couldn't help smiling. "Uncle Joe, you didn't have to."

He winked and held the screen door for her to head back in.

The pile of waffles proved he'd been cooking for a while, and he poured them each a cup of coffee as Jocelyn sat at the little round table. The floral tablecloth made her smile.

They ate in silence as minutes crept by, the time marked off by the sleek, minimalist clock that hung in the corner of the room. The minute hand caught the light, glinting a soft golden color that matched what touched the barn she could still see just outside the window over the sink.

There was hope in this little kitchen, all gleaming counter tops and refinished cabinets reflecting the morning light.

She turned to her uncle, waiting until he'd chewed down his most recent bite. "What made you decide to get sober?"

He didn't seem bothered—or surprised—by the question. Sitting back with a sigh, he gave his head a shake. "It just don't feel good to need something that bad."

A note of anger rang in there, and maybe that was part of it, too. A person needed to hate the thing that had them so locked in its grip to break its hold.

Was that what Mama had done with her father? Why she'd been so unkind to him that last time Jocelyn had seen him come around? Though she'd never known Bonnie to give him an inch, Jocelyn knew her mama's heart had held onto him for longer than she'd ever wanted it to.

Joe took in her pensive expression. "What's your plan, Jossie?"

"Probably talk to Sally Anne again. I already asked her about Ned Turner."

"Turner?" That name came chewed up as Joe spat it out. A history there, for sure. "Your landlord, back then, right?"

She nodded. "Do you know him well?"

Joe's mouth pinched. "Worked with him for a bit. 'Fore I lost my job for bein' drunk on the clock. He's a mean old badger." His beady eyes shifted to suspicious. "You think he had somethin' to do with your mama's fire?"

"It's crossed my mind."

He rubbed his palm over the white grizzle on his chin. "What do you need with Sally this time?"

"Aside from this new fire?"

His mouth tipped up.

"She was Mama's best friend back then. She might know something I don't. I've been digging, Uncle Joe. Digging deep, looking at old reports, making notes. But nothing beats talking to people who were there."

Understanding lit in his gaze. "True enough."

"Before seeing Sally Anne," she said, "I want a shot at Ned Turner. Start with the harder case. You know where he lives?"

Joe's lips pursed. "I do. But, Honey, I don't know about you goin' after him."

She bristled but managed a tight smile. "I'll be nice."

"It's not you bein' nice I'm worried about."

"I'll be alright, Uncle Joe."

He grunted.

When she rose to clear the dishes, Joe stopped her with a shake of his head. "You got stuff to do, Jossie, and you're my guest. Let me handle it."

She shot him a soft smile. "I'm family, not a guest."

He gave his head another firm shake. "No, ma'am. I have a lot to make up to a lot of folks, you and your nan most of all. Please, let me take care of 'em."

The earnestness in his face made her relent, if reluctantly. "Alright."

She bent to kiss his cheek, and he smelled of sandalwood and menthol cigarettes.

"Give that old porcupine hell," Joe said with a raspy chuckle as she headed out.

TWENTY

"Do not let your fire go out, spark by irreplaceable spark..." - Ayn Rand

Cole pounded down his usual running route like he was trying to outrun the mess inside his own head. Normally the looping roads and sloping hills burned the edge off, but today his mind ran faster than his legs.

And every one of his thoughts boiled down to one thing: Jocelyn.

He wondered how she'd slept after the fire. Hell, *if* she'd slept. Wondered where she'd laid her head. Wondered if she'd thought about their last fight, or if she was preparing to shut him down when he offered help again.

Finally, he wondered if she'd given up. But, no. Her reaction was burned into his memory—that was the kind of mad that didn't cool off. The kind that kept you moving. She hadn't come back here to fold. She came hunting answers, and she wasn't leaving 'til she had them.

He barreled through the old mill district, the dead brick factories crouched like watchmen in the shadows. Felt like a ghost town these days.

He pushed harder, lungs heaving as the road tipped uphill into the canopy of trees. Sun and shadow striped across his skin like paint strokes, carrying him out toward the crooked cluster of homes on the other side.

That's when he heard it. Voices sharp enough to cut over the bass thumping in his headphones. Arguing.

He might've kept on—small-town drama wasn't his business—if not for the car in the drive with North Carolina plates. Jocelyn.

A jolt of electricity shot through him, and he was veering before he'd even thought about it. He tugged his earbuds out, stuffing them in his pocket, and cut up the gravel drive. And there it was: Jocelyn's voice.

"I just wanted to—"

"I said get off my damn property!" That was Ned Turner, plain as day. Old and mean, all bile and bluster.

"Mr. Turner, please," Jocelyn said, desperation in her voice.

"I ain't repeatin' myself, girl," Ned growled. "You wanna know about that fire, talk to your daddy. He was there that day."

She lurched forward, hands outstretched. "What do you mean?"

"What I said. I saw your daddy's fancy car, sittin' slick in the driveway like it belonged there. Now get off my damn property. This is a stand-your-ground state, and I got my shotgun right here."

Cole's blood surged. His jog broke into a sprint. "Hey!"

Both of them whipped toward him.

"You best watch yourself, Ned," Cole barked, clenching his fists around air instead of Ned Turner's bloated neck.

"Watch your own self, Hauser." Ned glared, but he backed into the house, slamming the door so hard the windowpanes rattled.

Jocelyn's face was drawn with fury—and not a little bit of fear. Cole slipped a hand around her arm, tugging her back toward the car.

"That man is crazy," she sputtered, voice jagged with leftover adrenaline.

"Nah," Cole muttered, keeping a keen eye on that front door. "Just an asshole. But assholes with guns aren't worth stickin' around for."

She let him steer her to the car, that healthy fear doing its job. Her hair caught sunlight like embers, and she wore the same clothes as yesterday, though freshly washed. She looked fierce, and worn, and damn stubborn.

Cole guided her to the driver's side then went to the passenger side door, yanking it open.

She stopped short, glaring. "What the hell are you doing?"

"Ridin' back with you." He arched a brow, daring her to argue.

Her mouth pinched, but she said nothing and slid behind the wheel. He climbed in after her, relief loosening his shoulders as she threw the car into reverse. The tires crunched over gravel too fast, and his hand went to the overhead bar as they shot out onto the road.

"Why were you at Ned Turner's?" he asked, voice steady despite the way she was whipping around the curves.

"Same question," she fired back, focus trained on the asphalt like it might buck her if she blinked.

He let out a slow breath, deciding to give her his truth first as a peace offering. "Out for my run, heard him jawin' at you. Figured I'd better check."

"Felt like rescuing me, you mean." The teeth she put into the words didn't have the same bite when her nerves gave her away.

Still, his hackles rose. "Give me a break, Jocelyn. He threatened you. You're damn lucky I came along when I did."

That earned him a sharp look, her lips pressed tight.

"Turner's always been mean as a snake, but you got him riled." When she didn't respond, Cole pressed, "Get any answers?"

"Besides that jab about my father, no. He shut down the second he saw me. Looking like my mama doesn't exactly help my case."

She meant it serious, but the sulky tilt of her words made Cole bark a laugh before he could stop it.

Her glare had his humor drying up. "Sorry. Bad timing."

She whipped the car to a stop in front of the Nail, dropping it into park but leaving the engine running.

"Come inside," he said.

She sliced him with a look, apparently not keen on the invite.

"Don't open for hours yet. Just—come inside, Jocelyn. I wanna talk."

She studied him a beat longer before killing the engine. Purse in hand, she followed him in.

Cole flipped on the low lights, and led her upstairs. What hit him inside his apartment was something he wasn't prepared for. It was the sight of her in his own space. She wandered, gaze touching details and taking in everything like she was cataloging evidence. When her eyes slid back to him, softer now, it damn near knocked the air out of his lungs.

For a second, he wanted nothing more than to cross the room, drag her close, and kiss her until the world burned out.

Her head tilted when she caught his expression, a puzzled look dancing across her face. "What?"

Cole grunted, tearing his eyes away. "Nothin'. Gimme five minutes."

He ducked into the bathroom before he lost all his sense, showering quick and cold, yanking on clean clothes as quick as his damp skin allowed.

When he came back out, he found her standing over by the island that separated the dining area from the kitchen, running long, slender fingers over the counter top. It was another slab of cedar, the twin to the bar top downstairs.

Awe was painted across her face as sunlight blazed in, caressing her cheek and setting her hair on fire, pulling out the red. He wanted to release it from the braid she'd pulled it into, watch it drag across the counter top as she leaned down to inspect the swirling grain in the wood. He wanted to tangle his fingers in it, brush it back over her shoulders, let it fan out around her as he laid her down on his bed.

No.

With effort, he shook the image from his mind and stalked into the kitchen.

"What'd you wanna talk about?" she asked, voice as unsteady as he felt.

Cole busied himself with the ritual of pouring coffee, taking comfort in the familiarity. He lifted the pot to offer her some.

She shook her head. "I had some at my uncle's."

That raised his brows as he replaced the pot. "Your uncle's."

He heard her smile and turned to drink it in. There was disbelief in the layers of her expression, buried under all the history that belonged to her and not him. He'd heard just enough from gossip to have an inkling, but the details were out of his reach.

The craving to be invited there, to know it *all*, was as strong as the one he fought daily for movement and busy-ness.

"I went out to Joe's last night, after..." She shifted and cleared her throat. "I couldn't believe it." She gave him a hard look. "Did you know?"

He leaned back against the counter. "Knew he got sober a while back. Wasn't until recently that I saw how he did it."

She shook her head. "It's incredible. I wish Nan could see it."

"Why can't she?"

Jocelyn snorted. "A lot of people have let her down, and Joe was the last in a very long line. Old age and experience have robbed her of a forgiving heart."

"Hm."

She squinted at him. "You keep distracting me."

Same, he thought wryly.

"So?"

He cleared his throat. "I wanna help with your investigation."

Her fingers tightened on the edges of the island. "You want to help." Those words—flat, dangerous—warned him of the risk he was taking.

"Yeah," he said, standing his ground. "You already shared some of it with me. Why not go one step more? Figure having somebody local, you might have some better luck."

Her eyes flashed. "You think I can't handle it alone. That I'm too much of an outsider."

Heat flared through him, but his voice stayed level. "Not what I said."

"It's what you meant," she bit out, leaning forward.

He leaned forward, too, frustration sparking. "Jocelyn, Ned Turner threatened you today. What if I hadn't been there?"

"I would've left," she shot back. Her voice didn't waver, but her eyes did.

"And what if he hadn't backed off?"

The space between them shrank again. The island wasn't wide, and suddenly her gaze dropped to his mouth. His blood roared in response, fingers tightening on the handle of his mug.

"I suppose you think that because your dad saved me back then, it's your turn now?" Those words were warning smoke over his lips because what she said next burned: "You've got a savior complex, Cole."

The words hit hard, and he jerked back, hot coffee splashing out of his cup to scald his chest.

He hissed.

Jocelyn scrambled around the island for the paper towels, swiping at his shirt until he caught her wrist, holding her hand still.

"That hurts," he ground out.

"Sorry." She pulled her hand from his grip and took a step back.

He pulled his shirt over his head, tossing it aside. Her gaze followed, cheeks flooding pink, her expression caught between apology and something else he couldn't afford to dwell on.

"All I need's a new shirt," Cole muttered, brushing past her, heat in his skin from more than just the burn.

When he came back, she was by the window, arms wrapped around herself as she stared out over First Street. For a moment, he just watched her, unsure what the hell to say next.

She felt him there and turned to give him a rounded stare. "I'm sorry. For what I said."

"Is it what you think?"

"No. Yes." Her mouth twisted. "Maybe. I just hate feeling... like I can't do things for myself."

Cole shook his head. "No one's saying you can't. And I sure as hell don't think that."

"Then why offer to help?"

"Because if that fire was on purpose, someone's still tryin' to bury the past. And I don't like the thought of you without somebody watchin' your back."

Twenty-One

"This is how the fire starts. This is how we burn." - Libba Bray

Jocelyn's doubt was a fortress built over years of let-downs and being chosen last. But the earnestness in Cole's expression sent a tremor through its foundation, and she wasn't sure she could patch it back up if it cracked.

Having him along on her investigation *could* be a boon. People weren't exactly forthcoming with her. No matter her roots, in their minds, she was not the prodigal returned. More like a traitor slinking back.

She'd thrown a lot of suspicion toward Cole's family, so his motives might not have been as clear-cut as he claimed.

It kept her doubt deeply entrenched. "Do you even want to know what really happened?"

She expected a reaction, but Cole only crossed the room to retrieve the coffee he'd splashed on himself. To buy himself time?

He even sipped before answering. "Like you said, there are some big question marks."

She shouldn't have been entertaining this. Finding out about his father's secret had rattled him badly, and despite what he thought, she didn't want to hurt him.

"What if you don't like the answers?" she challenged.

He lowered the mug, steady though the faint flicker in his eyes betrayed him.

"This is your town," she insisted. "The people here are *your* people, your community."

Cole set the coffee down and moved closer. "You think I'd rather protect this place and let a murderer walk free?"

There was something feral in the way he closed the distance between them. It sent a shiver down her spine—part unease, part attraction. She expected a smirk to dance around that sexy slash of a mouth, but it never appeared as she backed up. The window sill stopped her, and still he kept coming.

"I don't know, Cole," she said, breathless. "People always say they want the truth, but not when it hurts."

He stopped only inches from her, but there was no victory in his expression, only intensity.

"I'm no stranger to pain, Jocelyn," he said, voice rumbling and low. "I'd rather dig it up myself than have it hurled at my back."

She searched his face for the proof that he meant it. "Just make sure you know what you're yourself getting into."

His gaze narrowed just a fraction. "Oh, I know what I'm getting myself into."

The air thickened between them, and a foolish, impulsive part of her brain whispered it wouldn't hurt to just push up on her toes, lay her mouth over his, put a match to the gasoline swirling between them. It was such a blistering heat that seared in the sliver of space that separated their bodies that she stupidly thought giving in might make it easier to douse the flame after.

Cole seemed locked in his own violent war with himself. He didn't step back, but his muscles were clutched so tightly, the energy to keep them frozen made a warmth radiate off of him, adding to the building pressure.

Her mind screamed, *Just kiss me*—and maybe she'd whispered it, because suddenly his mouth was on hers.

He pressed against her, hands firm but not wandering, only cupping the back of her head as his tongue tangled with hers. She clutched his shirt as the fire caught low in her body, flaring every nerve ending to screaming life. She was dangling at the edge of a precipice, and he was the only thing keeping her from falling.

A knock at the door snapped them apart.

"Cole?" A man's voice called, dousing Jocelyn in cold reality.

"Shit." Cole's mutter brushed her ear before he called, "Hang on, Heath."

Heat still burned in her cheeks when Cole opened the door to Sally's husband. Heath stood there, exhaustion etched into every line of his face, the acrid smell of smoke clinging faintly to his clothes. His gaze snagged on Jocelyn standing across the room.

"Oh. You have a guest."

Cole redirected by asking about the hotel.

"Yeah, that's why I came by," Heath said, attention shifting. "Wanted to see what you and me could do ourselves before we get quotes from contractors."

"Oh, sure." Cole glanced at her. "I'll be there in a half hour."

Heath nodded, looking dazed, like he didn't know what his life was any more. Tragedy could sure do a number.

"We can walk over with you," Jocelyn offered. "I want to chat with Sally anyway."

Heath shrugged, relief evident in his expression.

She ignored the look Cole shot her. He wasn't done with what had just happened between them. Neither was her body, but logic dictated that she put distance between them before she lost all sense.

"We'll meet you over there, Heath," Cole amended pointedly.

Heath's brow furrowed, but he nodded and headed back down the steps.

After he shut the door, Cole turned on her, the same wild light in his eyes as before.

Before he could say a thing, she headed him off. "If we do this—"

"This what?" His demand cut sharp through her words.

She pretended not to hear him. "There can't be any more kissing."

His jaw clicked shut, then he exhaled through his nose. "Fine."

She studied him, suspicious. "You agreed quick."

He scowled. "The investigation's what matters, isn't it?"

"Yes..."

"Then there's nothing to think about." He held the door for her, surly but resolute.

They decided to drive separately, the tension between them loud as thunder as they got into their vehicles. Jocelyn replayed their conversation over and over, wondering if the regret she felt stirring was from letting him in or putting up such strict boundaries.

The Hollow Inn came into view, leaving no more room to analyze.

On the outside, little seemed damaged. But inside, with the tarp covering the ruined wing and the smell of smoke clinging to every surface, Jocelyn stumbled under the weight of old memory. Cole seemed to falter, too, but he recovered quicker as they approached the front desk, where Sally and Heath's daughter Remy sat. She looked older than her seventeen years at the moment.

"Your mama around, Rem?" Cole asked. "Jocelyn's here to see her."

Jocelyn tried not to be annoyed at his take-charge attitude as Remy nodded. Her blonde ponytail bobbed as she slipped from her stool to head into the back, returning a moment later with a frazzled Sally Anne in tow.

"Oh, Cole, am I glad to see you," Sally Anne said. "Heath said you'd be by. He's off that way with the insurance man."

Cole nodded at her gesture and tossed Jocelyn one last look before he went in search of Heath.

"Let's talk in my office," Sally said, brushing loose curls from her face. "Oh, Jossie, it's so awful. I've been canceling reservations all morning, rearranging accommodations, and refunding all the guests stayin' in the right wing. Oh, I need to refund you for your stay!"

Jocelyn waved her off. "I used the room, didn't I? I've got a place to stay from here on out, so you just worry about everyone else."

Sally Anne eyed her as she led her into the cramped office, its walls crowded with family photos, licenses, and awards. "I heard you went up to Joe's."

Of course she had. Jocelyn squeezed into the lone chair, knees bumping the desk, while Sally Anne slid behind it, her hands lacing neatly together.

"It's amazing what he did with the place," Jocelyn said.

"It is." Sally's smile was faint and brief. "So, what is it you wanted to talk about?"

Jocelyn took the hint. "Any guesses how the fire started?"

Sally Anne's mouth flattened. "Electrical's what they're sayin'. But they're still lookin' into it."

"Electrical," she repeated. "Does that sound right to you?"

Sally Anne hesitated, wary. "When we renovated, we re-did everything—wiring, plumbing, the works. Paid special attention to it because of the buildin. But the fire started in a utility room where all that's hooked up. Could've been something we missed. Modern don't mean perfect."

"Who was the last person in there?" Jocelyn pressed.

"We got a maintenance guy, but Heath's just as nosy about that stuff as anyone." Sally Anne tilted her head. "Why are you askin' me this, Jocelyn?"

Jocelyn made a face.

"You think it wasn't an accident," Sally Anne said flatly.

"I don't think anything yet," Jocelyn deflected, though they both knew it was a lie. "But it's suspicious this fire happened now. In the hotel where I'm staying."

Understanding dashed across Sally Anne's face. "That's why you were askin' about Ned. You really don't think your mama's death was an accident, either."

Jocelyn didn't answer. She didn't need to.

"But why?"

"You were her best friend, Sally. Didn't it ever strike you as odd? Mama never drank that much. She never would've left a candle burning next to those curtains."

"They found the wine glass." Sally Anne's voice carried doubt, but not conviction.

"One glass, on the windowsill. They think it was wine on the curtains that made them torch so fast. But how did it spill there when she was found across the room?"

"Even if there was somethin' off about that fire, why would it be connected to this one?" It sounded like she was mostly asking herself the question.

Something like triumph lit inside Jocelyn then. "What do you remember about that night?

Sally Anne faltered, her gaze drifting upward as if memory lived in the ceiling. "Lord, it was so long ago. I was workin' at the Nail back then—before I met Heath."

"The Nail?" Jocelyn asked.

"Way before it was Cole's, it was this beat up old place. Had its regulars. Still does. Some of those guys still give me a little nod when we come in for dinner sometimes."

"Who?"

"Donny Shankman, Jack Friedl, Frank Leone..." Her voice slowed.

Jocelyn sat forward at that. "Was Frank there the night of the fire?"

Sally Anne nodded. "Soon as he got off work, like usual."

"Except when he was with Mama," Jocelyn murmured.

Sally Anne considered. "True. And now that you say it, I remember thinkin' it was odd. It was her night off."

Jocelyn's pulse raced. "How did he seem?"

"He was... down. Wouldn't say why. Just seemed off. Sat there sulkin' most of the evening, suckin' a beer."

"Talk to anyone?"

"Not really. Lydia Abbott said somethin' to him that lit him up for a minute." Sally Anne rolled her eyes. "That woman could chap the hide off a fence post."

Jocelyn didn't smile. "Then he left?"

"Must've. I wasn't payin' close attention, but he wasn't there when I got the call about the fire."

The eagerness under Jocelyn's skin nearly had her bolting out the door to find Frank. Instead, she forced her focus back. "Thanks, Sally. Do you know if I can get my things from my room?"

Regret painted Sally's face. "No, Honey. Your room took heavy damage. Most of that wing did. We'll get you money from the insurance—help you replace what you lost."

"I've got it covered."

"But—" Sally Anne stood just as Jocelyn did.

Jocelyn touched her arm. "You just focus on getting this place back on its feet."

Sally Anne still looked dazed when Jocelyn slipped past her, the weight of new information burning hotter than the fire that had started it all. The cramped air had been stifling, but stepping into the hall didn't loosen the knot in her chest. If anything, it cinched tighter.

Frank Leone.

He'd been there. Acting off. And Sally Anne had remembered enough to make Jocelyn's suspicions sharpen to a point. It flew in the face of what he'd told her.

Cole was waiting near the desk, his arms folded, that steady gaze locked on her when she came out. He didn't ask a thing, but the weight of the kiss still lingered between them, humming in the air like static.

She pushed past it. "I need to find Frank."

His jaw flexed, a muscle twitching in his cheek. "Now?"

"When the hell else?" Her voice came out clipped, urgent.

For a beat they just looked at each other, the air charged, not with heat this time but with something heavier—determination, maybe even fear. Cole's hand brushed along her elbow, light but anchoring.

"Then I'm comin' with you," he said.

The words should've steadied her. Instead, the mix of his nearness and the urgency burning in her veins left her even more off balance. Still, she didn't argue. She couldn't. Frank was the thread she needed to pull, and Cole had just tied himself to it.

Twenty-Two

"Her heart was tinder, and he the match." - Unknown

"I'm drivin'," Cole said.

She opened her mouth to argue.

"You know where to find him?" he challenged, tugging his keys from his pocket.

Her mouth snapped shut as she went to the passenger side of his truck.

"You said I could help," he pointed out as they slid into their seats.

She didn't like being reminded, but she sighed as she buckled up.

"So, why do you need to talk to Frank so bad?"

"Aside from the fact that my conversation with him the other day wasn't that helpful?"

He gave her a wry smile. "Yeah. Aside from that."

"Well," she started, "when I *did* talk to him, he was very vague about that night, which—fine, it was traumatic for us all and a lot just goes fuzzy—but he led me to believe he'd been out with my mama that night."

"But he wasn't."

"Not according to Sally Anne. She remembered him at the bar when *he* said he'd taken Mama out."

He shrugged, deciding to play devil's advocate again. "Could be he has a bad memory."

She clicked her teeth, frustration a simmer between them. Probably could tell he was baiting her on purpose.

"Sure," she ground out. "Except he said he couldn't remember. He only agreed that he'd probably taken her out at my suggestion because he almost always did on Mama's nights off."

It seemed straight-forward to him, but there was a reason she was bothered. "You don't believe that, then?"

"Sally said he was there, and I would tend to believe her. She was certain."

"Alright."

Despite the acceptance in his voice, she kept going, intent on the road before them. "Sally said he was upset about something, and she noticed that he didn't take Mama out when he normally would."

He considered that. "Maybe they'd had a fight."

"That would explain some things, but if that was true, why wouldn't he say that?"

"Makes him look bad," Cole suggested.

"And why would it make him look bad if her death and that fire were both accidents?" She raised a brow at him.

"You said yourself they aren't."

She whipped her head to look at him.

"And I already told you I agree."

"That's all they were to everyone else," she said, brows folding. "So he's either lying or he really doesn't remember."

He heard the steel in her voice. The pain under it, too. "And you need to figure out which."

She was quiet a moment, something bubbling below the surface. "I might've hedged about why I was in town, and I..."

So there was some guilt there. Part of him felt the twinge of resentment about that, about the fact that she'd feel bad misleading Frank when she came out swinging at his pop. But he also knew the questions had been chasing her for decades, and he was supposed to be helping.

"You deserve your answers, Jocelyn."

"Do I?" she murmured. It was like she knew what he'd been thinking.

And he found himself forgiving her for asking the questions because he couldn't shake the sadness in her expression just then. It wasn't quite like she regretted any of it or like she wanted to give up, and he could admire that. Two decades was a long time to wonder about something so traumatic, and there sure had been a lot to rattle her cage the last twenty-four hours. Unfortunate, his had to get rattled right along with.

"Frank was the closest thing to a father to me, and he was still so kind to me the other night." Her voice rolled over him like a mist, soft and gentle, as he turned into the parking lot of the auto shop where Frank worked.

He put the truck in park and turned to her. "It won't matter what you ask him if he cares about you, Jocelyn. But you have to ask. You have to know."

His own words landed heavy. Came from knowing they were for himself, too. Because it was true. If he cared about her—which he couldn't deny anymore—he had to let her do this, keep asking, keep digging, even if it hurt. She'd warned him, hadn't she?

He'd said the words, but this was a moment when he had to decide if he believed them.

Jocelyn studied him, her posture edgy while she searched. And maybe she could see how he had to fight himself. But she finally nodded, satisfied with the grit she saw him shoring himself up with.

Cole trailed a little behind her as she headed for the shop's front door. Not much activity was going on, though the sign told them the place was open for business. Slow day, apparently.

A bell above the door announced their arrival, and the smell of engine grease and warm metal hit him hard. It was something familiar and foreign, tying him to other memories—taking his first truck in for an oil change because his daddy didn't have time to teach him. When he'd rolled that same truck and sat sulking after they'd told him it was totaled.

Instead of sitting, Cole leaned against the wall near the door, the memories making him edgy.

"Help you?" a man's voice, grizzled and worn, called as he walked out from a back office.

Robbie Clayton had graduated with Cole, an all-state football player who'd run with the high and mighty crowd. Cole hadn't been interested in sports, though he heard plenty about it. In a small southern town like this one, football was a religion.

Looking at Robbie's craggy face and thin hair, the greasy coveralls over his paunch, Cole didn't suspect it had gotten him far once they'd gotten out of school.

The other man looked from Jocelyn to Cole, his squint going tighter.

"I was looking to talk with Frank," Jocelyn said. "Is he here today?"

Robbie jerked a thumb behind him. "Was on his lunch break. I'll send him out. You that Hill Drive fire girl?"

Cole watched the muscles snap tight along Jocelyn's back.

"Heard you was hangin' around the Hollow, askin' questions." Robbie set his scrutiny back to Cole, sizing him up. "Heard you was runnin' with Hauser, here, too."

Something about the look and tone had Cole's hackles rising, but he didn't move a muscle. People always talked, always embellished. And he sure had plenty of experience with it taking on a negative spin. Was plain Robbie meant it that way, too.

"Jealous, Clayton?" Cole asked.

Robbie's mouth pinched, but he didn't move. He might've been a heavyweight and stacked with muscle in high school, but he'd gone soft and round over the years. Even back then, though, he'd been all air. Some things never changed.

Jocelyn gave Cole a warning look.

Frank's rangey frame came into view behind Robbie before the conversation spiraled further. He froze when he spotted Jocelyn, and Cole saw the flash of fear in his black eyes as they shifted to him.

"Jossie," Frank said, voice tight. "What're you doing here?"

Jocelyn looked at Robbie, whose attention was slow to move from Cole.

But then it finally did, and he turned to Frank. "Take it outside. Don't need y'all's drama botherin' customers."

Frank looked at Robbie like the other man had betrayed him, but he headed around the counter toward the door, Jocelyn and then Cole following him out.

"I had some questions," Jocelyn said as soon as the door closed, her voice too hard, like she was covering the guilt or the hurt.

Frank shrank down like someone had battered him. "Alright." His gaze slid to Cole.

"I'll be right over here," Cole said, shifting to lean against the tailgate of his pickup. Close enough to hear, far enough to seem uninvolved, especially when he turned his face away. Frank was uncomfortable enough.

"What'd you want to ask?" Frank's voice was still wound tight, like he suspected what she might have to say.

"I had a chat with Sally Anne this morning."

"Heard about their fire. That where you were staying?"

From the corner of his eye, Cole caught her nod. "I was just checking in on them. We got to talking about that night."

She didn't have to say which one. The way Frank's expression shuttered made it clear he knew exactly where she was going.

"She worked at the bar back then," Frank said, heading her off.

Cole didn't bother hiding his interest in the conversation now.

Jocelyn didn't relent. "She said you were there that night, not out with Mama."

He rubbed his chin. "Wasn't I?"

Cole tracked the movement, the change in his expression.

"She remembered you seemed pretty down."

"Aw, hell, Jossie. That night runs in with all the rest back then. Your mama, your daddy, all of it..." Frank turned to pace away from her but froze at the reminder of Cole's presence. He made a point to turn back to her. "Not much of it's clear anymore, but you think I lied to you about it?"

Jocelyn's arms wrapped around her middle. "I don't want to, Frank, but you told me a different story, and it's not close to what she said."

"It was twenty years ago," he said through his teeth. Then his shoulders slumped. "The woman I loved died. You expect me to remember exactly what I was doin' when my world came crashing down?"

Cole saw the toll those words took on Jocelyn, and he pushed himself upright, waiting for the sign she needed support.

"I don't know." Her voice was stronger than Cole thought it'd be. "My world fell apart, too. And I never got all the pieces. So I thought..."

"I'm so sorry, Jossie." There was a fault line in Franks words then. "You've no idea how sorry I am, will always be, that she was taken from you. I wish to hell things were different. Been wishing all these long years."

Cole could see that, too. They all knew that his life had never moved forward. He'd never been with anyone else long enough for anyone to learn her name, lived in the same old house, worked at the same place. Stuck.

"I gotta get back to work."

Jocelyn took a breath. "I'm sorry to bother you here, Frank. I'm sorry for stirring up ghosts and old pain."

"Can't be helped, Jossie. They're all over the place," he said, turning to head back inside. His eyes flashed one last time to Cole before he disappeared inside.

Jocelyn's pain scraped the air as she stood there, attention tight on the faded asphalt at her feet. Hurtin' Frank had hurt her, and Cole's urge to fix it nearly overpowered him. But all he had were his two hands, and he'd promised to keep those to himself.

"Joss," he murmured, pulling her gaze back to his face.

She didn't say a word, simply walked toward the truck to get in, so he had no choice but to do the same.

He let the silence hang heavy for a few minutes as he drove them back, waiting for her to roll through her feelings about the conversation. It did a heavier number than either of them had anticipated.

But maybe that'd been Frank's goal. He sure hadn't admitted a damn thing, and that stuck out to Cole like a city slicker in a corn field. The question was whether Jocelyn saw it yet or not.

When he couldn't stand the quiet anymore, he asked, "Wanna talk about it?"

"Not particularly. But I probably should."

She fell silent again for another stretch, and Cole just let her be, watching the big green trees fly by them as the highway brought them from Whitley back to Cedar Hollow. Whitley had always been a little depressed in comparison, its population much smaller, the way of life even slower. It barely had a business to its name. Meant most of their folks headed to Cedar Hollow for anything worth doing.

"Ned Turner made a comment about Daniel Abbott."

Cole turned a surprised gaze on her. She sure avoided calling him her daddy at every opportunity. But Cole didn't remember the comment. He'd been too busy keeping his eye on Ned and that shotgun.

"What comment?"

She kept her face toward the window. "He said he saw Daniel's car in our driveway that day."

Suspicious for sure, but he was her daddy. "That wasn't usual?"

She shook her head. "He never publicly acknowledged us. There was no custody agreement, no relationship between us to speak of."

There was pain here, too, deeper, more raw. He hadn't known that. Sure, he'd made connections about the situation—given that she and Natasha were so close in age and Daniel had only married one of their mamas. But he hadn't realized it was some well-known secret. What a self-absorbed jerk he'd been back then.

"He'd come around before," she continued when he said nothing. "But not to see me. To argue with her about giving us money."

"To help take care of you?"

She scoffed. "Yeah, if we moved away."

Cole sucked a breath in through his teeth. "That what he said?"

She hesitated, brow folding. "It's what Mama told me he said."

"Hell of a thing, no matter who said it."

"Yeah," she agreed, looking out the window. "But something Frank said... he mentioned Daniel, too."

He let that sit for a moment. The question was there, waiting to be asked. But it would probably hurt, too. And he was tired of seeing her hurting when he couldn't do a damn thing about it.

He finally dredged up the guts. "You gonna confront him about it?"

Those arms went around her middle again. Trying to keep herself together, seemed like. "Eventually."

God, he wanted to hold her. "Nobody says it has to be now."

She sighed and turned to the window again. "Can you drop me at Joe's?"

She could use the rest. Hell, he needed the break from fighting himself so hard. He wanted too damn much.

"Sure, Darlin'," he said, making a turn.

As he headed up the driveway, he thought about the one thing he might be able to do for her.

"You still got that note with the threat?"

Surprise flashed across her face, but she dug in her big bag. "It wasn't really a threat."

Same thing she'd claimed the other day. But he said nothing as she met his eyes.

"What for, Cole?"

"Gonna see if I can match it to what Ma's got in her stores. Maybe eliminate one of your questions for you."

He pulled to a stop, and she handed the scrap over before reaching for the handle.

"What about your car?"

"I'll have Uncle Joe bring me to get it later. Maybe tomorrow."

She sounded so sad, and that slammed him hard. He kept his hands on the steering wheel obediently, but he felt like dirt doing it.

Twenty-Three

"When one burns one's bridges, what a very nice fire it makes." - Dylan Thomas

U ncle Joe dropped Jocelyn at her car around lunchtime the next day.

The sidewalks of downtown Cedar Hollow stirred with life as people took advantage of a day with cooler weather. Another storm had blown in the night before, teasing people with the faintest taste of autumn, and Jocelyn moved among them.

She'd been around almost two weeks, and the gazes didn't linger as much as they used to, like she'd become a bit more of a fixture. Some folks even offered her a nod of friendly acknowledgment.

It was odd, though. That ache in her middle kept throbbing, reminding her there were answers still to be found, a line that kept her from settling.

That thought stopped her. Settling wasn't the point.

And yet, she found herself drawn across the street, lured not only by practicality, but also some measure of connection. It would've been easy to seek it out with Cole, whose presence still clung to her like heat, pulling at her even as she fought to steady herself. Her body remembered his touch too easily, craving more than she dared allow. The very thought sent warmth into her cheeks.

But she kept on toward Natasha's boutique. The bell above the door chimed as Jocelyn slipped inside. Natasha was bent over the counter, blonde hair spilling forward as she studied a sheet of paper. She glanced up, her polite smile breaking wide when she realized who it was.

"Jocelyn!" Natasha said, then she gasped, her hands flying to her mouth. "Oh God, you were staying at the Inn, weren't you?"

Jocelyn sighed. "Yeah. I'm basically out of all my clothing."

"Oh, no!" She met Jocelyn halfway across the store and linked arms with her. "Well, let's get you a few things. On me, of course!"

Jocelyn waved her hands, a pit forming in her stomach. "Oh, I couldn't."

"No, please," her sister said. "I can use it as a write-off, and I order these tall sizes just in case, so they end up sittin' here unless I get them for myself. And I certainly don't need them!"

She ushered Jocelyn to a dressing room and bustled into the back, returning with an armload. "At least three out-fits," she said, voice stern. "There's a pajama set in there, too."

She dumped them into Jocelyn's arms and pushed her into the stall, hushing any protests. As before, everything fit like it was tailored to her.

It felt flat wrong to watch Natasha place the outfits into big bags and hand them over, but she continued to shut down any of Jocelyn's attempts at denying the generosity.

"Now," Natasha said brightly, folding her manicured hands on the counter. "Tomorrow night's the big bonfire. You comin'?"

Jocelyn cocked her head. "What bonfire?"

"A tradition they started a few years ago. It's for locals and tourists, a lead in to the Festival. There's an apple dessert contest." Natasha's eyes sparkled like she had a vested interest in that event. Still, it sounded like something no one but her would be happy to find Jocelyn at.

"I don't know..." Jocelyn shifted the bags on her arm.

"Please come!" Natasha clasped her hands like she was praying.

"I'll try," Jocelyn said, mostly to appease her.

It was enough to satisfy Natasha, and Jocelyn headed for the door, pushing through the guilt that she might've been lying to her sister. But, then again, maybe she wasn't.

Her waffling thoughts fell right out of her head when the door opened before she could reach it, and Daniel Abbott stepped into the store.

His smile faltered as soon as he saw her. It was only one breath before he pushed forward with a practiced resolve.

"Jocelyn," he said. It was almost a question, and the sound of her name on his lips seemed foreign.

They'd so rarely spoken to each other. She remembered the sharp arguments he'd had with her mama, how sometimes his expression softened when his eyes drifted to Jocelyn—as if seeing another life in her face—only to wrench his gaze away again.

"D-Daniel," she managed, scooting past him.

He grimaced, his attention shifting to Natasha. "You ready, Sweetpea?"

The words pelted Jocelyn, leaving her breathless. She didn't look back at Natasha, who called her name, only shoved through the door into afternoon light, her chest heaving until she could finally drag in oxygen.

She had thought she was ready, that she could face him. Thought she could ask her questions, maybe even repair something fractured long ago. But as the air pressed heavy around her, Jocelyn knew she wasn't strong enough—at least not yet.

And when she found the newspaper clipping caught in her windshield wiper, she almost dismissed it as trash blown in on the cool breeze. But its location, and the timing, made her reach for it with a stone heavy in her stomach.

It was just a sliver, but one sentence was circled in red ink.

Even so, fire officials at the scene emphasized there was no immediate evidence of foul play, describing the incident as "nothing but a sad accident."

Funeral arrangements for Murphy are being handled

"Nothing but a sad accident," she muttered.

Somebody was going a little heavy-handed.

And it was just one more damn thing she didn't need.

Twenty-Four

C ole dragged one of the long folding tables from his parents' garage, muscling it up to the tailgate before shoving it into the truck bed. Hauling six-foot tables wasn't his idea of a Saturday morning, but it kept his hands busy.

Didn't do a damn thing to keep his head clear.

He hadn't seen Jocelyn for near on two days, and he was lucky Friday nights at the bar were chaos. He hadn't had more than thirty seconds to breathe, let alone brood about the fact that he hadn't caught sight of her anywhere. By the time he finally surfaced between the dinner rush and the late-night stragglers, it'd been too late to go in search.

Something about that seemed odd. She'd been aching, sure, but she'd still had that stoniness about her that promised she'd keep digging for her answers. He'd nearly asked his mama for her number but didn't want to invite that woman's questions or Jocelyn's anger for overstepping.

If he didn't see her by lunchtime, he'd eat his pride and ask his mama. Worth checking in to make sure Jocelyn was alright, even if it stirred her up. He'd've considered inviting her to go to the bonfire, but maybe she'd had too much of flames.

He dropped another table onto the stack and turned back for the last one. Might've still been too warm for a fire, considering it wasn't quite fall yet, but it was close enough that folks would turn out for anything that smelled like tradition, especially with the Harvest Festival around the corner.

"Hey, Sugar."

That syrupy drawl cut through the thick morning air and put a ready smile on his face.

He swiped sweat from his brow and turned to the neighbor leaning on the fence. "Miz Lu. Love of my life."

Luann Polk was pushing eighty, with silver curls tight against her head, arthritis stiffening her hips. She wore it all with pride.

She tsked, wrinkles deepening with her smile. "You're liable to make ol' Gentry jealous."

His brows wiggled. "Hope so. When you gonna ditch that old geezer and run away with me?"

"Oh, Honey, I'd love to. But these hips don't run any-where."

"I'll carry you." He winked. "Just say the word."

Her chuckle warmed him like always. They'd been running that joke for over a decade.

"You'd break your back, boy," she said, waving him off. "You goin' to that bonfire tonight?"

"Droppin' tables for the dessert contest." He lifted a brow. "You better be bringing those apple fritters."

"You know I don't break tradition." Her gaze sharpened then, cutting right through him. "That Murphy girl gonna be there?"

He blew out a breath. "How would I know?"

"You didn't invite her?"

Felt like an accusation, and heat crawled up his neck. "No, ma'am," he said, keeping the sass in check. She'd ream him if he let it fly.

She clucked her tongue. "You flirt with me all day but don't snatch up that sweet girl? Shame on you."

"It's complicated."

"I don't see how. The second I saw her, I knew she belonged here. She's got roots. Been too long neglected."

He pushed the garage door closed. "Not everybody thinks she belongs."

"Some people got sticks up their butts."

That made him laugh. "Miz Lu spittin' truth."

"Damn right. Now, go invite her. Let her know some of us knew and loved her mama."

That pulled him up short. "You taught Bonnie?"

"Oh sure. Had half this town in my classroom. Jocelyn's mama was kind. Always helping somebody, the light in every room. I see it in her girl, though life's dulled it some." She winked. "You could bring a little of that shine back. You did alright gettin' your own."

He walked over to slam the truck's tailgate so he could dodge both the compliment and the charge.

She squinted at him when he didn't respond. "You been alone a long time, Cole Hauser."

That was not a reminder he needed. But he knew what to say to shake her off. "Only 'cause you won't run off with me, Miz Lu."

She flapped a hand at him, her laughter following her as she shuffled toward her house.

He tapped his thumb on the tailgate, chewing on her words. Maybe a few folks wanted Jocelyn here. Plenty wanted her gone. They hadn't been shy about it.

His glance drifted to his parents' place. The scrap of card stock Jocelyn had handed him sat heavy in his pocket. Wouldn't take two minutes to see if Ma had paper to match it.

His mama swore Jocelyn deserved answers. He wanted to believe her. But his folks had hidden a truth from him for twenty years, and that wound still throbbed.

Inside, the kitchen was quiet and cool, a sign his mama hadn't been around for a while. His pop's truck sat in the garage, but the house felt empty.

He took the stairs two at a time, ducking into the old office. Scrapbooking central. Shelves of albums lined the wall, every year neat in a row. Ma's projects-in-progress sat in plastic totes he'd seen many times. But he went straight to the scrap bin.

The lid popped loud when he opened it, and he froze for half a second, then shook it off and dug through the piles. Spreading a handful of scraps on the clean table, he compared them one by one to the jagged note. Some were easy to rule out. Colors off. Textures wrong. Edges didn't match.

Didn't rule it out. Didn't ease his mind, either.

The handwriting... close enough to his mama's looping script. Too close. Made his gut turn.

"Cole?"

His daddy's voice snapped his spine straight.

He shoved the note into his pocket and headed down. "Hey, Pop."

The old man stood at the base of the stairs, sweat dripping, shirt damp. "What were you doing up there?"

His lie came easy as he made it to the bottom step. "Lookin' for you."

"Out for a walk," Pop muttered, tugging his shirt.

"This time of day?"

"Best time. What'd you need?"

"Just grabbing the tables. Got it figured."

John nodded, setting his hand on the bannister. "Your mama'll be back from her scrapbook swap soon. Might want to wait. Say hi."

That stopped him cold. "Scrapbook swap?"

His daddy rolled his eyes. "Yeah, bunch of 'em trade paper and stickers. Saves money, so I say what the hell? Just one more thing to get her out of the house." He shrugged.

Book club. Scrap swap. Recipe circle. All the same crew, Cole knew. And half of them had complained about Jocelyn to his face. Edith Wetzel. Harriet Munson. Kiki Womack.

And Lydia Abbott, who hadn't outright spoken against Jocelyn but had every reason to want her gone. Jocelyn had mentioned a comment—what was it? Some snide, backhanded thing. And that matched down to the ground with that torn piece of card stock. Not quite a threat but certainly no friendly warning.

The scrap could've come from any one of them.

Cole's mind was already wandering down new avenues. "Well, gotta get those tables to the square. You goin' tonight?"

John barely paused as he started up the stairs. "Depends on your mama. Dunno."

"Alright. Later, Pop."

"Son."

He left his daddy at the stairs, chewing on things as he loaded up and drove to the square.

He parked half on the curb, knowing nobody in uniform would ticket him. Most of 'em had grown up with him or had dragged his sorry teenage ass home themselves. All of them knew he was solid now.

With tables unloaded, he set up where the dessert contest would run. The fire pit was ready in the center of the square, wood stacked high. Still too hot for it, but it would be a pretty sight.

"Speakin' of pretty," he muttered when Jocelyn's car rolled in.

She pulled up behind his truck, sunglasses hiding her eyes. Didn't matter—he felt it when her gaze landed on him, and he headed over.

"Hey, Darlin'," he said, leaning against the car.

She smiled at him like the nickname amused her. "Hey."

It warmed him to see she'd shaken the sadness from the other day. "Was wonderin' where you'd been."

Her attention shifted toward the road. "I was working."

Wasn't the whole story, but he didn't need to pry. Not yet, anyway. Miz Lu's words rang in his ears, and why not? It would give him the opportunity to dig later.

"You know about the bonfire tonight?" he asked.

She swung her head back to him. "Natasha mentioned it. Why?"

He rubbed the back of his neck, stomach dropping like he was on a roller coaster. "Thought maybe you'd want to come."

Her brows lifted. "You thought I'd want to come?"

"Yeah. With me. Maybe."

Her head tilted, smile threatening. "Like a date?"

He rocked back like she'd landed a right hook and buried his hands in his pockets. Let his eyes land on the building across the street. "Or just... somethin' to do besides interrogating locals." He squinted against the sun. "Let folks see you here. Get used to it. You might even enjoy yourself."

"Cole."

"What?"

"Is it a date?"

His breath locked, and he forced his eyes to hers. "Doesn't have to be."

A wrinkle cut between her brows.

Mercy, he was tense. "I'll be a gentleman. Hands to myself and everything." He held them up as proof. "Unless you want somethin' different, the agreement stands."

"I want a lot of things," she said softly, like he wasn't meant to hear. Then, firmer: "How about I come, and we see how it goes?"

Relief trickled in slow. Not the answer he wanted, but not a no either. "Alright."

Her lips twitched. "Alright."

"Starts at eight."

She let him have the smile then. "I'll meet you here."

He stepped back, shoving down his own grin as she drove off. But his lungs felt empty, like she'd taken his damn air with her.

Twenty-Five

"Desire is a bonfire that burns with greater fury, asking for more fuel." - Sri Sathya Sai Baba

The sky had faded to pale blue, stars just beginning to glimmer like the sparkles from a princess costume she'd worn once. Jocelyn remembered her mama spending hours bent over the sewing machine, specks of glitter dusting her cheeks like metallic freckles.

The air still carried the day's heat, trapped like an oven long since shut off, heavy and stifling. But it wasn't the weather that made Jocelyn falter—it was the sight of townsfolk and tourists laughing together in the square. For a moment, regret at agreeing to come twisted inside her. She could've been at Uncle Joe's house, buried in notes, chasing answers.

She had plenty to dig into, especially after that newspaper clipping she'd gotten. And that was reason enough to turn right back around. She hadn't told Cole about it. The opportunity had been there earlier, but something had stopped her. Maybe it was his nerves about asking her to the bonfire. Or the way her heart had reacted to seeing him.

But she hadn't figured out where the newspaper clipping was from, even though she'd spent hours the day before searching. And because of it, the investigation continued to feel unfinished, making her itch for progress.

That almost made her turn back to the car. Almost. Then Cole appeared from amid the crowd, moving with purpose, his gaze locked on her. He crossed the street without hesitation, and the heat under her skin surged. Every rational part of her screamed that this shouldn't be a date. But the way the bonfire's reflection burned in his eyes made her pulse stutter, and—oh, crap—a much larger, and less wise part of her, wanted this to be a date.

He stopped in front of her, closer than comfort but careful not to touch. Relief and disappointment warred in her veins. Her fingers twitched with the urge to clutch his shirt and pull him near. She shifted back instead.

"Thought about makin' you chase me through the crowd," he said, mischief in his gaze, "but figured you'd just turn around and leave."

The teasing eased her nerves a little. "Smart man. I would've."

He gave her a half-smile. "Ready?"

Time to dive in, she thought, taking a breath. She stepped up beside him, and her hand brushed his.

He arched a brow. "Careful, Darlin'. I'd almost think you want to hold my hand."

Her breath caught, and she felt that tug of war again between date and not date, wisdom and desire. "You promised to keep them to yourself."

He nodded, solemn. "I did."

"But I didn't." She slid her hand into his, making the decision, even though her stomach flipped. The callouses of his palm scraped hers, sending a tingle straight up her arm.

His expression softened with wonder before he squeezed her hand. "Not a date, though, right?"

She rolled her eyes, trying to hide her smile. "Shut up."

He grinned as he led her forward.

The bonfire roared high, unnecessary in the clinging heat but mesmerizing all the same. Shadows danced through the crowd and across Cole's face, making him look caught between light and dark.

"So, this is the bonfire night," Jocelyn murmured. "Can't imagine what kind of hootenanny Harvest Fest must be."

Cole's mouth tightened. "It's more important to them than it should be."

She frowned at his tone. "But this is nice. To have community." Her voice caught on the word, touched by a longing she couldn't quite shake. Her mama hadn't had this—not really. Not after Daniel Abbott's family pushed her out.

The thought of her father hit her like a bolt. What if he was there? The memory of their brief encounter the day before made her stomach pitch. She still wasn't ready.

"You doin' okay, Darlin'?" Cole asked, nodding at a passerby as he walked her in an easy loop, letting the crowd get used to her presence—or maybe the other way around.

"Fine," she answered automatically.

He lifted their joined hands. "My numb fingers say otherwise."

Her face flooded with heat, and she loosened her grip. "Sorry."

"You don't always have to say 'fine,' you know."

She squinted at him.

He smirked. "Might feel better if you just said what's really botherin' you."

"I am fine," she insisted, her voice too even.

"There's that word again."

She glared at him, and he laughed.

"It doesn't have to be me," he said. Then he winked. "But I am good at keepin' secrets."

Her chest warmed in a way that felt a little dangerous. But surely he was safe, far enough removed from her family drama to handle what was on her mind. Maybe that's why the truth slipped out before she could snatch it back.

"I was thinking about Daniel Abbott. Worried he might be here."

Cole hummed. "You can relax. The Abbotts rarely bother with this."

She cut a dark look across the crowd, taking in the revelry, the smiles. "Beneath them?"

"Lydia, yes. Daniel's too busy cuttin' deals and pushin' folks off their land." His tone matched what she felt.

"Land? Why?"

Cole shrugged. "Developers want acreage. As the big real estate guy around here, he's approached a lot of locals. Even me."

"You?"

He shrugged. "Fifty acres makes for a nice-sized, cookie-cutter neighborhood."

"Fifty acres." She shook her head, still struggling to picture it. And, damn, could she. The roughness of his palm against hers told a story of hard and loving labor, and she could see him pouring it in.

"It's small." He shrugged.

She snorted.

"The house," he clarified, drawing a full laugh from her.

He gave her a grin as they drifted toward the dessert table.

Jocelyn eyed the selection, lingering over a classic lattice-top apple pie. "If only there was ice cream," she murmured.

"A damn shame," Cole agreed.

"If it needs something with it, it ain't worth the vote." The older man proctoring the table scooted over to them, leaning over as if sharing some secret.

Jocelyn didn't recognize him, and he smiled at her like he hadn't the faintest clue who she was, either. Or maybe he just didn't care.

"That's my cousin Ellie's pie," the man continued, his wrinkled brow folding. She expected him to beam with pride, but he looked concerned. "I worry she mixed up the sugar and salt when baking this thing. Don't taste right."

Jocelyn laughed, drawing a smile from both men.

"What's your favorite then?" Cole asked.

"Uh-uh!" A new voice chimed in, a woman Jocelyn also had never met.

"You're in trouble now, Clyde," Cole said under his breath.

"You can't sway anyone's vote. That's called cheatin'."

"How's it cheatin', Dottie? It ain't like I'd win if I give my opinion."

Cole and Jocelyn exchanged an amused look as the woman marched over.

"It's voter tampering," Dottie retorted, planting her fists on rounded hips. Thin, wispy hair was twisted up at the back of her head, the shiny silver locks held in place by a rhinestone barrette.

"I'm just saving them a little time," Clyde argued, turning back to Cole and Jocelyn. "The five toward that end are the only ones worth votin' on."

"Clyde Johnson!"

The pair continued their bickering, and Cole's hand landed lightly on the small of Jocelyn's back so he could nudge her down the table. She glanced back at the couple, who were now engaged with a new set of taste-testers, and Jocelyn caught the way Clyde surreptitiously gestured for them to head on down the table as well.

Cole's hand pressed against her back again so she turned back to what was before them. But it was impossible to taste the desserts when all she thought about was the way her skin ignited under his touch. She scrawled a vote blindly, spinning to face him just to break the contact and give her nerves a break.

He leaned close to grab his own slip, his smile soft enough to steal her breath. For a moment, she thought he might kiss her. She sidestepped instead.

He looked up from writing on his paper. "You keep dodgin' like that, folks'll think I'm trouble."

It took her a moment, but she found her footing, even if it was a little unsteady. "Aren't you?" She raised a brow.

He straightened, folding his paper as a sly grin curved his lips. "Definitely."

A breathy laugh escaped her, and she turned to search the crowd as a distraction. She recognized some faces; others were foreign. To her surprise, not many glances lingered on her the way they once had. Maybe they *could* get used to her being here.

"I, uh, hate to break the mood," Cole said, drawing her attention back. "But I took that note of yours up to my folks' place."

She took a slow breath, letting her arms wrap around her middle and watched his hand as it reached to rub the back of his neck.

His face twisted in a grimace. "Didn't find a match. But didn't rule it out, either."

The words dropped like stones into her stomach, disappointment and dread mingling.

"But," he went on, squinting toward the fire, "Pop mentioned a scrapbook swap."

That had her puzzled. "What's that?"

"The group of ladies my ma gets together with to trade their scraps and designs and books. Or somethin'."

That sparked a little hope. And more disappointment. Because she still wouldn't know who was leaving her these little gifts—though it took the weight of all the suspicion off of Ellen. "Who's in this group?"

Another grimace. "The usual suspects. Notably Kiki Womack and Lydia Abbott."

Her intake of breath was sharp, and her hands squeezed her elbows. "Could be either of them."

"Could be," he agreed.

Lydia Abbott had come up more than once lately. Knowing she'd spoken to Frank Leone that night, worked him up, made it clear she sure knew how to stir the pot. Writing passive-aggressive notes seemed like her style. So did that article left on her car.

With the opening there, she figured she'd better take it. "I got another one."

Cole's gaze snapped to her face.

"It wasn't a note this time. Newspaper clipping. I haven't matched the article yet, but it was one about how it was ruled an accident. Circled nice and bold so I wouldn't miss it."

"Son of a bitch," he muttered. He looked ready to throttle someone.

She put a hand on his arm. "It's alright, Cole. Nothing we can do right now."

"But someone sure doesn't like what you're up to."

"We knew that already," she said grimly.

"Don't have to like it," he growled.

That almost made her smile. And made her want to kiss him.

The thought was barely formed when Natasha's voice rang out. "Jocelyn, you came!"

"Hey, Natasha," she managed, heart twisting as her sister's arms wrapped around her before she could react.

Cole stepped back while Natasha divided a bright smile between them. He managed to mask his frustration with a half-smile.

"Are you having fun?" Natasha asked, turning to look around. An extra measure of nerves filled her voice, as if Jocelyn's answer would be a judgment on her and not the town.

Jocelyn went with the safest answer she could muster. "How could I not?"

Cole's hand landed low at her back again, a silent support.

"It's a lot," Natasha said knowingly. "But this has always been my favorite night before Harvest Fest."

"Why's that?" Jocelyn asked, forcing her voice steady.

"It's cozy. Less about sellin' to tourists." Natasha grinned.

"Free food," Cole threw in.

Natasha laughed. "There's that," she agreed, then her smile went shy. "I made one of the desserts."

Jocelyn's brows shot up. "Did you?"

Natasha shrugged. "It's a recipe from the internet. My mama would never touch a kitchen. Neither would Granny. I'm learning on my own."

"I have a great recipe, if you want it." The words slipped out before Jocelyn could stop them. Her throat tightened, regret sparking instantly.

But Natasha's eyes lit up, bright as the fire. "Really?"

Cole's fingers brushed her back again in reassurance, like he knew she was second-guessing her offer.

Baking had been her mama's passion. It'd started with Nan, but it was Mama who'd been magic with it. The diner Bonnie worked at used to sell her homemade treats, and Jocelyn remembered sitting at the counter when people would stop in just to buy whatever she was offering that week. Truckers went out of their way off the standard route to get one of Bonnie's Baked Beauties.

After she died, when the pain hadn't been quite so sharp—or maybe because she wanted to keep her daughter's memory alive—Nan had taught Jocelyn, too, passing down the magic and a recipe book of Bonnie's favorites.

Jocelyn bit back her hesitation so she could answer Natasha. Her sister. A practical stranger. The representation of all the things she'd never had. But she couldn't go back on her word.

"Sure," she said, sounding more certain than she felt. "I can email it to you."

Natasha practically bounced. "That would be amazing!"

And Jocelyn, aching for connection, let herself give in. Just one recipe. For her sister.

Twenty-Six

"Words are only painted fire; a look is the fire itself." -
Mark Twain

Cole watched firelight flicker over Jocelyn's face as Natasha introduced her to some of the folks she often ran with. Jocelyn might've had an interaction or two from back when she was a local, seeing as most were natives, but he couldn't be sure if she knew them.

Didn't matter when twenty years were stacked between then and now.

He kept watch as he absently polished off Jocelyn's plate of her sister's apple crumb cake. She'd passed it off to him, saying she was too full, though he suspected it was nerves more than anything. They all seemed friendly enough, but the discussion about two "non-threatening" notes sat heavy in his mind, and everyone deserved his suspicion.

"That's a right pretty thing you've had on your arm this evening."

Cole cut a glance sideways as Clyde came to stand next to him. "That she is."

Clyde folded his arms across his chest. "Bonnie Murphy's girl, ain't she?"

"Yep." Cole took the last bite of cake, dropping the plate into a trash can.

"Heard she went up to see old Joe."

Cole eyed him, though it wasn't a surprise he'd've heard. Small towns and all that. It wasn't a stretch, either, given that he and Joe were about the same age. Probably ran together at one point.

"What else've you been hearin', Clyde?" Cole asked as he folded his arms across his chest.

Eyes twinkling, Clyde grinned. "Oh, lots of things. Plenty from those folks ridin' your tail about running that Murphy girl off."

There was that. "Doing a bang up job of it."

Clyde gave a raspy chuckle. "That you are, Cole." He rubbed a hand over his chin, the sound like sandpaper. "Dottie and I are just tickled about the tizzy they got up in about it."

Cole straightened, pursing his lips as he glanced at Dottie near the dessert table. "Y'all don't think she ought to get run off?"

Clyde rolled back on his heels. "Heavens, no. We need a little intrigue around here. And the Murphys have always provided that. 'Sides, it's good for you."

Cole slanted a look in Clyde's direction. "Oh, sure, gettin' harassed by gossip mongers and my mama's bookclub is good for me."

"We all know Jocelyn's been asking folks questions." He tipped his head. "Just tryin' to understand, seems like."

Cole shrugged, not keen on confirming or denying. "Was a tough thing, what happened."

"Sure was." Clyde nodded sagely. "Don't blame her for the askin', whether it ruffles feathers or not."

Ruffling feathers. Was that all it was? The notes didn't seem to say so.

"Anyway, a man needs to be harassed now and then." Clyde caught his wife's eye. Dottie was staring him down with a glint as sharp as it was deadly. "Speaking of bein' harrassed. I've been gone from the voting too long."

Cole grunted as Clyde moved along back to the table where his wife stomped her foot at him. Maybe more people didn't mind Jocelyn bein' back as much as it'd seemed at first, and that sent a measure of relief through him.

Hell if he could explain why he cared so much so fast.

Maybe it was how her hand had fit in his like it belonged there. Or the way she carried that fire in her, sharp and restless. Or maybe it was 'cause the busted-up parts of her looked a bit like his, like maybe they could fit them together if they angled them just right.

It wasn't just about her mama's story or his making wishes, and it damn sure wasn't for show. He wasn't fooling anybody—least of all himself. He decided there was no use trying to.

He spotted Jocelyn just as she finished talking to Natasha, leaving her to her friends. She was scanning the crowd, looking for him. He could tell 'cause the second she caught sight of him, she smiled.

Something tugged at his center like there was a rope looped around his chest and she'd grabbed hold, pulling him in slow, hand over hand.

She didn't move. Just stood there waiting like she knew he'd come to her. But there was something different in her face. A look he hadn't seen before. It shot straight through him, sharp and fast, rattling up his spine like a jolt from a live wire.

He was nearly to her, hands halfway out like they had a mind of their own—and from the look in her eyes, she was ready for it, too—when a sound cut through the air, clean and sharp like a blade through ripe fruit.

His hands dropped back as they both turned toward the firehouse. The crowd's energy vanished like smoke in the wind, sucked clean away by the sudden rush of movement over there.

"A fire?" There was something laced in Jocelyn's voice, a knowing that chilled him.

He didn't think. Just slipped his hands around her waist and pulled her in close while he scanned the sky, looking for the telltale orange glow or a smear of black smoke cutting through the night.

"Might be somethin' else," he said, but the lack of conviction bled through. Even if the fire crew was called out to every emergency, always tag-teaming with the medical side, that knowing sat in his gut, too.

And then he spotted it. "There." He nodded east, where a faint glow shimmered low on the horizon—out past where town gave way to fields and trees.

The firetruck screamed to life, siren howling as it peeled off in that direction. It laid on the horn as it barreled out of the square, the sound low and mean.

Jocelyn's fingers curled into the fabric of Cole's shirt as voices started to cut through the fog in his head—sharp, urgent. Words like "Joe Murphy's place" snapped into focus, slicing through the rumble of the crowd, the buzz in his brain.

Jocelyn's grip tightened as she looked up at him. She'd heard it, too.

"I'll drive," Cole said, tugging her toward the Nail so they could cut through the back to get to his truck.

"My car's closer." Her voice was too soft, too small. She pulled the keys from her bag and shoved them into his hand without looking up.

He just nodded and jogged with her across the street, keeping a grip on her as something hot and electric cracked through his nerves. Outwardly, he kept steady. Inside, he was all fire and kindling.

Joe's place wasn't far past city limits, but it wasn't exactly easy to find, either. Nearest neighbors were a good half-mile off, tucked behind thick trees that offered privacy most days, but tonight they were a risk. One strong gust and that fire could jump the line, set the whole ridge ablaze. Tennessee usually got enough rain to keep wildfire fears at bay, but it wasn't unheard of.

Jocelyn didn't say a word the whole ride. Just sat there stiff as stone, eyes flicking to the speedometer every few seconds—even though he was already riding the edge of too fast. She was so still, he might've thought she wasn't breathing if he couldn't hear each tight breath scraping through the thick silence between them.

If it was Joe's place, she'd be thinking it was intentional. The rest of the town? They'd chalk it up to her drunk of an uncle screwing up again. Sure, he'd cleaned up lately, but folks around here didn't trust change until it held steady for a decade or two. Even then, plenty still clung to the worst version of a person.

Cole didn't know where he landed on it. Didn't really matter. Her opinion outweighed his a thousand times over. But he'd been watched for slip ups long enough to know how established opinions could linger.

Jocelyn leaned forward, bracing her hands on the dash as they turned onto Joe's drive.

The glow was impossible to miss. Hell, he could see it before the car cleared the last bend, like the earth itself had split open and swallowed the place whole. It didn't take more than a glance to know there was no saving it. All they could do now was try to keep the blaze from jumping to the trees.

The truck's tires slid on loose gravel as Cole slammed to a stop, and Jocelyn hopped out before he'd even put the car in park. He cursed under his breath as she sprinted toward the house. He was still trying to get the keys out of the damn ignition.

He shoved his door open, stomach lurching into his throat until a firefighter jumped forward to catch her, stopping her from getting closer.

It took only a few seconds for him to catch up, and when he did, he nodded at the crewman, sliding an arm around her shoulders to hold her in place.

"Oh my God, Cole." She jerked forward again, but he held fast.

"You can't, Jocelyn."

"But Uncle Joe!" She turned wide eyes to him, flames dancing in the tears gathered there.

It was hell to say what he had to, but she needed to hear it: "If he's inside, there's not a damn thing anyone can do for him."

Her face crumpled at the words, and he ached to carry the weight of her grief, to lug it until the end of time. But he made do with pulling her against him as they watched the crew scramble around the blaze.

There were dozens of yards between where he and Jocelyn stood and the house, but the heat nearly blistered his skin. He knew it was wasted effort to try to get her to move farther away, though. Tears spilled steady, but she searched window to window, looking for some sign of a miracle.

Wouldn't be too good for anyone if Joe came running out now. If he made it through the first twenty-four hours, he would've been in for a mess of torture.

Experiences with burn victims had always haunted Cole's daddy.

"Jocelyn!"

She stiffened in Cole's arms then craned her neck to look at the man behind them who'd called her name. As soon as she recognized who was jogging their way, she pushed out of Cole's arms. Relief hit Cole fast and hard at the sight of Joe Murphy.

The older man glanced toward the house for only a moment before Jocelyn had him in a hug so tight, she might've squeezed the air from his lungs.

She released him. "Thank God you're not inside that…" Jocelyn looked at the house, the flames dancing and distorting in the new tears that brimmed.

Joe shook his head, lips going colorless as he held in a reaction. "Was at the neighbor's. Heard about my own damn house bein' on fire 'cause someone in town decided to call and warn them."

"Oh, Joe." She put her hand on his thin arm. "I'm so sorry. All that work."

He pulled in a long inhale, staring at the old house. "It's ain't nothing more than stuff." He patted her hand, offering a grim smile.

Felt like he was saying it more for himself than her, and it struck Cole that this could derail his sobriety. Might check on him in the coming days, make sure someone had his back.

By Jocelyn's expression, it was clear she was thinking something similar as she met Cole's gaze.

A man's voice cut across the din of crackling wood. "Joe."

They turned as one, locking onto the firefighter jogging over. He was suited up head to toe. Full gear weighed at least seventy pounds, but he moved like it was nothing.

"Have some questions," Kyle Lambert said. He was newer to the station, but Cole knew him well enough.

"Sure," Joe said, following Kyle to the incident commander.

Cole's daddy had run point on fires before, talked his son through the process when he was a kid and still interested. There'd be questions about others in the home, when Joe'd last been there, hazards inside, and whether he could guess how it had started.

The dazed look on Joe's face said they wouldn't be getting their answers tonight.

Jocelyn was tight with nerves beside Cole as she watched, waiting for Joe to head back. He did slowly, shoulders slumping as he walked toward them.

"Uncle Joe, you have somewhere to stay tonight?"

"My folks have a guest room," Cole offered.

Joe rubbed a boney hand over his chin, that sunken look to his face common to decades-long alcoholics. "I got a place. Thanks."

"Well, let me at least sit with you awhile," Jocelyn insisted.

"I'll be alright." He sent her another of his grim smiles. "You go on. Take Cole up on his folks' guest room. I'm sorry about the..." He trailed off, gaze going to what was left of his house.

"Oh, Joe," she whispered, tears in her eyes again.

He smoothed a hand down her arm. "Go on, Jossie. Get you some sleep."

"I'll call you in the morning," she promised, and he nodded before turning back to his pickup parked at an angle right behind her car.

He was gone before the first beams started collapsing, and it was a mercy only she and Cole were the ones watching the place come crashing down instead of him.

"Come on, Darlin'. There's nothing more we can do." He put his arm around her shoulders to lead her away.

She didn't fight him.

TWENTY-SEVEN

"Kiss me with fire in your mouth." - Unknown

J ocelyn held her silence like a sacred relic as Cole drove them away from the wreck of her uncle's house. She didn't look back. Didn't ask where they were going.

A hundred years of memories had been burned to ash. Some good, some not—but Joe had been fighting to tip the scales toward hope. Now it was all gone.

Downtown was deserted. Whatever spirit the festival had carried, the fire had smothered it. Cole's grip on the steering wheel was iron-tight, his jaw set in grim silence. He swung into the alley behind his restaurant and parked her car beside his truck.

Wordlessly, Jocelyn followed him through the back door, past the hum of the now extra busy restaurant, and up the stairs to his apartment. She had no energy left for questions. Both places she'd been staying at in the past week had gone up in flame. It was only mild consolation that her new clothes and all of the notes she'd painstakingly put together were safe in her car.

Cole flipped on the light, and silence filled the small apartment, pressing on her like smoke seeping into her lungs. It was too loaded, too toxic, and everything was starting to spin. She needed something in her hands, something to anchor her, to keep her from unraveling. She had to find a clue, a link, an explanation. She needed to understand why.

Her purse hit the kitchen island, and her hands speared inside. She dug past her laptop to yank free the battered journal that had started this whole search. Pages rustled beneath her frantic fingers, the notes and clippings a blur as she hunted for the articles about the old fires, flipping faster and faster. She didn't notice her trembling until the paper tore under her urgent hands.

The sound broke her, and a sob clawed its way up her throat.

Cole was suddenly there, his hands sliding gently down her arms until his fingers wrapped around her wrists. His touch was firm but careful as he pulled her away from the chaos of the journal. The heat of his skin seeped into hers, solid and grounding.

She collapsed against him as he cocooned her in his arms, holding on when she tried to retreat, his steady warmth keeping her from shattering.

The smoke was back in her mind. The pain. The choking. The heat at her bedroom door when she was nine. Crawling toward the window to the man who'd saved her—but not her mama.

That had been no accident. Someone had done it on purpose, had set the blaze that robbed Jocelyn of her childhood. And now they were sending her a message. These fires weren't random—they were warnings. But she'd survived the flames once. She wouldn't bow to them now.

The sobs tapered as resolve slowly replaced grief, brick by brick.

Cole loosened his hold as her breathing steadied. He had clutched her as though he could keep the pain from spilling out, and for the first time, she let herself admit she'd needed that, that she didn't have to push him away.

Turning in his arms, she leaned back against the counter to look up at him. He didn't step back as he studied her face. Worry etched itself into his forehead. He wasn't the man who'd saved her back then, but he'd saved her just now—from breaking apart.

Lifting her hand, she brushed her palm against his cheek, the scruff tickling her skin. "Thank you," she whispered. Her fingertips lingered longer than they should have, tracing the line of his jaw as if testing how much temptation she could get away with.

"For what?" The words rumbled low and soft, like he was worried someone might overhear.

It drew a smile to her lips. "For being here."

His hand slid over hers, thumb brushing lightly over her knuckles. "Anytime."

Silence poured over them again, but it was different now, heavier, slower—charged in a way that had her skin crying out. Her heart hammered against her ribs, her breath tangling with his as every inch of her screamed with the awareness that they were too close, too still, too dangerous. His gaze traced her face like he was committing it to memory, and Jocelyn felt herself unfurling like a flower to the sun, despite every warning she'd ever carried. Murphy women were disasters with love, and she should remember that.

But Cole was right there, warm and solid, and she didn't want to be careful anymore. Not tonight, not after watching Joe's place burn.

Her fingers curled into Cole's shirt, and before she could second-guess the decision, she tugged him closer until his body pinned her against the counter.

He tipped his head forward, bringing his face centimeters, millimeters—a breath—from hers. "You told me not to kiss you again." His words skimmed along her mouth, dancing the temptation over her lips.

She arched a brow. "What if I changed my mind?"

"I need to hear you say it." His voice was rough, snapped tight from the effort of holding back.

"I want you to kiss me, Cole."

His name barely left her lips before his mouth crashed against hers, taking what she was more than willing to give. The solid weight of him pressed into her, stealing the last of her resistance.

This wasn't like before. Their first kiss had been reckless and consuming, and all she could do was hold on. But this? This was slow-building desperation, a pressure pulling her deeper with every brush of lips and tongue. Every time his mouth moved against hers, she felt herself unraveling, her body arching into his like it had been waiting for this exact heat all her life.

She got lost in the journey of discovering what he tasted like—the sweet cinnamon from the pie earlier mixed with something like bourbon, smooth and intoxicating—and beneath it, something purely him, wild and dark and impossible to resist. His scruff scraped along her chin, marking her, branding her, until she thought she'd carry the memory of this kiss on her skin forever.

There was some kind of knowing in the way they connected, inevitability in every touch, and she knew it wouldn't just be one night. It couldn't be when it felt like everything had been leading to this moment.

She broke the kiss with the realization, trembling at the knowledge. She wanted to choose the scary thing, to let herself fall into his kiss, even his bed. Cole searched her face, patient as he waited for her to make the choice, because that's what he was giving her.

"Murphy women are cursed in love," she whispered, more to herself than him.

His nose brushed her cheek. "Curses can be broken."

She tipped her head back so that his lips could graze her throat.

"Just call me the curse breaker." His breath danced along her skin, making promises she willed herself to believe. Her body wanted her to, even if it meant lying to herself.

But maybe, just maybe, it wouldn't be a lie. She was desperate for it to be true, for something to be real and honest and... permanent for once. His eyes were telling her it would be, that he wanted that as much as she did.

"Alright, curse breaker," she said, voice shaking only a little. "Prove it."

He growled, the sound rumbling through her as he took her mouth again. He turned them, walking backward without breaking the kiss. But then he lost patience and slipped both hands behind her thighs to scoop her up. Her breath hitched, the world spinning as he lifted her like she weighed nothing. She clung tighter, nails digging into his shoulders, the primal thrill of being carried toward his bed burning away the last of her hesitation.

Her logical mind still tried to force some sense of self-preservation to the forefront. But she was too far in now. Her body would destroy her if she let her mind take control. Her skin ached with want, her senses lit by every press of him. She had survived fire once before, but this time she was the one fanning the flames, begging them to consume her.

She couldn't stop now even if she wanted to, and she did not want to.

When he laid her down, lowering his body along hers, it was no longer even a choice. Every shift of his hips, every scrape of his jaw along her throat, stoked the heat spiraling lower, winding tighter, until she thought she might combust.

His lips claimed hers again, slower now, deeper, exploring, tasting, demanding. And as their breaths mingled, as hands roamed and pressed, the line between comfort and desire blurred entirely. She tangled her fingers into his hair, the silky curls softer than she expected, and his eyes slowly shut.

"Feels amazing." The words vibrated against her mouth like a secret meant just for her, his breath hot on her skin, and she arched up into him, desperate to be closer, to erase every barrier left between them. She clawed at his shirt, impatient, aching to feel the bare heat of him against her.

His eyes shot open to meet hers.

"I need you now, Cole." It wasn't embarrassment that painted her cheeks red. It was pure, unadulterated desire.

A wicked grin spread across his face. "You got it, Darlin'."

Some time later, as she lay tangled in him and his hand moved lazily along her spine, sleep tugged at her like an eager friend. Instead of dreams, though, memory met her. In the twilight of consciousness, she found the hallway of her childhood home, the nightgown clinging to her as the creak from the front porch chased her back to her room.

And then there was heat.

The distant crackle of fire.

A spark leaping from shadow.

And the fabric of the nightgown flared with flame, igniting across her body like she'd been covered in lighter fluid.

She jerked awake, her breath coming in lurching gasps.

Cole's hand was steady on her back. "Jocelyn?"

She sat up, brushing the hair from her face. Faint light from around the edge of a curtain drew her eye, kept her from looking at him while her heart beat steadied.

"Joss?" he said again.

She sighed. "I'm fine."

"That fucking word," he growled, sitting up next to her. She turned to look at him, startled by his tone.

"I'm tired of hearing it. You throw it out like I can't handle the truth. Or like I don't care."

"I—" she started, but she had no defense. She looked away. "I'm sorry."

"Damn it, don't be sorry." His hand cupped her chin, forcing her to meet his gaze. "Don't be sorry that other people have made you feel like you can't say what's botherin' you. Just don't treat me like I'm one of them."

She pulled out of his grasp, but not to hide from him. Not anymore. She would make herself say it because he was right, and after everything, he deserved the truth.

"It was a dream. About the fire."

He must've known which one she meant because he didn't ask.

"I've always had them. But they've gotten worse this past year," she admitted softly. "That's why I started digging."

His hand found the bare skin of her back again, tracing in that tender way that brought tears to her eyes. It took her a moment to let the emotions roll through her, and he just sat with her while they did. Patient. Steady.

"It's not the whole thing," she finally said. "Only snippets. Just enough to throw me."

And sometimes, things that never happened—scarier things that reminded her how fragile survival could feel.

After a long silence, he kissed her shoulder. "Tell me somethin' else. Not about the fire. Somethin' no one else knows about you."

She glanced sideways at him.

"Besides those little noises you make," he teased, a sly grin breaking through.

"Cole!" she gasped, swatting at him, and he caught her wrists with a laugh—low and loose, sweeter than anything she'd ever heard from him before. Maybe she'd unlocked something in him just as he had done to her. The warmth he radiated made something coil tight and hot down deep, the kind of heat that made her pulse thrum and her skin tingle.

He tugged her closer, leaning back to pull her on top of him. Then, without warning, he flipped them, and she gasped as she was pinned by the delicious weight of him.

He nuzzled into her neck. "Tell me all your secrets, Darlin'."

"I don't have secrets," she said, breathless.

"You have plenty," he rumbled against her throat. "Let's start easy. Your favorite color?"

She laughed. "Maroon."

"Favorite food." It was a demand now as he moved downward, brushing his lips along her collarbone, back and forth, soft and tender and teasing.

"Um." Her thoughts stuttered as he started a trail down her sternum. "I can't—I don't—"

He looked up at her from his position near her stomach. "Favorite food," he repeated.

Her hands gripped at the blankets as he shifted lower, lips still brushing skin. "Anything Italian," she managed.

"Mmmm," he rumbled, the sound vibrating through her until she melted beneath him, ready to burn all over again.

Twenty-Eight

"Most people guard against going into the fire, and so end up in it." - Rumi

Cole wanted to see Jocelyn sitting at his kitchen island in the morning light every damn day for the rest of his life.

Even with her distracted, just having her there settled something in him. The way the sun caught her hair, pulling out the auburn tint, or how it kissed her skin so she looked like she was lit from the inside... It about wrecked him.

She had one leg tucked up, looking real easy in her body, but her eyes said she was someplace else entirely. She'd called her uncle to check in earlier, so might've been the fire weighing on her.

Could've been their night together, too, and fear twisted a fist in his belly at the thought that she might've been sitting there, hoping it'd stay a one-time thing. Or worse, that she was wishing it hadn't happened at all.

Because he sure as hell wasn't.

He used to be a one-and-done kind of guy, back when he was still trying to outrun all that heat burning him up inside. But he wasn't that kid anymore. Now he knew, every time his eyes had landed on that photo of her on the mantel, it wasn't just habit.

It was him waiting.

Waiting for this, for her, sitting in his kitchen after a night tangled up in his sheets like she belonged there. Because damn if it didn't feel like she did.

He set a plate in front of her, drawing her mind back.

Her brow loosened as she smiled down at his creation. "What's this?"

"Taste it," he challenged.

Her gaze slid to his as she cut herself a bite, watching him the whole time she brought the fork to her mouth. She only broke the contact when she looked down, surprised. "Is that—"

"A frittata," he confirmed.

"How...?"

"Experimenting is my thing. The recipes on that menu downstairs? Mostly came from me." He shrugged and straightened. "Frittata is kinda like an omelet."

"Kind of, but not exactly," she said, eyeing him. "This is amazing, Cole. You sure you don't want to turn the Nail into an all-day eatery?"

He blew out a laugh and shook his head. "Nope. What I got is plenty to keep me busy."

Her mouth curved slow. "I thought you liked staying busy."

He turned back to the stove to get some grub for himself. "Noticed that, huh?"

"You seem to have an endless supply of energy."

He turned and grinned at her. "You'd know."

She rolled her eyes. "Speaking of busy…"

"Oh no." He groaned, dropping his head. It wasn't a surprise; there was plenty he needed to do that day, like building some more of the booths for the festival at the end of the week. But he'd wanted to bask in this for a while yet. "Can't we just act like nothin' else matters? Just for one day?"

She smiled at him grimly, and then an uncertain look glimmered in her dark eyes as she looked down. That, he knew, was related to them.

He wanted to pull her in close, tell her he wasn't going anywhere. But she already looked like a spooked horse, and the last thing he wanted was to make her bolt. So he kept his hands to himself, walked to the island like it didn't cost him, and sat down to eat his breakfast, pretending it was just another morning.

"What's on your docket, then?" Didn't sound like he was rattled, thank God. Even if he was.

She pinched the edges of her plate. "I've been putting it off, but I know I need to go talk to Daniel Abbott." Tension had her stung tight, and it bled into her voice.

"Sure you're ready for that?"

She shrugged, but the movement sure wasn't casual. "It doesn't matter. This is what I came here for, and if my uncle's house burning down taught me anything, it's that someone in this town has something to hide."

Didn't surprise him that her mind went there. His had, too, while they stood there watchin' that fire eat through her uncle's place like it had her mama's. But now there was a new kind of fear sitting heavy in his gut, turning his breakfast to dust before he could even swallow.

"And what if they've moved past warnings?"

She glanced up so fast, she might've snapped her neck. "You think they might do something to hurt me?"

He played over the conversations he'd had with folks about getting rid of Jocelyn. Felt like townie nonsense—folks with too much time on their hands making a big deal out of a festival that didn't much matter in the grand scheme. Might've been something more buried there, though, some bad blood somebody was hiding under a concern about the town.

"Jocelyn, your mama died. Even if it was an accident, somebody still lit that match. And they know damn well what they did."

They know. Those words echoed in his head like somebody else had said them. She looked just as shaken. But deep down, she knew, too. Hell, it was why she came back—to dig into what really happened that night. 'Cause even if nobody said it out loud, there was always something that didn't sit right.

"No way you didn't think it'd be dangerous." He worked at keeping his voice from rising.

"I knew people wouldn't be happy," she started, her mind clearly spinning.

But he was close to spittin' now to think she'd never considered the danger of it all. "It was just revenge on your mind, not a killer covering his ass."

"His?" she repeated, voice already dark.

"Figure of speech." A pit opened up in his stomach, threatening to swallow him whole. The notes, the fires, the things that didn't add up.

"You think I'm here for revenge?" she asked now, soft and low.

Dangerous ground. But the accusation was there in her voice, and it made him stiffen.

"I don't know."

"That's a bullshit answer, Cole, and you know it." She stood then, slim hands balling into fists at her sides.

He planted his palms on the counter top, the cold surface cooling his overheating skin. "Seems like it sometimes. The way you go off half-cocked at people."

She reared back. "Half-cocked? All I want are answers! You agreed that things were suspicious. Your own parents said to find out who did this."

"If that's all you were doin'—"

"To hell with you, Cole." She snatched her purse and sandals off the floor and made straight for the door. Didn't even stop to put 'em on—just stormed out, barefoot and burning mad. The door slammed behind her hard enough to make his teeth clack together.

Twenty-Nine

"Fire and gunpowder do not sleep together." - Proverb

Jocelyn rode the high of rage all the way across town, passing boxy brick homes that harkened back to the sixties and seventies and the little craftsmans from the early half of the 1900s. She was hellbent on reaching that long road that wound along the rolling hills to the huge estate up above town.

An unseen force had kept her from driving up that lane before—a mix of fear and resentment. It was the anger that gave her the courage now as her car wove its way up, passing under gnarled old oaks stationed like sentries along the gravel.

It was anger, too, that kept her from admitting part of what Cole had said was true. She wasn't ready to acknowledge it yet, let alone look in the mirror and see where she might've been wrong. She'd spent her life painting this town as her enemy, but how much of that had been fodder fed to her by a bitter old woman and a mama who hadn't always made the best choices?

And what of this blooming relationship with her sister? And... Cole? Thinking of them made it harder to hang onto the fire and the steel it had forged in her spine.

So she shook those thoughts from her mind as she pulled into the circle drive, stopping in front of the house. The massive facade seemed to watch her—columns stretching two stories, aged but well-kept brick shaded by double-decker wraparound porches. What a place to grow up. She could picture ladies from a century and a half ago in wide hoop skirts, fanning themselves through the blazing summer heat.

When she rang the bell, a deep gong reverberated through the stately house. While she waited, she traced the length and width of the porch. The sheer size seemed like overkill, but its age reminded her it needed to be wide enough for those skirts to pass two by two.

The creak of ancient hinges drew her attention back as the ornately carved wooden door swung inward. She was surprised to find it was her biological grandfather who peered out at her.

Errol Abbott released a breath like it'd been sitting in his lungs too long. "I wondered when you might show up." His words were elongated in the drawl that was familiar for this region, though it was different than Cole's. It was more stretched and rounded, whether from age or from his perceived station, she couldn't tell.

Despite her still-simmering rage, her southern roots had never fully left her. "I hope I'm not disturbing you."

He swung the door wider as answer. "Come on in." There was no grandfatherly warmth, but he was polite enough. Maybe even resigned.

Inside, her shoes made no sound on the thick rug that covered the shiny wood floors. A massive staircase loomed to her left, tall doorways lining the high-ceilinged hall. A chandelier glittered above. She could imagine the rooms beyond—family room, a library, a dining room, the kitchen.

Errol led her through the first doorway on the left into something like a parlor. The windows stretched floor to ceiling, the swath of light diffused by gauzy curtains framed by heavy, embroidered drapes. Gilded portraits stared down from the walls, the solemn faces belonging to ancestors she was possibly tied to by blood.

"Have a seat." Errol gestured to an antique-style sofa of carved mahogany and cream upholstery.

She lingered in the wide doorway, watching him lower himself into a wingback chair with an old man's weary grunt.

"You are welcome to make yourself comfortable, but if you'd rather stand, be my guest."

She studied the room, pausing on the dour-faced man whose likeness hung in an ornate frame above the fireplace behind Errol.

"That is your five-times great-grandfather," he said, steepling his fingers. He gave her an academic appraisal she tried to ignore. "Lewis Abbott. He built this house."

Her eyes slid back to his, dulled gray with time.

"You're surprised. These are modern times. I have no reason nor desire to deny who you are to me, child."

Something twisted in her stomach. If he had no reason to deny it, why pretend she didn't exist all these years?

He sighed. "Now, my dear wife—God rest her—had old-fashioned ideas about things."

On the surface, he seemed so benign. But there was still something in his tension, the way he sat so tightly, she suspected there was something underneath.

"And since she's no longer alive, she's a convenient scapegoat," Jocelyn said, testing him.

A flash lit in his gaze like the glint of light along a blade. "You are quick to think the worst of people."

"Can you blame me? The way my mama and I were treated for all those years—"

"Your mama," he interrupted, "had a chip on her shoulder, and pride a mile wide." The kind of authority he was used to wielding edged his words. He leaned forward, ready to say more.

"Dad."

The voice came from behind her, sending a bolt of electricity up her spine. She turned.

Seeing Daniel Abbott struck her even more than a few days prior, when she hadn't been ready for it. He had the leanly muscular build of a high school jock. With his clean-shaven face, the lines from smiles and frowns were more evident, but it only served to make him appealingly distinguished. No doubt it gave him an edge in the real estate industry. A handsome face, clean-cut lines, well-cared for body, and charm that was second nature went a long way.

Though his hands hung loosely, the line of tension was obvious when he walked into the room. Stepping from the dim hallway into sunlight, he was like an ethereal being, and it made Jocelyn realize how easily her mama must've fallen for him all those years ago.

Daniel looked more like a whipped dog at the moment, though. Nothing like the imperious, if muted, older man who sat across the room from her.

"I'm sorry to hear about Joe's place," Daniel said, looking at Jocelyn.

The sentiment stirred her anger. "Are you?"

"Your mama passed on the gift of that chip, I see," Errol cut in, and Daniel shot him a look. He curled his lip and stood. "I see I am no longer wanted here. In my own home," he added dryly as he swept by his son.

Daniel moved to the far side of the room as soon as his father was gone, keeping distance between himself and his daughter.

His daughter. The one he'd pretended didn't exist for decades.

She wasn't ready for the heart-stuff yet. Fear of rejection steered her elsewhere. "I heard you've been trying to get locals to sell off their land to your developers."

He went still, light catching in crystalline blue eyes—the same eyes she remembered wet with tears after his last argument with her mama.

"Is this your way of asking if I set the house on fire?" He twisted the shiny gold band on his left ring finger.

A coldness seeped into her stomach. "Did you?"

He didn't react or seem offended. Just kept spinning that ring, his head bowed low. "No."

That one-word answer landed hard, flat. Honest. And it sent a measure of relief through her.

"Do you think I started the fire that killed your mama?" His voice held resignation.

Emotion came back full-force, and she blinked several times, hating that this was a conversation she had to have with her own father. "Sometimes I wonder."

He didn't miss the present tense and lifted his head. "I wish I could say having her gone made things easier."

The words seared the space between them, and she stepped forward, lip curling as vitriol coated her tongue. "Is that supposed to prove you didn't?"

"No!" He took a breath to steady himself. "No. I have no proof to offer you."

"But you did come to the house that day," she pressed.

His jaw tightened. "Hours before it happened."

"Why?"

He looked away, shame coloring his cheeks. "To this day, I can't shake the hold your mama has over me. I will always love her."

Her blood burned hotter. *Good*, she thought. *You should be miserable without her.* "That's not an answer."

He swung his face back to her. "Your mama and me—we argued."

"About what?"

He was no longer twisting his ring, but he held it between his fingers like he had to keep reminding himself it was there. "We'd... had a... tryst."

She fought the poison of his words, refused to believe it. No way her mama would wreck a home. "Bullshit."

He grimaced. "Your mama regretted it almost immediately and kicked me out after, told me never to come back, to never speak to her again."

Jocelyn spun away, trying to fit this in with the woman she knew, the one who'd always been so faultless in her mind. The circumstances around her conception were a little less black and white but definitely not to this level. Nan had said Daniel made her mama believe he was free, or would be shortly. And then he'd come back to tell her that Lydia was pregnant, and that he was going to marry her.

Bonnie had fled town after that only to find herself pregnant, too. She'd tried to stay away, to start a life somewhere else. But for Nan, she came back.

Jocelyn was desperate for that story to be true because believing different would mean a whole shift she wasn't ready for.

"We never stopped loving each other," Daniel continued. "And it was a weak moment."

She turned back to glare at him. He was staring out the window, only his profile visible, limned in bright light.

"I felt like I couldn't live without her, so I begged her not to end things."

Another wave of cold washed through Jocelyn. "Were you planning to leave Lydia for her, then?"

He stiffened but didn't answer right away. The coward.

Her mama would've hated being the one who'd ended a marriage, but at least that might've been more honest.

"I couldn't," he said softly, his mind distant. "I had a daughter."

Those words ignited within her, a new kind of burning that scorched, and that cold was suddenly gone. "I was your daughter, too. But I hope to hell you were a better father to her than you were to me."

He spun and stepped toward her. "I didn't know! She didn't tell me!"

Incensed, Jocelyn moved forward, too, one finger stabbing in his direction. "Because you chose someone else! Why do you think she left? Why she didn't tell you?"

He looked away, the muscle in his jaw jumping again.

"She only came back because she had to." Her voice softened as the pain touched her words. "And they all treated us like the trash you left behind."

He took a breath. "She never was going to tell me. But she didn't have to. Everyone knew the second she showed back up with you." He turned his sad face to her. "I didn't want that for you. I tried..."

When he didn't finish, she prompted him. "Tried what? Paying her to take me somewhere else? To hide?"

"You would've had a good life! I would've made sure everything was taken care of, and you wouldn't have had to deal with the whispers."

She'd overheard the conversation, lying on the floor coloring while they'd argued on the front porch. She remembered how mad her mama was that he never looked at his own child, never tried to be her father.

"She didn't want your money."

"No, she didn't. She wanted what I couldn't give her." Regret softened his tone. "What I wasn't willing to give her at the time."

Jocelyn wrapped her arms around herself as he rubbed a hand down his face, looking less and less like the golden boy of Cedar Hollow. He was a pillar of regret, of bad decisions and miserable circumstances.

"I was just trying to do the right thing. But every decision I made was wrong. Everyone has suffered for it. And I don't know what would've been better for any of us. Because you and your sister... If I hadn't married Lydia, where would they be?"

She wanted to hold onto the fury, the righteous indignation, but she couldn't when he put it like that. Natasha deserved to have a family, too. And Jocelyn realized she could never fully understand his motivations or the circumstances that led him down the path he'd walked. She knew nothing of who he was, nothing of where he came from. Her short conversation with Errol had been the most she'd ever talked to the man, or anyone on this side of her family.

What history formed the man before her today? He'd been young when all of this happened. Stuck between two women, and only one who'd told him he'd fathered her child.

"You did the best you could." It cost her to say it, the words bruising and scraping at her throat as they went.

He glanced up at the acknowledgment.

"But she still died that day. And you were there."

Moisture shimmered in his eyes. "I'm so sorry."

She slashed at the air as if to knock his useless apology away. "I need to know if you remember anything that could help me find out why."

Something shifted in his expression, like it was the first time he'd considered it might not have been an accident. Her accusation earlier had probably seemed like a wounded child throwing out barbs to cut her absentee father down a peg.

"You don't think it was just an accident." It wasn't a question, and she could see him flipping through the event in his mind with a new lens.

That sense of intensity skated through her as it always did when someone gave her a platform. "The reason I came back was to find out what happened and why. It's been suspicious from the get-go, but no one is willing to look into it."

His face hardened. "You talked to Eric?"

"Eric Ward?" She snorted. "Fat lot of good that did me. He promised to give me more information then blew me off."

He sighed. "He's going through a divorce."

"So I've heard."

"Not really anything new." He shrugged and continued as if this was important to the conversation. "They've separated many times."

She squinted at him.

He waved the unspoken question away. "Sorry. He's Lydia's brother."

"Lydia's brother," she repeated. Something about that felt significant, though she couldn't pinpoint why at first. But her own thought about firefighters being the perfect arsonists because of their understanding of fire rolled back through her mind.

Could the reason Eric Ward had dragged his feet be that he wanted the culprit to stay buried?

"Lydia—your wife?"

Daniel went unnervingly still, as if that was an accusation in itself.

There was no denying that Lydia hated Jocelyn's mama. She had a fair enough reason, even if the person she should've hated was the man across the room from Jocelyn. Was it possible Lydia had hated her mama enough to hurt her—accidentally or intentionally—and then she'd had to find a way to cover up what she'd done?

Natasha had mentioned driving by their house more than once. But who didn't? It wasn't in the back woods. But she'd said *many times*, like it was an unusual amount. Jocelyn turned away from Daniel's intense gaze, brushing her fingers over her lips as she replayed that conversation. *One day it was there; the next day, it was gone.*

Jocelyn had taken it as a turn of phrase, a child's observation of things without true knowledge of the frequency or the time that had passed. But if driving by was a regular occurrence, maybe they'd driven by that day. Could it have been when Daniel was there, trying to convince her mama to keep their affair going?

Had Lydia gone back later?

Jocelyn pulled the newspaper clipping from her purse, staring at it again. The person had highlighted the phrase "sad accident," but just above that, a sentence cut in half she'd missed before was visible if she really studied it: "consistent with a blow to the head."

Jocelyn swallowed, her mind spinning and spinning. "I-I have to go."

Daniel's hand stretched toward her. "Wait. Please, Jocelyn."

She'd taken two steps back, but that tone, the plea in it stilled her movements.

"Will you forgive me? For-for everything I did and... didn't do?" His voice broke a little. "I wish to God things had been different."

There was that little twinge inside her, the knowledge that, damn it, she didn't really know what had led him to make the choices he had. But her mama had suffered for it, and it wasn't something she took lightly.

"I don't know," she answered truthfully. "Maybe someday."

His lips flattened as he nodded acceptance of that answer, but his shoulders slumped.

She turned to go, ignoring the pull of sympathy.

Thirty

"If this is to end in fire then we shall all burn together."
- Ed Sheeran

Cole was mad enough at himself over what he'd said to Jocelyn that he rage-worked through half the morning, knocking out so many tasks for the Nail that he left himself with nothing else to do before the rest of the crew rolled in for shift. And that was still a couple hours out.

He hated it. Hated himself. Hated what that conversation had done to her—done to them. Because, damn it, he cared if there was a them. He didn't know what that would mean for her, or for him, or for this town.

She was just as reluctant to put down roots here as folks were to welcome her, but it seemed like a few people had started warming up, her sister in particular.

Would she consider staying?

Would he consider leaving?

He'd been chasing the approval of the locals for so long, not giving much thought to what *he* wanted. And what he wanted was that house he was building outside of town. The quiet in those trees. The serenity of the creek that cut along the back of the acreage. The history in that land.

But asking her to stay felt like a mighty big request—especially when whatever this was between them was still fresh.

He knew he was getting ahead of himself.

And he was fixing to drive himself clean crazy.

He headed back to the supply closet, checking inventory again even though he'd already made a list of what he needed to order soon. Maybe he oughta go ahead and order everything while he had a minute.

His fingers itched, and he rubbed them along his thigh, unable to quit thinking about the way Jocelyn's skin had felt under his hands. His mind circled back to the curve of her body as he'd traced it, the taste of her on his tongue, the way her fire called to his.

He thought about her humor. About how tough she was for surviving what she had. About the kindness she'd shown Natasha, who represented just about everything she'd never been given.

His gut twisted at the thought of this being the end of them. He knew he couldn't let her go. Hell, he'd sell the restaurant and the land and start fresh somewhere else if it meant being with her.

Lord, he was in over his head. Farther than he'd ever planned to go.

He should've known the moment his body had reacted that first time he'd seen her back in town—even before that, really. The way her picture on his parents' mantel had caught his eye every single time he'd been there.

The urge to fix what he'd broken that morning was so strong, he found himself with a hand on the back door-knob before he realized what he was doing.

A knock at the front stopped him in his tracks.

He crossed back through the restaurant, too hopeful that it was Jocelyn on the other side of that door. It made his palms sweat just knowing what he'd been thinking about before—a future he had no reason to grasp for, no right to.

When he opened the door, his brows folded low. "Chief?"

Eric Ward wasn't in uniform, but he sure as hell wasn't dressed for lounging either. That set Cole's nerves twitching as he glanced behind the older man.

"Hey, Cole. Jocelyn around?"

Cole scratched the back of his neck. Strange question. He and Jocelyn hadn't exactly been advertising themselves, but he supposed folks in town had eyes. Kiki Womack sure had made some insinuations before a damn thing had happened.

"No. Why?"

Ward nodded, glancing past him into the empty restaurant. "Looking into the fire out at Joe's place. Heard she'd been stayin' there. Also checking some of the older buildings on First. Lot of electrical issues lately."

Something tugged at the back of Cole's mind. "You think Joe's fire was electrical?"

Ward snorted. "Not likely. Man's a drunk—probably his own negligence. But the Inn's fire could've been prevented. Don't want another one cropping up."

Cole stepped aside. "I've got a few minutes."

Ward walked in, gaze roaming over the bar like he owned it. "How's your pop liking retirement?"

"Seems alright. Still settling in. You know he has trouble sittin' still."

"Don't we all," Ward muttered, his voice carrying something Cole couldn't place.

"Is that what this is?" Cole asked. "Keepin' busy?" Gossip wasn't his thing, but it always found a way to him, and Ward seemed to be lookin' for more than just wiring issues. He'd asked about Jocelyn after all.

"Official busywork." Ward's smile was tight, quick, and wrong. He disappeared into the back before Cole could say more.

Cole frowned, noticing a few misplaced glasses behind the bar—leftovers from last night's stragglers. He reached for them just as Ward reappeared.

"You redid the apartment upstairs, didn't you?"

Cole straightened. "Yeah. Don't know that you'd find anything. I pulled permits. Had the wiring inspected proper-like."

"Mind if I check? Safer that way."

A weight pressed into Cole's chest. "Are you just stalling for Jocelyn?"

Ward laughed, too loud. "Might be. She's been asking questions about her mama. I finally got around to diggin' into some more of the old files for her."

Cole's jaw clenched. "I'll let her know you stopped by when"—if—"she gets back."

Ward smiled at the dismissal. "I'll be gone soon as I check upstairs."

The hairs on Cole's neck stood up. Eric Ward was no longer asking, and under different circumstances, he might've been curious about why. But something was off.

"Go ahead," he said, turning to reach for his phone on the bar top. "I'll meet you up there."

"Sorry, Cole." The man's tone had shifted—stone heavy and dark. "Leave the phone where it is. I'd like you to come with me."

Cole turned slow. The gun in Ward's hand wasn't a surprise, but his gut still dropped.

He forced a shaky laugh. "Eric, come on."

Maybe it was a joke. God, he hoped it was. But the ice in Ward's gaze said otherwise.

"Upstairs," Ward ordered. Then added as an afterthought, "Know what? Go on and hand me that phone. Might help us make sure that Murphy girl comes back in a timely manner."

Ice hit Cole's veins. That Murphy girl.

The words slipped out before he could stop them: "You killed Bonnie."

Ward's eyes hardened, cold now. "The phone."

Cole didn't move, his mind racing. What would Eric Ward have against Bonnie Murphy?

"Why?"

"Why what?" Ward snapped.

"Why kill Bonnie?"

"I didn't—" He huffed, snatching the phone himself.

He dialed a number, pressing the phone to his ear.

That stumble of denial—*I didn't*—told him plenty. Even if it was an accident, Ward had been involved.

He spoke into the phone, but he watched Cole. "Meet me at the Nail. I have a job for you." So he wasn't calling Jocelyn. Not yet. He hung up without saying goodbye and jammed the gun into Cole's side. "Up the stairs."

Cole swallowed, legs carrying him forward. He wasn't stupid—he'd play along for the moment. Ward was strong, trained to haul bodies out of burning buildings. Cole couldn't take him head-on, not yet. But he might get an opening if he paid attention, and that meant biding his time.

As they reached the stairs, Cole glanced at the phone in Ward's hand. One chance, maybe. Dangerous with a gun in the mix, but he'd take whatever edge he could get.

His only comfort was that things between him and Jocelyn had been left unsettled. Maybe unsettled was enough to keep her from walking straight into the trap Ward had waiting.

THIRTY-ONE

"He who sits by the fire and thinks he is safe is the most in danger." - Plautus

J ocelyn's mind circled as she drove back toward town, her grip so tight on the steering wheel it hurt.

She should've asked Daniel where Lydia was. Should've asked him where his wife had been that night. But she hadn't been able to think clearly.

We drove by a lot.

Natasha's words echoed in Jocelyn's head.

One day it was there; the next day, it was gone.

Lydia's brother was the fire chief—just a lowly member of the crew back then, but he knew fire. Would Lydia have picked up enough to start that fire? Or had she asked him to cover for her?

Motive, means.

We drove by a lot.

Opportunity.

Sally's story was that Lydia had said something to Frank, and that had put Jocelyn's eye on him. Knowing what she now did about the bar back then, it wasn't exactly Lydia's scene. So why was she there?

An alibi?

She needed to talk to Cole. Resolving things from their fight that morning could wait. Once she got another look at her notes, they could talk it through. He wasn't so tied to the whole thing, someone with a clear head. Too much was swirling in her mind to do it herself.

She pulled to the curb in front of the Nail, hoping Cole would be in there, would open the door for her despite everything. She pounded on it just in case he was upstairs and wouldn't hear her, but it wasn't necessary. It swung open after only a few seconds.

"Cole, I—" She stopped dead. "Frank?"

"Hey, Jossie." He pulled the door wider, looking briefly behind her.

Her heart stuttered. "Where's Cole?"

"Upstairs. I asked if I could talk to you about some things. Said I could wait here for you."

Her stomach flipped, but she figured it was the heaviness in his demeanor about what he wanted to talk about. Their last conversation hadn't exactly been warm and fuzzy. Cole wouldn't have let Frank in if he didn't think he was worth listening to.

Jocelyn stepped inside. A scent she couldn't place hung in the air, tugging at her attention, but the hollow quiet pressed harder—an emptiness that echoed in the cage of her ribs. Her heart still pulsed with the urgency she'd felt on her way here, but whatever Frank had to say might help her clear things up. After all, he was the one Lydia had singled out that night.

"What did you want to talk about?" she asked, peeking back toward the stairs.

He was breathing hard when she turned back, his hands hanging limply at his sides. He looked thin and hollow.

She pulled in a breath. "Frank?"

"Jossie, I'm so sorry."

Pressure was a fist against her sternum. "Why are you sorry, Frank?"

Frank stared at her, looking so resigned that she knew she would hear something she wasn't going to like.

She moved toward the stairs, but Frank moved with her. "Cole?" she called up, not letting her gaze leave Frank's.

"Jossie—"

"Don't." She held a hand up to stop him, her throat threatening to close.

This man couldn't be a murderer. She didn't want him to be the one responsible. Maybe it was something else, but surely he didn't do anything to harm her mama. If he had done something, Cole never would've let him inside. She just knew it.

"I loved your mama so much," Frank said, the strangling sound of a sob threatening to break through.

The words scored her. It sounded too much like a confession of something more. *No, please, no.*

"But she didn't love me. Not as much." Frank swallowed. "It was always Daniel for her." A bitter edge crept into his voice, and the shock of it snapped up her spine.

He looked at her then. "He was there that day. Did you know?"

"Yes."

He rubbed a hand over his mouth. "When I found out, all I saw was red."

Her pulse throbbed. "Did you confront her?" she asked, everything she thought she knew teetering over an edge. She'd been asking the questions, but she wasn't sure she was ready now. Not when she was alone.

Where the hell was Cole?

Frank looked away from her again, but he was between her and the front door. "I went to the house that night. She was crying." This through his teeth: "Daniel broke her heart again."

Could she make it to the back door? The stairs? Why hadn't Cole heard her call?

"She slept with him." Frank turned to face her again. "She told me she was sorry, that I deserved better."

Jocelyn hadn't wanted it to be true, but here was her confirmation of what her mama had done. It sparked just a snapshot of pity for the man before her.

Frank shook his head. "I was angry." His expression turned imploring. "I didn't mean…"

Those words pelted her, and her heart twisted. "You didn't mean what, Frank? What did you do?"

His nostrils flared.

"Did you start the fire?" Her fingers became claws. She wanted to grab the front of his shirt and shake him.

"No!" He hurled the word then shrank. "No, I didn't start the fire. But…" He licked his lips, his eyes flashing away, hands curling and uncurling.

"But what? Dammit, Frank. I need to know." Her voice wobbled. She couldn't tell if she was about to cry or scream at him. So much emotion burned through her body she might've even slapped him.

"We fought." He swallowed. "I hit her. I'm not proud of it. But I was so angry, so hurt."

Her mouth dropped open. It was impossible to reconcile what he was saying with the gentle, soft-spoken man she'd known as a child.

He kept moving forward with the story, though, his words hollow. "She fell. Oh, God. And she hit the dresser."

Jocelyn's heart hammered against her ribs, but she didn't dare speak, didn't want to disrupt the truth as it poured out—even if it twisted up inside her.

"I didn't know what to do when she didn't get up. But she was alive. I swear, she was breathing."

Jocelyn covered her mouth with a hand, vision blurring with the tears she hadn't noticed building.

"I knew it looked bad, so I ran."

She backed up a step.

"I'm so sorry, Jossie." His hands started to reach for her.

"Don't!" Her finger sliced at the air in front of his face. "Don't you call me that!"

"I'm so, so sorry." He dropped to his knees, the sound against the wood floor painful to her ears. "I hurt her, I know. But I didn't start that fire."

Rage, unholy and nearly blinding, scorched through her. "But she's dead because of you! And you never said a damn thing! Twenty years, Frank!"

He fell to his hands, literally groveling at her feet. "Please forgive me. I never could. I never could forgive myself."

Her hands balled into fists, her arms trembling with the violence of her fury. But he was pitiful before her, sobbing into the floor. She wasn't sure she could ever forgive him, but she decided he didn't deserve to hear it even if she could. Forgiveness would be for her, herself and her mama only.

"Please," he sobbed when she didn't answer. "What can I do?"

She wanted to tell him to rot in the hell he'd created for himself. She wanted to break something. She wanted... too much. There was too much pain.

But this whole thing was supposed to be about answers... and justice.

She forced the words out. "You need to confess. You have to own up to what you did."

"Isn't that what he's been doing?"

The voice behind her sent a trickle of fear down her neck and silenced Frank's sobs. She stood frozen for a moment, watching Frank lift his gaze to the man standing at her back.

She turned then, her eyes snagging on Eric Ward's gun first.

Thirty-Two

"The fire you kindle for your enemy often burns yourself more than them." - Chinese Proverb

E ric Ward ushered them both up the stairs, his steps and breathing steady as he followed after them. Jocelyn didn't look back, but her awareness of his gun kept a constant tingle on the back of her neck, her pulse jumping at her throat.

Where was Cole?

The fear coiled in her stomach, and she cringed at every creak of the stairs as they walked. Maybe Cole wasn't here. Maybe they'd lied to her, and he was out preparing for the festival that would kick off in a few days.

The hope was faint, but she fought to cling to it.

"Go in," Eric directed as they reached the door.

Frank stumbled through first, and Jocelyn scanned the apartment as Eric pushed her in afterward.

She spotted Cole by the couch, curled on his side with his hands tied behind his back, feet bound. There was blood on the wood floor beneath him, and panic clawed through her insides, threatening to rip her apart.

Ward snagged her arm just before she rushed over. "He's alive."

She jerked to look at the older man, taking in the hardness of his expression. But there was also resignation and a bone weariness that made no sense.

"What did you do to him?" she demanded.

"Won't matter soon enough." He shoved her forward, and she stumbled, catching herself at the island to keep from falling.

Ward locked the door behind him before turning to Frank, who wiped his running nose on his sleeve. His grief and pain still marred his face with blotchy patches of red, his eyes puffy from crying.

"I did what you asked," Frank said, his voice weak. "Now let her go."

Ward frowned like Frank's words disappointed him. "That wasn't our agreement. But you did play your part nicely."

Jocelyn looked from Ward to Frank, who refused to meet her gaze. "What is he talking about?"

The weight of Ward's stare made her skin prickle, but she kept her attention on Frank.

Realization dawned when the two remained silent. She'd thought Lydia had started the fire, and at most, Ward might've helped cover her tracks. But it was him all along.

It didn't make sense. He'd never been anything to her mama. Jocelyn had never even heard of him before her investigation.

"Why?" she asked.

"I like fire. Always have." Ward spoke through his teeth like he hated the fact. "All it took was a perfectly placed candle near a curtain splashed with a trace amount of accelerant. Didn't know then that Bonnie'd be lyin' half-dead in there later that night."

"When?" Frank cut in.

Ward rolled his eyes. "Before either of you were even there, Leone. After my sister had come to me about the affair."

So Lydia *had* known about Daniel and Bonnie. And it was *her* anger that had been the catalyst. But was she in on it? Had she begged her brother to help her get revenge on the woman who threatened to end her marriage, ruin her reputation, and destroy her family?

Jocelyn's heart ached for Natasha. "Does Lydia know what you did?"

"No," he snapped. "And if I'd known she'd baited Frank, here—" he tipped his head—"I might've done things different."

Jocelyn glanced at Frank, who seemed to get smaller the more her shock and horror grew.

"When I found out she'd died in it, it didn't take much to figure who might've been responsible for her bein' there at all."

As if she wouldn't be. They lived there, hardly ever stayed anywhere else. But maybe Ward had banked on Bonnie seeing the fire and getting them out before it became a problem. Or maybe he hadn't cared at all.

Frank's hands became fists. "Sure sat on it, lettin' me believe it was all my fault for *years*."

"It *was* your fault, damn it," Ward snapped. "*I* didn't kill her."

"Didn't you?" Jocelyn asked.

Anger flashed across his face. "It was an accident. And I covered it up nicely for you, Leone. No one's come to bother you except your own conscience."

"She still died because of you," Jocelyn accused, drawing Ward's attention back.

"I didn't know!" He slashed at the air with his gun, then took a breath to calm himself. "If you hadn't come back here asking those damn questions..."

The sentence hung in the air as he glared at her.

Chest heaving, he gestured at Frank with the gun. "Tie her up."

Frank's red-rimmed eyes went round. "What?"

"Tie. Her. Up." Ward stepped forward with each word, pressing the gun to Frank's temple.

Jocelyn's stomach lurched up her throat.

Frank hesitated, then took the zip tie from the counter behind him, shoulders slumping as Ward walked with him to Jocelyn, keeping the barrel at his temple.

There was an apology in Frank's eyes as he took her wrists. Then he spun her, tying them together, pulling the plastic tighter. But not tight enough. Her heart stuttered as his fingers squeezed her arm like he was communicating something. Like he'd left the tie loose on purpose.

Before she could turn around to confirm it in his face, though, the blast of the gun had her flinching as a scream ripped up her throat. She spun as Frank hit the floor at her feet. Blood sprayed her shoes, jolting her backward.

She jerked to look at Ward, stomach heaving. His mouth was pulled into a tight line of displeasure as he stared down at Frank.

When he shifted back to her, she caught the determination that edged out the desperation in his eyes. "Sadly, Frank's guilty conscience got the better of him." His voice was flat, overly controlled. "What a sad ending to the story of that Murphy girl."

Each word dropped into her stomach like a stone, heavy and jagged. A sad ending. He was going to kill them and pin it all on Frank. She cut a look at Cole across the room. Was he even breathing?

When she focused on Ward again, she tried to find the psychotic glint that had to be in there somewhere. But he looked resolved, grim. Burdened.

Pulling ever so slightly at her bound wrists, she asked, "So what's your plan? Make it look like murder-suicide?"

"Covered by fire. I've got his confession all written up." He gestured to the couch. "Have a seat."

Despite Frank's body at her feet, she struggled to believe that this was really happening, that Ward would go through with it. And maybe he wouldn't if she resisted. He didn't seem happy to be dealing with the whole scenario. Maybe he could even be reasoned with.

He moved toward her when she remained where she was. The threat in the movement made her step back, which seemed to incite his anger.

"I'm not a violent man, Jocelyn." The edge in his voice chilled her. "It didn't have to come to this. *You* left me no choice." His gaze flicked to Cole. "You couldn't just let it go."

He shuffled forward again, and she recoiled, expecting him to hit her or throw her onto the couch himself, but he'd stepped up to Cole, the gun poised at his head. Her stomach torqued as his finger shifted to the trigger, violence a prickle in the air, his intent clear.

"Sit."

A vice tightened around her chest as she complied. Air seemed to grind through her lungs like it was filled with gravel, and she fought for every breath. Ward's gaze scraped along her skin as he moved toward the door. A bag rested on the floor there, and he crouched beside it, his eyes never leaving her as he reached inside.

A big bottle of lighter fluid came out of the bag, and it slid home what was going to happen, that this was real. That this man had killed her mama, and he was going to kill her, too.

Her chest hurt from how hard her heart threw itself against her ribs, and her blood pumped hot and fast through her.

Looking down at Cole, so still, she saw the rise and fall of his chest that proved he was alive. Her eyes squeezed shut as she counted the seconds that ticked between his inhale and exhale, tuning herself to him. If she didn't concentrate on his breathing, she would hear the splashing of the fluid as Ward poured it around the room.

It helped a little, though the scent of the chemical bit at her nostrils, snapping her back to reality easily enough. She recognized that smell from downstairs, the scent she hadn't been able to place. Oh, God, he'd already doused it down there.

She opened her eyes to find Eric standing across the room from her, pouring the fluid in one spot like he'd lost track of his thoughts.

Think, Jocelyn, she told herself. She couldn't let this happen, couldn't let this be the end of her life, of Cole's.

As Ward turned in a slow circle, drenching all of Cole's furniture, she began working at the zip tie around her wrists again. Ward looked less like a man reveling in chaos and more like someone carrying out a sentence he shouldn't have been saddled with, but he was still her enemy, the thing standing between her and life.

He lit a match; the sound of it catching made his pupils blow wide like a shark scenting blood. They were out of time.

She yanked at her ties more violently, desperation clawing up her spine.

The plastic zip tie gave with a sharp snap against her wrists, and Ward's face jerked to her just as she lurched to her feet. With a cry torn from somewhere deep and desperate, she slammed her shoulder into him before he could react.

Ward staggered on the slick floor where he'd poured the lighter fluid, his eyes flying wide with shock more than fear. Her stomach dropped out as they both went down.

The crack of Ward's head against the edge of the coffee table eclipsed the sound of flame catching the accelerant coating the floor, but she didn't miss the sight of the fire as it curled up the curtains, licking higher with every second.

She scrambled off of Eric, who didn't stir, and crawled toward Cole.

He still lay unmoving on the floor as the blaze raced across the room, igniting Jocelyn's panic.

Thirty-Three

"Fire that's closest kept burns most of all." - William Shakespeare

Pain dug through the back of Cole's skull, spreading like tree roots clawing for soil. It dragged him up toward consciousness, slow as being hauled out of deep water.

Footsteps on the stairs jolted panic through him. Fear didn't make sense—only folks he trusted came to his door. But his gut told him there was a reason. Something was wrong.

His eyelids fought him, heavy as lead, and the pain seared. The dark yanked him back under until a chemical stench hit his nose, sharp enough to twist his stomach. He groaned as the agony gripped him again.

"Cole!" someone called.

That voice cut through the haze, straight to his gut. But he couldn't place it, not yet. Not when his head was under attack like this.

"Cole, please!" Desperation cracked the voice, nearly breaking it into a scream.

It's her. A brief taste of that realization tinged his tongue. It was a woman calling to him. Someone who mattered.

Her whimper stirred him closer to the surface.

Something was damn sure wrong.

His eyes shot open, and sunlight stabbed through his skull like a pickax. Darkness swallowed him again.

"Cole, wake up!"

The words yanked him back, this time with the burn of smoke flooding his nose. Wood and chemicals cooking together, acrid and heavy. The woman was coughing now. He felt her hands on him.

"Cole!" she screamed.

It rattled in his skull, and he wanted to go back under. But the shape of a name formed. *Jocelyn.* The fear in her voice tore at him harder than the smoke.

"Please wake up!"

He tried to answer, tried to move, anything to calm that terror in her throat. Only another groan crawled out. But this time he stayed awake, awareness anchoring when he felt his hands bound tight behind him, his feet tied together. Memory slammed back—Eric Ward, the gun in his face. The lights going out with the explosion of pain in his head.

If Jocelyn was here, Ward had her, too.

The smell of smoke. The faint growl of fire. Heat all around him.

Cole cracked his lids, just enough to see. Light still seared, but it didn't drop him flat this time.

"Jocelyn," he rasped, her name sluggish on his tongue.

Her sob broke like glass. "Thank God, Cole."

He wanted to pull her in, shield her, carry her out through the flames if he had to. Instead his thoughts slid around, half-formed, fighting the pounding in his head. How long had he been out?

"Your place is on fire." Jocelyn's voice was strained, her body shifting.

Cole blinked through the haze. She was pulling at his bound ankles.

"We have to get out of here. If I get these, will you be able to walk?"

Heat licked at his neck—indignation or fire, he couldn't tell. It was a fair question, though. His head felt split open.

"I think so." He tried to look around, hissed when pain clawed at his skull.

Jocelyn hacked as the smoke thickened around them.

Cole craned his neck but couldn't see past the couch across the room. "Where's Ward?"

"Down. Or dead. I don't know which." She gritted her teeth, glancing over her shoulder as the smoke curled lazy but heavy around them, the fire roaring louder by the minute. Cole's lungs bucked against it, every cough stabbing his skull.

"Bedside table," Cole rasped. "Knife."

Her gaze met his. A beat of hesitation. Then she stumbled across the room holding her arm over her face against the heat. She fumbled at the drawer, fingers frantic.

Flames clawed higher—curtains, walls, his TV stand. Everything he owned turning to fuel. He glanced at the door, only a few feet away, useless fury grinding in his chest.

She scrambled back to him. Without a word, she slashed through his bindings. The second the ties snapped, she hauled him upright. His legs buckled, nausea gnawing at his gut, but he forced himself forward.

The fire was faster. A wall of flame burst up near the door, heat driving them back for a moment.

"The door's on fire!" Jocelyn screamed.

Cole clenched his jaw, shoved forward anyway. The windows were worse. This was their shot. He drove his boot hard into the door. The wood cracked, buckled, gave way.

Outside, flames raced down the steps, bright orange, greedy. Ward hadn't just lit the apartment—he'd fed the whole place to the blaze.

Cole's chest seized at the sight. His apartment. His restaurant. His whole damn life burning. But none of it mattered except the woman at his side. He wrapped Jocelyn close, shielding her with his body as he forced them down the stairs.

The fire chased, hungry. Heat blistered his back. Jocelyn shrieked. Cole didn't let go, didn't slow. The back door gave after a desperate shove, and daylight poured through. He pushed her out first, stumbled after, the two of them spilling into fresh air and autumn sun.

He shoved her farther, clear of the flames, until the back fence blocked them. Smoke and pain took their toll, sending him to the asphalt.

"Cole!" Jocelyn dropped beside him, hands clutching at him.

"I'm okay," he rasped, hauling her in tight against him, anchoring himself with her weight. "I'm okay now."

And with her safe in his arms, for the first time since waking, he believed it.

Thirty-Four

"The blazing fire makes flames and brightness out of everything thrown into it." - Marcus Aurelius

When Cole went down, a fresh wave of panic spider-webbed in Jocelyn's chest. She wouldn't have thought she'd have the capacity to be scared after everything that had just happened, but watching him lose all color and sink to the ground terrified her more than anything in her life.

There'd been blood on the floor beneath him, and he'd struggled to stay conscious when she'd called his name.

"Where are you hurt?" she asked as he clutched her to him, thankfully not passing out the way she feared.

He didn't answer, just reached for the back of his head as if only then realizing he was injured.

Jocelyn gently pulled his hand down to check for herself, leaning close to inspect the dark, matted curls. The blood was tacky and drying—a good sign—but the gash was still deep enough to make him flinch when she carefully probed it.

Thank God sirens were already wailing closer, but the reminder that Eric Ward was still in the apartment jolted her attention upward.

Flames burned hotter inside, punching out windows with the rising temperature, making her flinch. The brick structure would stand, but everything inside—everything that had been Cole's—was another story.

She glanced back at him. His gaze seemed unfocused, but he was staring at the building that carried the weight of all his work, and her chest ached for him. A sharp edge of guilt twisted inside her, too.

Before it could take root, Cole's grip on her tightened as emergency vehicles rolled into view, lights splashing against the alley until they pulled close to where they sat. He buried his face against her neck with a sigh, his breath brushing her collarbone.

"It's a damn relief seein' you in one piece," he muttered.

"Me?" Jocelyn gave a weak, wobbly laugh. It threatened to turn into a sob.

"It was hell not being able to do more in there. If somethin' had happened to you..." His words trailed, rough against her skin.

She smirked faintly. "You don't have to rescue me, Cole."

He lifted his head, wincing at the movement but managing a playful glare. "It's not about playin' hero."

"No?" she asked, cupping his face in both hands.

He gave the slightest shake of his head. "I couldn't live with myself if I lost you."

Her breath caught at the words, lodging somewhere in her chest, but she didn't get a chance to say anything, to ask what he meant.

Two fire fighters had made their way over, separating them. The first—introduced himself as Holt—started asking about possible injuries, pain, checked her eyes.

"I'm fine," she said, drawing Cole's hard gaze, but she didn't look over.

"Others in the building?" Holt asked, slipping a blood pressure cuff onto her arm.

"Frank Leone," she said numbly, staring down at the gauge as the needle danced. "He's already dead. Ward shot him."

Holt's hands stilled. "Ward?" he asked.

She nodded. "Chief Eric Ward. He started the fire."

Holt exchanged a glance with his companion, who'd paused his appraisal of Cole. Then he turned to call for another crewman, who jogged over.

Holt waved his hand at the new guy. "Get on your radio. The lady says Chief Ward started the fire. Where is Ward now?" he asked her.

"Inside, too." She swallowed, the full weight of what had happened, what she'd *done,* taking shape along her shoulders. The air suddenly felt thin as the men around her stared. "I tackled him. He hit his head. Didn't move. I don't know if he was alive. I didn't check." Short sentences were all she could manage. "We had to get out."

The men exchanged a glance again, then looked at Cole, who was intent on Jocelyn's face. It was the first he was hearing this part, too.

"Ward pulled a gun on me. Knocked me out," Cole said, reaching for the back of his head.

"Eric Ward?" the firefighter kneeling before him said again, disbelief plain in his voice.

"Yes," Cole snapped.

"Radio this in." Holt said to the new guy, face edged with shock.

"Got a head injury here," his companion said. "Concussion likely."

"And call for the ambo," Holt said to the radio man. Then he looked at Jocelyn. "I need you to come with me."

He helped her to her feet and tugged her away from Cole, toward the mass of bodies crawling through the alley.

The fire still roared, burning through its rage.

She felt the heat along her skin, but inside, all she felt was cold.

Thirty-Five

"To love is to burn—to be on fire." - Jane Austen

They'd kept Cole overnight. Only released him because he fought them on another day.

His mama had fretted over it, over him, but he managed to shake her so he could take Pop's truck to drive to the Nail and see the damage himself.

There was still too much heat coming from the building for him to stand on the sidewalk in front, so he stood across the street, hands slung low on his hips as he processed the sight.

Too many feelings tore at him at once to pick one, so he just stared. His head still hurt. Body ached, too, but he was alive, damn it.

His place, though. Looked like a charred skeleton. Lifeless. Creepy. Didn't look like it ever could've held life.

"Should've known you'd be up on your feet already."

Her voice soothed the sad that threatened, and he glanced over with a ready half-smile. She was a picture, even with her tired eyes and sad smile.

"Where'd you come from?" he asked, reaching for her.

"Police station." Jocelyn let him tug her into his side. "I had to answer more questions. They found the note Eric planned to plant to frame Frank. Found a lot of his arson supplies, too. They're going to reopen a lot of investigations."

Her arms wrapped around his waist, and they both looked back at the rubble of what he'd built that was now just an empty husk.

Didn't look as bleak when she was wrapped around him like that, lending him her quiet strength. He would've been part of the ruin in that building if it hadn't been for her. She'd handled Ward on her own, refusing to let the man who'd taken so much from her take her all the way down. And she'd kept Cole from being taken down, too. Hell of a woman to be able to do all that and still be standing, and no tears to boot.

"It's awful. Your whole life, Cole." Her voice was heavy with sadness, and he wanted to lift it off her with his own two hands.

"It's nothing but stuff, Darlin'," he replied, remembering Joe's words from—shit—only a few days before? Felt like lifetimes.

She tucked herself closer against him, as if she wanted to dig in and bury herself inside him. He'd let her. Hell, she was already so deep under his skin, he'd never get free—not that he wanted to.

"Will you rebuild?" she wanted to know.

A sigh sawed up from his chest. "Could."

She tipped her face up to study him.

"Could just give it up." A shrug. "Could sell my place outside town, too." He said it toward the building, feeling the intensity of her stare, the question she pressed into him with those dark eyes.

Her words came out small. "Why would you do that?"

Finally, he looked down at her. "I'd do it if you asked."

Her brows folded. "But this is your home."

He shook his head. "It's just a place."

Quiet settled over her as she looked out across the street, but he doubted she saw any of it. He hoped to hell she was considering what was behind his words. He meant them. There was no question he'd go if she did. That house and the land didn't matter much if there wasn't someone out there with him.

The someone he wanted was her.

"It's a nice place," she said after a beat, sparking a little hope in his chest.

"It is," he agreed, holding steady. "But you and this town have a history. And not a pretty one."

She frowned, chewing on that. There was that history, and her family that'd been torn up by what'd happened the day before—a scandal that had rocked the town and their place in it. With all that drama and all those memories, he wouldn't blame her at all.

"You're right," she finally said. "But I also have the possibility of a future—one I can shape myself." Tilting her head up, she offered him a slow smile. "And I know I'd have some help."

"Damn right you would," he said, his voice rough. "You're sure?"

She laughed. Maybe she could hear his doubt, the fear in the question. "I'm sure of you."

He cupped her chin, smiling like a fool. "Should be. If I make a decision, it sticks."

"Long as you stick with me."

He brushed her mouth with his, just for a taste of those lips before he said, "You got it, Darlin'."

EPILOGUE

"Love in its essence is spiritual fire." - Seneca

ONE YEAR LATER

Cole paced in front of the steps, painted a smokey blue, energy pinging through him. It was later than he'd planned, took longer than it should've. Cicadas hummed from the trees surrounding him, the constant buzz adding to the unease in his bones.

Natasha had been and gone, helped him set everything up, gave him an encouraging hug before she headed off, laughing about the scowl that haunted his face. She gave as good as Terra, and that was all he needed—more people to bust his balls.

What he had needed today was Natasha's touch, her eye for detail, for pretty.

When he heard the crunch of tires on the gravel drive, his lunch threatened a reappearance. He swallowed it down and stopped his pacing, trying to school his features as Jocelyn's car eased up to the small concrete slab he'd had poured in front of the garage.

She got out of the car and turned, the sun painting her hair. But nothing could outshine the smile on her face as she looked at him.

That eased his nerves some, and he grinned. "Hey, Darlin'."

She walked forward, straight into his arms, and damn if she didn't smell like his dreams. Her long hair brushed over his arms as he held her. She left it down almost always now because he preferred it.

"Tash said you had somethin' to show me." Her accent was thick and strong now, teased out from being back in Cedar Hollow a year.

He let her step back but snatched her hand before she got too far. "Pull you away from anything important?"

She shook her head, a soft grin on her face that lit him up. "I'm glad for it. Nan and Joe were arguin' about whether to add square footage to the floor plan. County allows half again as much as what was original. Even at their age, they bicker like school children."

"Siblings," he said. Not that he knew from experience, but she did, at least a little these days.

She gave her body a quick shake as if to rid herself of the mild frustration. "So what'd you want to show me?"

He tipped his head toward the house. "Inside."

One dark brow arched up. "You showed me the new counters the other day. You can't go draggin' me out here for every update."

"The hell I can't," he said, tugging her up the steps with a grin.

Now that he had her there, the nerves had died down. With her hand in his, all was right in the world, even if everything in it was about to change. Or maybe not. It was just the next step in the line he'd been walking toward anyway.

Jocelyn eyed him with suspicion and even tried peeking through the front window. He'd expected as much and asked Natasha to do up some curtains.

"Cole Hauser, what're you up to?"

His grin stretched as his hand landed on the knob. "Quit askin' questions. That's how pretty girls get themselves into trouble."

She glared at him. Joke might've still been tainted with pain, but his whole plan hinged on turning this time of year around for the better. He'd timed it for redemption.

The damn ring had sat in his pocket for a month or more while he waited to see how Jocelyn's reconnection with her daddy went. And it was promising. She might very well have someone to walk her down the aisle. Providing she said *yes*.

He opened the door and guided her inside, knowing he'd nailed it as soon as her breath caught.

More like tapped the right person to nail it for him.

He hadn't checked it himself, so his own mouth dropped open a second.

Natasha had organized movers to set the dark suede couches, the sleek metal and wood coffee table. They'd hung the black and white stills above the couch, warmed the corner up with a indoor palm plant he didn't know the name of.

It touched on Cole's style and added in the soft flavors of Jocelyn's with the blue-striped throw pillows and tiny bouquets of flowers, tying everything together like he planned to do with their names.

"Cole," Jocelyn breathed, hands going to her mouth. "You did this?"

He shrugged when she looked at him. "Tash mostly."

She laughed, though it was breathy.

"It's just this room for now. But the rest is comin'. We can move in end of the week."

She gasped. "This week?"

"Aren't you tired of shuffling between places?"

They'd been bouncing between a hotel room at the Hollow Inn, his folks', and Natasha's until he finished the house, until the contractors finished The Hammered Nail rebuild. Only at the Inn did they get to stay together. And it'd been hell, though he'd given her the space to build the relationship with her sister because it mattered.

But he was done. Done not waking up to her every morning, done waiting to make her his like he was already hers.

And so, as she turned in a slow circle, taking in the details of what her sister had done up for them, he did the traditional thing and lowered himself to one knee.

She caught the movement and spun to him. "Cole," she breathed as he dug the box from his pocket, cursing when it took extra work.

Should've taken it out before he'd knelt.

His nerves rioted back into his gut, but her smile told him it was a done deal already. He wanted to say the whole thing, anyway. Wouldn't count otherwise, and his mama would ream him if he didn't.

"House is done, Darlin'," he said, voice jagged with emotion. "But it ain't home until you're in it with me, with a ring on your finger tellin' the world you're mine." He opened the box. "What do you say? Wanna marry me?"

She dropped to her knees before him, grabbing his face to plant a kiss on his mouth. "You got it, Darlin'."

His laugh was damn wobbly, so he focused on taking the ring out to slide it onto her finger. At least his hands were steady.

When he looked back at her, catching that shine in her eyes, certainty solidified in his chest.

"Welcome home," he said, and a long, slow kiss was her reply.

ACKNOWLEDGEMENTS

First and foremost, I want to thank my Lord and Savior, Jesus Christ. Without Him, I would be nothing. He gave me the talents, and I'm just trying to be a good steward of what He's given me.

Then there's the usual suspects: Shiny, for always encouraging me and talking plots and taking notes and reading my books and helping me make every design decision. Also for buying me sushi every time we hang out. Lyssa, for being the best best friend who ever best friended, who supports and loves me, who encourages me and does this mom life with me, even long distance. Meredith and Danielle, my go-to betas! You guys should know by now I can't put a book out without you two.

I want to thank my family—my husband particularly because of how gracefully he handles my eccentricities and for how he supports this career of mine. To my babies, Bennett and Tessa, you are the light and the joy of my life, and I love you both so much. I'm so grateful that I get to hang out with you guys all day and that you both willingly share me with my stories on occasion. To my mama, who reads every one of my books and encourages me and makes me laugh and helps me enjoy life—thank you!

And lastly, to my readers! You make this whole thing possible. Without you, I wouldn't have a reason to put these books out, and it means so much to me that you're here!

ABOUT THE AUTHOR

Tracey began writing at age 13, when there wasn't much for kids who loved adventure and weren't into the drama of everyday teenager-hood. She has always loved romance with a side of danger, and she has a hard time writing anything else. She really likes to read it, too. *Kiss, kiss, pew, pew,* and all that jazz.

In January 2022, she took a leap of faith and published her first book, *The Alternate End of Cassidy Marchand.* Since then, she's published the full trilogy, a side novel, a co-written book with C.H. Lyn, *Love Undercover,* and the first book in *Secrets of the Unborn.* And she ain't stopping. Except when she has to teach her kids for homeschool. Or when she has to answer her 800th *why* question. Or when she has to break up a fight between her two kids. But, you know, when she's not doing those things... she's not stopping!

Check her out on socials @authortraceybarski (honestly, she mostly does stuff on Instagram) to find out what shenanies she's up to, like book info, new releases, sneak peeks, and weird reels.

Go to traceybarski.com for all other info, to sign up for her very infrequently sent newsletter, and see what events she might have set up.

ALSO BY Tracey Barski

The Alternate Chronicles

The Alternate End of Cassidy Marchand
Resurrecting Cassidy Marchand
Cassidy Marchand Unraveled
Heart in Parallel

Compromised

Love Undercover

Written with C.H. Lyn

Love Is Murder

Kiss Or Kill
Secrets of the Unborn

www.ingramcontent.com/pod-product-compliance
Lightning Source LLC
Chambersburg PA
CBHW021210310726
48971CB00006B/1508